Victoria El Henawy is an archaeologist specialising in 12-15th century Egypt. She is passionate about the art, architecture, culture, and history of the Islamic world. She has worked with several charities supporting women and children of the Middle East. A mother of two children, she is especially interested in the promotion of rights, health, and education for girls. She earned a graduate degree in Islamic art and architecture from School of Oriental and African Studies, University of London. This is her first published title in a series of books on great Muslim women and girls through history.

FRONT COVER ARTWORK: by Dina Wassif – Proud Egyptian artist, Wife, Mother, Artist and Biker.

I would like to dedicate this book specially to my daughter, Zara, who inspired me with her confidence and magical energy; but more broadly to all the girls who dream of achieving greatness. Also, to Amr and Faris who supported me with love and my parents for their endless encouragement.

Victoria El Henawy

TREE OF PEARLS

The slave girl who ruled Egypt

AUSTIN MACAULEY PUBLISHERS™

LONDON * CAMBRIDGE * NEW YORK * SHARJAH

A CIP catalogue record for this title is available from the British Library.

ISBN 9781398442184 (Paperback)
ISBN 9781398442191 (Hardback)
ISBN 9781398442207 (ePub e-book)

www.austinmacauley.com

First Published 2022
Austin Macauley Publishers Ltd®
1 Canada Square
Canary Wharf
London
E14 5AA

Chapter 1
Cheated

'There is no god but God, and Muhammad is the Messenger of God' – the beautiful words which summed up the Muslim faith boomed from the *Muezzin*'s voice. Walking past a large jasmine vine heavily scented with white blossoms, Shajara heard the muezzin from the mosque calling out the *adhan* or call to worship. The muezzin's melodious voice was loud enough to be heard all over the western part of the city, and Shajara loved to listen to it.

The morning air was sweet with the promise of spring, but a chilly breeze was blowing from the east and carrying with it the faint odour of baking bread. Down the road, a bird was singing on the highest branch of a tree, and she could see that it was a shrike with its black and white feathers and a blushing of red. She had learned the names of many birds and could recognise their song for Anatolia, the country where she lived, was home to many birds, some from Africa to the south and some from Europe to the north and west. Konya, her hometown, was one of the largest trading cities in all of Anatolia and sent local products to places as far away as the homes of the migrating birds. In this year of 1210 CE, it was often said it was one of the largest trading centres of the world!

As Shajara walked along, she sang a verse of one of her favourite songs. It would help cheer her before entering the baker's shop. Shajara had never liked the baker, but it was the only bakery near her master's house and she sometimes had to go there for the bread for the household. Always, the baker served her last. Always it was the people he knew and their families and then, last of all, the slaves. She thought the bakery a dirty place with its crusted surfaces. She loved the spotlessly clean kitchen at home with its counters that she and her mother, Rehan, scrubbed clean every day.

Today, as usual, many customers in the baker's shop had brought their own dough to be cooked in the baker's ovens, and their clay pots lined the counter. The baker's wife was busy stacking the flat bread for sale on the counter. Shajara waited till the baker finally made eye contact with her, for there was never a queue, just a gathering, pushing crowd. She made her order, took the warm bread and felt in her pocket for the large, slightly bent, copper coin, the one the cook had given her that morning. The baker tossed it into a pot filled with other coins and threw back at her two much smaller, thinner copper coins. Without a word, he turned his attention to the next customer.

Shajara was immediately incensed. The baker had cheated her. He should have given her one medium copper and two small copper coins, not just two small ones. She shouted, "Hey! You gave me the wrong change!" He ignored her and continued to serve. She raised her voice and tried again, "You cheated me, do you hear, you cheated me!" Shajara saw that people were staring at her, so she continued, "And therefore you are cheating my master – Master Osman Balabar the Trader!" She raised her voice very high, because she knew that her Master was one of the wealthiest and most pious men in Konya, and therefore, one of the most respected.

She had caught the baker's attention by yelling out. More importantly, she had drawn the attention of the crowd of customers and often a crowd gave a judge's verdict. She knew she had only seconds to make her point, before everyone's attention would turn back to bread and daily duties. So, she went on quickly.

"I gave you the largest copper coin. You owe me one medium and two lesser copper coins."

The baker, now looking much taller and larger than Shajara had first thought him, directed his blackening glare at her and boomed, "You little lying slave girl. You handed me a midsize copper! Now get off with you!"

The crowd was standing still, everyone looking towards Shajara, waiting for her response. She felt the room go quiet. Her confidence was a little shaken but anger at the injustice stirred in her heart. Pushing her way across the grimy counter, she leaned over it to the pot of coppers just by the baker's hand. He made a movement towards it, but she was far quicker. She grabbed the large copper coin and waved it threateningly in the baker's face.

"This! See this? This is the copper I gave you. I know because it's the bent one our cook handed me this morning." She waved it higher for all to see. There was only a moment's pause, but it was sufficient for the baker to realise that he was beaten, for the crowd, unanimous in their disapproval, was murmuring and glaring at him. With a murderous look and grumbling, he handed over the one medium copper coin she was owed. She turned and ran out of the bakery.

Feeling a warm glow of victory and with a new spring in her step, Shajara hummed her favourite song. She knew she was a slave, and a girl, but she wasn't stupid. But should she have challenged the baker like that? After all, he was not only very much larger and older, but a freeman and a business owner. To make such a public scene could have disgraced her Master. But then, in fact, it had all worked out well and, if the Master should hear of it, then he would be proud that she had not allowed his money to be stolen. And with that thought in mind, she burst into song.

She had sung only one verse when an outstretched hand landed firmly on her shoulder. Immediately, the thought flashed into her mind that someone had followed her from the shop. Was she to be scolded?

When she turned, it was not the furious baker but a kind-faced woman in a blue dress with a matching silver embroidered scarf draped over her head and shoulders. Her face wore a crinkled smile and her hazel eyes danced with amusement. Standing behind her was a young man, with an equally friendly smile, but circled by a sparse, dark beard.

These people were definitely not servants. From their clothes alone, she could see they were wealthy. But what did these rich people want with her?

"Peace be upon you. That was quite a performance, my dear. That baker won't try to cheat you again." The woman chuckled. "You argue as well as you sing!"

Shajara with her eyes cast slightly down to the dusty street murmured the correct reply, "And upon you be peace." The package she saw in the young man's arms was probably bread from the baker's and that was where they had seen her. She had taken a risk in challenging the baker, but these people were from a class and position far above bakers and other tradesmen. To offend them could bring shame to her Master and bring her harsh punishment.

"My name is Mumina and this is my son, Jalal." The woman's sparkly eyes had been inherited by her son and both were smiling. Shajara's eyes drifted slowly up to meet theirs and she began to feel less threatened.

The woman's foreign accent was intriguing. Shajara had heard endless tales of journeys beyond the sea and across the mountains, but she had never been

9

more than a few streets away from Master Osman's house where she had been born.

Perhaps these people were from the country where her father, Musa, had been raised. In the evenings, he would often tell her tales from his youth, from the time before he had been captured by the Sultan's army. Although unable to read – in fact because he could not read – Musa had memorised stories from his parents and grandparents and their stories from generations long before, all in great detail.

The woman was looking closely at her. "We want to talk with you, but the street is dusty and soon will be crowded. Come to have some bread and tea with us in my home? It would be a delight to hear you sing again." Mumina encouraged her with another warm smile. "Your voice is a gift from God."

This was not how rich people addressed slave girls in Konya. Shajara's curiosity was aroused and her instincts told her that there was nothing to fear. Yet Rehan, her mother, had often warned her that children, even adults, sometimes disappeared in the street, never to be seen or heard of again. These two, smiling people, obviously rich, would not do her harm. But the warmth of the bread in her arms awoke her to her duties.

"I must go home quickly before the bread is cold. Forgive me, I do not have time."

A flash of disappointment crossed Mumina's face and Shajara added, "I am very sorry." But as she turned to leave, the woman wanted to know, "Where do you work?"

There was no danger in letting them know. "In the house of Osman Balabar, the Trader," she said proudly. In case they had mistaken her for someone other than a slave, she added, "My parents are servants in his household." At this, Mumina raised an eyebrow, and surprise briefly registered on her son's handsome face. "Then how is it that you know so much about the value of money?" Shajara muttered a response. "I learned about it when the tutor was teaching my master's sons."

"You take part in their lessons?" The question shook her, and she simply shook her head.

It was unusual for servant girls to be in service with their parents, for one of the misfortunes of slavery was the break-up of families. Shajara was proud that Master Osman and Serine, his wife, had allowed her parents to remain in the same household and keep their child as well.

"Then Madame Serine is your mistress," the woman said. "And I know her well and will be seeing her soon. May the mercy, peace and blessings of God be upon you!"

Shajara responded to Mumima with the same blessing. As she walked away, she wondered what this fine lady would tell Serine.

ॐ

Chapter 2
Home

Shajara went home, almost running, eager to tell someone of her adventurous morning and to try to discover something about the strangers who had questioned her. When she entered the servants' hallway, she had barely removed her scarf and slipped on her house slippers when she heard Master Osman's booming voice and the shrill high-pitched voice of his wife. She could not make out the exact words but quickly understood that an argument was in progress and, from the sounds, it was getting more heated by the minute.

As she entered the kitchen to give the bread to Cemil, the cook, she saw her mother, Rehan, standing at the door, craning her neck to the hallway in order to hear every word. Her mother's job was to clean the house, and this Rehan did with steady, forceful strength and always in the same routine, first one room then the next in an unvarying order. But she had other duties to the lady of the house, for the Master's wife, Serine, often sought her advice.

Although a slave who had never learned to read or write, Rehan had learned much by keeping her eyes open to the ways of the world and she counselled Serine on matters as important as marriage, her children and parenting. She was a trusted confidante, for she had been at Serine's bedside at the birth of the children of the family.

Shajara waited for a few moments, hoping to gain her mother's attention. But as soon as the argument was over, Serine called Rehan to speak with her. So, Shajara went to find her father.

Musa was the gardener and gate man for the house. Short in height, quiet by nature, he treated his plants and flowers just as he treated people, with calm respect and gentle understanding. His face was worn and leathery, for when everyone else was taking an afternoon nap, he tended the garden. His war wounds had never fully healed, his health was uncertain and, because he would never rest even when sick, his wife and daughter worried constantly about him. He scoffed at their worries and scolded them when they fussed over him in the evening tending to each scrape or cut. Yet evening was the time of his day he prized most, and he always thanked God for sending him his wife and daughter, the treasures in his life.

Shajara found Musa on the roof terrace tending to the grape vines and a prolific scarlet bougainvillea, both planted in several enormous terra cotta pots.

"Good morning, my father! Are you well?" Shajara shielded her eyes from the morning sun as she watched him standing on a stool carefully intertwining the new growth from the vines onto the latticework structure.

"Thanks to God, I am well. May the blessings of God be upon you. How are you, my daughter?"

Shajara told the story of her morning's adventures under the bright morning sun, while swatting away the ever-buzzing mosquitoes. Her father was as good a listener as a storyteller and he was soon smiling at the baker's defeat and then wrinkling his brow at her description of the meeting with Mumina and Jalal.

Musa stepped off his stool and went to bougainvillea cuttings he had put in a woven basket ready for the bonfire. He plucked an especially vibrant blossom from the thorny cuttings and came to Shajara. "Look," he said holding the flower for her to see, "Look at its petals. They are like butterflies' wings, so delicate, so colourful and beautiful, and yet borne from a branch fierce with thorns."

Shajara took the blossom from her father's hands that were scratched and bloodstained from the morning's pruning. She grinned as she put the flower in her hair just as she used to do when she was a very little girl.

Musa's turban was dirty and had leaves caught in the folds. His shabby clothes were torn and patched; his face glistened with sweat from his morning's work; his frail body was bent; but he was smiling broadly. "Not unlike you, Shajara. A beautiful and clever girl, borne from slaves. A gorgeous flower from an unlikely branch. Your full name Shajara al Durr means tree of pearls and it suits you very well." He placed a kiss on her forehead.

They went down the stairs together to the inner court. "So, Shajara, these people you met are Hajji Jalal and his mother, Mumima, from Khorasan in Persia. He is a teacher of Islam, as was his father. They are living two streets away from here, near the new mosque."

Her father had been at the mosque on Friday and must have heard all about Hajji Jalal there. Shajara knew that the title Hajji was one of great respect for it meant that Jalal had gone on pilgrimage to Mecca, thus performing one of the five pillars of Islam. "People say he is very pious," Musa said approvingly, "and a scholar of the law, a student of the great mysteries, and a poet." Shajara, recalling Jalal's smiling face struggled to understand how so young a man, and one so handsome, could possibly manage to fill so many serious roles.

Musa's tone changed and he looked sadly at her. "I'm not sure what they wanted, but I think it may be to offer Osman money to buy you. They probably need a servant to work in their household."

Her father limped back to work leaving her alone in the inner courtyard. She stood lost in thought by the courtyard fountain. What would happen to her if the Master sold her? Would she be allowed to return to see her mother and father? Her morning's worry of causing a scandal at the baker's had now been replaced by something both exciting and frightening.

The fountain in the courtyard was built in the shape of a geometric star. Its tiles were vivid blues, greens and browns, ten tiles altogether creating the geometric shape. She knew from experience that it had a mesmerising effect if one stared for long enough. Now, for the first time she saw how truly beautiful it was. How could she leave this place that had so long been her home? Perhaps her life up to now was just one tile in the pattern of what would become her life.

&

Chapter 3
A Deal

Serine had been very pleased to be invited to Mumima's house, for although she had already met the newcomers, she was interested in getting to know them better. Visitors from foreign countries always brought interesting news. But she also had an important mission in mind with the foreign woman and her son.

Mumima greeted Serine warmly and immediately began to tell the story of Shajara and the baker. She made Serine laugh at her account of how the girl had outwitted the wretched tradesman. But when Mumima went on to praise the girl's great beauty and lovely voice, Serine sighed dramatically, and the laughter left her face.

"I see I've upset you in some way, Serine. Please accept my apologies."

"Oh, Mumima. It is true, you've hit a nerve, for I've a problem with Shajara, and I'm not sure what to do about it."

Mumima had experience in helping people with their troubles. She leaned forward and put her hand on Serine's, "tell me, my dear. Perhaps I can help."

"It's about my sons, Mumima, and my fears about that slave girl."

Serine explained that every time she saw her sons with Shajara, and every time she heard her singing around the house, her worries grew.

"The girl is reaching an age when boys look at her. My son Abbas is very a studious boy and Shajara, for whatever stupid reason, has a desire to learn. She memorises everything and Abbas is always praising the girl's mind. Sabry, my second son, loves playing games and sports and, because Abbas is always with his books, Sabry insists that Shajara play with him. I see him looking at her, joking and teasing her.

"I ask you, Mumima, what would happen if one of my two growing teenage sons fell in love with this beautiful girl? I tremble to think what could happen." She looked at Mumima with her eyebrows raised, looking for agreement.

"Yes, I see. That could cause problems." Mumima answered. She handed her guest the plate of biscuits stuffed with dates, and after Serine took one, she herself bit into the soft crumbly pastry with its sweet chewy centre.

"Shajara will soon become a young woman and even as a girl, she's already a threat! Of course, I care for her parents, and they are wonderful servants, but when it comes to my children, I take pity on no one. The time has come for Shajara to leave!" She shifted uncomfortably in her chair for she knew that Mumima, widow of a teacher of Islam, might remind her that the Quran requires masters to be kind to those in their households, whether free or slave.

Mumima took a long sip on her tea and then carefully put the cup on the copper table in front of them. She was not yet ready to suggest the deal she had in mind, for although she was looking for a girl like Shajara to help her in the house, she didn't want Serine to think this was the reason she had invited her for tea. That would drive up the price, and as a widow, she had to be careful with her money. It would take her son a few more years to establish himself with his career and make a good living. She also knew that in the delicate matter of buying slaves, one had to be extremely careful. She turned to Serine. "What do you know about Shajara's background?"

"Her parents were born as Christians and lived on the shores of the Black Sea until captured by the army of the Sultan of Rum more than a dozen years ago. And they count themselves lucky that they were bought in the Konya slave market by my husband, Osman. We were not aware of their relationship at the time, as their language differed from ours, but it became clear shortly after they came to our house that Rehan was already pregnant with Shajara!"

"That is quite unusual, Serine. I thought families are parted at the slave market and are sold separately."

"Yes, that is true, but you know my husband has a soft heart and after he purchased Musa, the man was in such a state – pleading and sobbing. Well, you can imagine the rest. Osman came home with both of them and I can tell you, I believed they would run away at the first chance, and I was wary about them until Shajara was born. Afterwards, you have never seen such a content family." Serine hoped Mumima would see that it was clear she and her husband had provided well for this little family.

"To be honest, I'm not certain where they came from exactly. Rehan claims Shajara's silky voice comes from her Kipchak grandmother. Her father boasts that her green eyes come from his Armenian grandfather.

"Rehan and Musa converted to Islam, and like many converts, they practice our religion with zeal. They taught the girl to be pious." Mumima nodded, for she knew slaves were not forced to convert but often did so.

"But Shajara is not a good servant? Is that what you're telling me, Serine?" Mumima inquired.

"Oh no, Mumima!" Serine began to see her opportunity. "The girl is polite, always thorough in her work and willing to do more. Her only fault is that she's curious and wants to learn to read and learn. We all know that will only get her into trouble and my husband says her interest in such things will soon die out." A silence followed and the ladies sipped their tea, their thoughts still on the story of Shajara's family.

"Mumima, what would you do in my situation? You must think me cruel to want to sell such a girl!"

"No, no! I understand your problem." Mumima could sense that Serine was anxious to make the sale of Shajara, but it was important not to rush matters, and she poured her guest another cup of tea.

"Oh, Mumima, their family has come to be part of ours – Rehan helps me in all kinds of ways, but I'm at a complete loss what to do!" Serine threw her hands up in the air, dramatising her frustration.

Mumima knew this was the time to make the proposition to buy the girl. Serine would surely see it as the solution to her problem.

§♪

Chapter 4
Leaving Home

That evening, Shajara learned the worst. Serine came up to her and said, not in her usual kindly way, but harshly, "Well, young Shajara, you seem to be worth more than we thought. Go tell your father that I have sold you. You leave this house in the morning."

The shock of the abrupt announcement and Serine's cold tone brought quick tears to Shajara's eyes; her cheeks reddened; and she felt heat stir in her heart. She was sad, fearful and angry – all at once.

Serine continued: "You're a very lucky girl. Any servant maid in Konya would want to work for Mumina and her son, the teacher. This is a good thing. *God Bless it.*"

At that moment, Shajara hated the woman and son she had met in the street outside the bakery. Why would they want to ruin her life? It was all because she had caused such a scene with the baker, and now, this was her punishment.

Shajara ran to tell her father the dreadful news. He listened gravely, stroking her hair as she sobbed her way through her account, but when Shajara could speak no longer and collapsed against him, his composure too was shaken and tears filled his eyes.

Rehan greeted Shajara's news in her practical, matter-of-fact way. "You're almost a young woman. It's time for you to stand on your own feet and this is a good and lucky thing. *God bless it.* Besides, it's only down the street from home."

At that last word 'home', Rehan's voice caught and she had to turn away to hide her own emotion. She had been told by Serine earlier and had understood that this was a good solution, for she herself had seen the growing bond between the master's sons and her daughter. Nothing good would come out of that. There was no possibility of marriage between a son of a wealthy merchant and a slave.

In fact, marriage itself was a luxury. She and her husband had been extremely lucky to have been bought by Osman Balabar.

Musa and Rehan knew that nothing could be done about the sale, and they left Shajara in no doubt of it. She was Osman's property and could be sold when and to whom he wanted. They tried to calm her by emphasising that Mumima and her son were known to be devout Muslims who would treat her well.

That night, Shajara slept hardly at all. The next morning, she woke early, as usual, to pray. She felt there was nowhere else to turn except to God. *Salat* or prayer five times a day is the second of the Five Pillars of Islam and prayers must be preceded by careful washing.

Shajara had memorised the words of the first five *suras* or chapters of the Quran. She loved to recite them, to hear the beautiful Arabic words, and she would let the words echo in her mind. She listened not only with the ear but inwardly to the message of the Quran as it spoke to her soul. It was a message of good news for all who believed and who lived good lives. She knew that God was the friend of all who believe, bringing them out of darkness and into light, and her spirit was lifted.

After her prayer, she started practicing words to say to Mumina, thinking how to manage her farewells and went down into the courtyard for the last time. It was time to go.

Musa went with his daughter to the door of Mumina's house. It was only a short walk but Shajara could see that it had tired her father: Fears for his health and the thought that she might never be able to spend time with him again added to all the other emotions stirring within her. She embraced her father, who turned sadly away.

Standing for a moment before the carved wooden door, Shajara prayed for strength, for she felt that her world was crumbling around her. She summoned up her courage and knocked at the door. There was no answer. She knocked again but again without answer. Where was Mumina? Where was her son? Were there no other servants? Her anxieties and fears built up as she stood at the unanswered door. It was still early and there were few people in the street. She looked behind her down the road and saw the slow hunched form of her father walking away. She wanted to run after him.

Shajara nervously wound her fingers around the ends of her shawl. She tried to remember her morning's prayer and to regain the feeling of calm it had brought her.

"What is this?" a voice asked. She turned to see Jalal, Mumima's son.

He looked gravely at her. "Why grieve, my child? What have you lost?" His voice was calm and kind. "Surely, what you have lost you may find in another place." He opened the door with a large iron key produced from the pocket inside his vest. She stood unable to move, her eyes cast down, afraid to speak.

Shajara supposed his words were meant to comfort her. But what did he mean that she would find what she had lost? It was this man and his mother who had made her lose everything. If only she could be at home! She remembered the love and joys of her childhood. Right now, she would have been sweeping by the fountain while the boys were taught by the city's best tutor.

Jalal continued to look gravely into Shajara's eyes. He saw a very young, worried but angry girl, and he understood that her feelings were for the family she had left behind.

"Do you remember the bakery?" he asked her. "We saw a very different Shajara there. We saw a girl so quick in wit and so bold in action that she carried the day against that crafty baker. We saw both courage and grace. And now? What do we see?" The corners of his mouth tilted ever so slightly up.

"You think my mother was wrong to buy your services from Serine. Perhaps you are too young to know that safety never comes from seeking safety."

What are these things he is saying, she wondered. He is speaking riddles, but she repeated the words in her mind, 'safety never comes from seeking safety'.

Mumina came quietly into the courtyard. "Why these grave words, my son and why your sorrowful looks, Shajara? Aren't you pleased to be with us?" Mumima approached Shajara slowly. Shajara knew this was the time to accept her new position with appropriate gratitude. But with her head bent, she merely mumbled thanks to Mumina for her kindness.

Jalal turned to his mother. "Osman Balabar the Trader is this girl's master and I know him as a good and kind man. Only such a master would have let his servants nest their family in his house. Now, we have broken into that nest before the chick is ready to fly."

"What would you have me do?" Mumina asked.

"Tell Serine we think Shajara still too young, too frightened, too given to tears, to be our servant. Send her back to Osman's house. Tell her that we are afraid her tears will ruin our carpets." Shajara's face twisted with horror, for she knew that such words would disgrace her in Serine's eyes, and her father and mother would share in her shame. She shook her head, her eyes silently pleading.

"What? Don't send you back? Or don't send you back with such words?" Jalal asked playfully, his smile growing. "Do you think we should send you back with praise?" Shajara finally understood that the man was teasing her, and she found the courage to say, "I will serve you happily. I will stay in this house and do what you wish."

Mumina took Shajara's hand. *"If God wills*, it will be a pleasure to hear your happy voice raised in song around our house. Welcome, my dear."

&

Chapter 5
Inspired

Most of Shajara's days were spent cleaning Mumima's house. She started with the bedrooms, opening the shutters and letting the fresh air wash the rooms with sunlight. She made the beds, dusted and then cleaned the floors. She washed the laundry and hung it in the strong sunlight to dry.

She would then roll up the beautiful carpets that covered the floors of Mumina's home, take them outside to beat out the dust, then carefully broom and mop the floors before laying them down again. She knew these carpets were precious to Mumima, for they had been brought all the way from her home in Khorasan.

Following her mother's example, she would work thoroughly until the house was spotless. She knew that the Prophet himself, loved cleanliness. Jalal and Mumima praised her often. "Someone who works with all their heart finds joy." After lunch, Jalal went to his study to read and Mumima went to her room for a nap. Then in the late afternoon, Shajara would start the cooking with the help of Mumima.

Shajara soon came to love and trust Mumima and Jalal. Often in the evenings, they invited her to sit with them. They asked her questions about Konya and her childhood and they told her stories from their homeland. She sang songs for them, and in return, they taught her new songs. There was always laughter and companionship.

One day, Shajara answered a knock at the door to find Serine standing there.

"How are you, Shajara? It is good to see you looking so well." Serine offered.

Shajara did not answer her and instead asked after her mother and father. "Thank God, they are both well. I am here to speak to Mumima about something urgent. Is she home?"

"Yes, of course, come this way." Shajara led her into the courtyard where there was still plenty of shade from the midday sun.

"I will tell her you are here." Shajara ran to find Mumima.

"Oh dear," Mumima sighed when Shajara informed her of her previous mistress's arrival. "I suspect she will want to hear more of the Mongols."

It was not the first time that Shajara had heard the word 'Mongol' or the whispered stories of the horror they were spreading across the world.

"But why has she come to you?"

"Because, my dear, it was the threat of Mongols that had us move before and now they are rapidly approaching the Sultanate of Rum. Naturally, people think we know something that they don't." This was the first time that Shajara had heard that the Mongols might be threatening Konya!

While bringing fruit flavoured waters on a tray for the two ladies, Shajara overheard Mumima confirm the threat to Serine. "Those heathens slaughter all, both those who resist and those who surrender," she said. "In the east, where we once lived, when they took a city, they would drive all its inhabitants out onto the plain. There, each Mongol warrior must execute a given number of captives until all are dead. They don't leave a soul alive – even the dogs and cats are slaughtered. The plains in our homeland are littered with skulls and skeletons, and the earth red from blood." Shajara stood stock still, frozen with fear.

"These heathens are a monstrous threat," Serine agreed with a sigh of despair. "There was a pause in their attacks when Genghis Khan died, but now his successor is turning his attention to the West and we will be under attack soon! God help us Mumima," and she reached out a hand to hold her friends! Shajara remained still holding the tray when she felt a hand on her shoulder. It was Jalal, he had also overheard the women's fears from inside his study.

"We fear these men for the wrong reasons," he said. "Perhaps, as people say, they are great horsemen and can fight with bow and arrow as they ride. Perhaps, as is also said, their use of Chinese gunpowder is a skill we have not yet fully mastered. But their most powerful weapon is terror. They litter the plains with skulls for a reason: it is to fill us all with fear and foreboding. To beat them, we need courage and, then, we need to outwit them. Courage and cunning can conquer every foe."

"But don't you worry? You have had to move so many times before because of the Mongols, maybe you will have to leave again?" As much as Jalal's advice had made sense, Shajara could not help feeling the panic of a possible Mongol invasion to Konya, or her new masters leaving the city without her.

"I will move if I want to, not because fear dictates me to do so." Jalal shrugged his shoulders. He studied Shajara's face for a moment. "You do not fear the Mongols. You fear change. You must understand that change is something you must learn to embrace, for we are changing every moment."

Shajara lay on her mat that night and repeated Jalal's words over and over. Courage and cunning can conquer every foe. She remembered with shame her lack of courage on the day she had come to work and vowed that in the future she would be a braver and a more cunning woman.

The next day, Shajara was sweeping the room where Jalal worked. He was holding a penknife with a glinting blade and she could see that it was very sharp. There was a bronze inlay of vines twisted around the wooden handle and Shajara came closer to admire it.

Suddenly aware that he was being watched, Jalal laid the knife down carefully and opened the first drawer of his desk. He pulled out a little cloth bag and slowly untied the knot which held the bag together. He smiled at Shajara, beckoned her to come closer and slowly opened the bag. Shajara was expecting something glorious – what a ceremony he was making of it – perhaps jewels, perhaps an ivory carving or a set of Jade prayer beads! But when she saw what was lying in the soft fabric, she could not contain her disappointment. "But they're just wooden sticks!" Jalal laughed heartily.

"Well, not exactly." He picked up the darkest stick which was a reddish brown and handed it to Shajara. It was a little longer than her outstretched hand and about the same width as her forefinger. It was a cane, not wood, its end was black. Jalal took the cane back from her. "This is one of my favourites. It comes from the banks of the river which runs through Dezful, a town not so far from where I grew up. It's not too brittle, but not too soft either." He took the knife and with a long hard stroke, shaved off the end that had most of the black on it.

"And this one comes from China. Imagine that, Shajara! Just one small cane among millions growing in China and it came all the way to Konya to make something for you today!"

"Make something for me?" Shajara owned nothing but her mat, her clothes and her scarf. No one had given her a gift before. Her father had given her many bouquets of flowers, and her mother had made her many wonderful things to eat, but she had only their memories now.

"Yes, and I'll tell you why after we've created it." Jalal pulled a piece of paper from the pile of papers that stayed always on hand at his desk.

"Can you feel the power this paper carries, Shajara?" She shook her head. Jalal waved his hands over the paper as if to perform a magic trick. "It has the power to be almost anything…it is of *our* choosing."

Shajara wrinkled her brow and tilted her head to the side. She eyed the yellowed and slightly creased paper with wonder and doubt.

"For example, we could turn this paper into a poem with a few words. We could make it a painting with a few strokes of colour. We could fold it into a boat with a few simple creases. We could cut it into the shape of a snowflake with a few snips of my scissors."

"Let's see." He eyed her thoughtfully. "What's your favourite animal, Shajara?" She had always admired birds best of all and told him so. Jalal smiled as if he already knew, but he asked her why.

"Because they sing beautifully, they're graceful, and they can take flight and go where they will!"

He reached for his cane pen, dipped it into black liquid, and with a long, slow, squeaking movement, drew what Shajara recognised as the Arabic letter *Beh*. He stopped briefly to re-dip his pen in the inkpot and then with more squeaking as the cane moved slowly along the paper the letter *Seen* began to emerge. Another dip into the bottle and Jalal's pen continued upwards and Shajara was shocked to see that the letter was forming the outline of a bird's body. Next, the letter *Mim* became the birds' eye. She knew from her Arabic studies that *Beh, Seen, Mim* were the letters that started *Bismallah Ir Rahman Ir Rahim* or In the Name of Allah, the Most Compassionate the most Beneficent, and that these words started every chapter bar one in the Quran. The Rahman and the Rahim became the bird's wings and the letters Alif and Lam became the bird's legs. She could not believe how quickly and how simply Jalal had been able to create something so beautiful and so full of meaning.

He blew on the ink to help it dry and then handed it to Shajara. "I want you to know that you too are like this piece of paper. You have the power to be whatever it is you choose to be!" She stared at the still glistening black ink as she tried to understand his words.

"You are also like the bird. You were born with wings, Shajara, why not fly?" He laughed at Shajara's face. "No? You don't think you have wings? Maybe you just haven't learned to fly yet…but there's a reason I'm giving you

25

this, Shajara. I want you to keep it to remember me and my mother. For we're leaving on a journey, and you will not be able to come. We don't know exactly when we will be back, but it may be as many as three months. This paper will help you remember us. My mother says that in the meantime, you are to go back to Osman Balabar and your parents."

"Where are you going? Why are you leaving? Why can't I come with you?" Shajara blurted out.

Jalal smiled. "All this from the girl who did not want to come work here?" But he did not answer her questions. "Don't worry, we'll be back."

"Remember," he told her, "you were not born to seek safety and comfort, but to fly, to dance, to sing and to live courageously. One of these days, *Inshallah*, (God willing) you will go on a much longer journey than the two streets you walked to our house. You will spread your wings and fly!"

"But are you leaving because of the Mongols?" Shajara tried to steady her voice.

"No, I am going to Damascus to study, and my mother is coming to see the famous Mosque there; we will return in a few short months."

᪥

Chapter 6
A Gift

Serine was sure Mumima would return to employ Shajara again, but months went by and there was no word of Mumima or Jalal. Meanwhile, Abbas had insisted that Shajara attend tutorials and study with him! Serine's worries grew. What if Mumima and Jalal never came back?

Serine was so busy with the house, children and her social duties that she had little time for her husband's flourishing trading business. In the evenings, Osman often came home tired and after dinner, he would tuck himself away in his study with tea and biscuits. But recently, Serine had become aware that Osman was unusually excited by a business deal with a certain Rasheed.

Osman had travelled to many foreign lands, even as far as the Kingdom of Sicily, and he had built a reputation as the most reliable and experienced trader in all of Konya. It was widely known, too, that he could provide large quantities of dried apricots, refined sugar, the best quality Konya-ware pottery and other local crafts and that he had access to a major source of alum, an important ingredient for dyeing wool. When Rasheed first approached him, Osman thought it would be for only a small consignment.

Then Rasheed revealed that he was an agent of the Caliph of Baghdad himself and offered to help trade the goods from Konya in exchange for the glass and silks of Baghdad. Osman told his wife it could be the deal of a lifetime that would begin a lucrative annual trade with the world's most important city.

Osman set about stocking up wares for the journey to Baghdad and recruiting camel drivers. His warehouses were filled to bursting and the courtyard of the house stacked with bales and packages ready to load on the camels.

Then one evening, Osman came home with the astonishing news that Rasheed had promised to arrange a meeting for him with the Caliph himself. He begged Serine to think carefully about a gift for the Caliph, for no merchant could be received in court without offering something very special to the great ruler. His caravan was almost ready to go, but he needed a gift that would please the Caliph so well that all future business between Konya and Baghdad would fall into the hands of Osman Balabar the Trader. He stroked his beard, long and mostly grey, and his tired eyes met his wife's.

"You're a clever woman and I'm sure you can think of something. This is very important to me and it's important to our family. Think of all the opportunities this could bring for us! Our sons will meet only the very finest of Konya's young women! Our future will be bright with many grandchildren!"

Suddenly, Serine saw she might have a solution to her problem with Shajara. The girl was clever; she could sing and dance and was undoubtedly the most beautiful girl in Konya. She would make the perfect gift. She was still a slave and the Caliph's harem was filled with the world's most beautiful and talented women, many brought as gifts, some from as far away as China. There was no more special gift in all Konya than Shajara.

Serine knew that some girls with talent were trained as singers or dancers in the harem, while clever girls were schooled in reciting poetry and Quran all were taught fine manners. They were fed sumptuous fruits and delicacies; there were fine gardens in which to spend their days, and in the evening, they settled down in the galleries above the Caliph's court to enjoy the same entertainment as the Caliph himself.

Serine had heard that Baghdad was the cultural centre of the whole world, the greatest place of learning and the arts. She told herself that this was a good thing. God bless this opportunity.

Serine sensed that Osman might be reluctant to send Shajara away. She had no such hesitations and told herself that it would be a blessing for a girl who had shown aptitude for learning with Abbas. Shajara's voice, already beautiful, might be further trained and she might be taught intricate dances. Embroidery and etiquette would add to her accomplishments. Shajara would no longer be a slave born to slaves in the household of a trader. She would be among the most envied women in the world!

In these ways, Serine persuaded herself that she was doing Shajara a great favour. She tried to keep from her conscience the reputation of the harem as a place of backbiting competition. She knew the stories in which the Caliph's mother and sisters tyrannised over the other women and the tales of brutal servants whose favour the women had to win. Serine told herself that Shajara would surely win favour and survive all the dangers of harem life.

Besides, Shajara's parents would be happy to know their daughter would not be working as a cleaner for the rest of her life. Shajara would no longer threaten to bewitch one of her sons. It was an ideal solution!

At first, Serine said none of these things to Osman, for these were harsh realities she feared her husband might not understand. He must be slowly led to realise that her solution was best. "My loved one, this is truly a dilemma. If you bring the wrong gift surely you will lose all future business." She paused and watched her husband's brow furrow more deeply. "It must be a gift to outshine all others." Again, she paused as she saw her husband's agitation growing. "The Caliph already owns the world's most beautiful things. He will surely just toss aside any pretty bauble, or it might even offend him! No, it will have to be something that will continue to give him pleasure as time wears on." Osman stirred uneasily. *Hmmm, I wonder,* Serine pondered dramatically.

"What? Did you think of something?" Osman roughly pushed the bowl of grapes from his lap and sat forward searching his wife's face for clues. "You've thought of something special! I can see it in your eyes! Tell me, my love!"

"Well no, I'm not sure if it is a good idea." She played her husband for a few moments longer, "Although…perhaps?" Osman was on the edge of his seat. "Tell me!"

"Yes, I do and it's one of the most beautiful things he will see and it's likely to get more beautiful with time. But Osman, it will make my life much more difficult here. You see, my dear, you must take Shajara to be your special gift to the Caliph."

Osman sat still as the idea of bringing his slave as a gift sank in. He didn't doubt for a moment that Shajara would please the Caliph, but he saw her as an excellent servant and did not like to give away the girl who he had seen grow up in his house. What would be the consequences of giving away Musa and Rehan's only child? They had been so sorrowful when she went to work with Mumima and he felt guilty to cause such loyal servants such pain. Things in his house ran smoothly when the servants were happy. How would he explain such a decision to them?

Yet, when Serine began to expound on the dangers to their sons, he sighed and agreed. He gave explicit orders to his wife that Shajara's parents must be shown the huge opportunity this would offer their daughter.

29

"You have always had a way with these things, my dearest, please don't be so brutal this time with her. I will only take her if there is a sincere wish on their part."

With this, Serine jumped into action knowing just the things to say to Rehan to make her wish this for her own daughter.

ঌ

Chapter 7
The Caravan

Shajara made her way to the old market where Osman was already busily organising his caravan. All her life Shajara had seen camels in the streets of Konya. Yet, she regarded the huge creatures with some distrust. Some people said that camels are bad tempered and can spit, bite and kick. Shajara had been quick to believe it. Osman, however, said that all his camels were mild in temper and gentle. He praised their milk as nourishing and sweet. He said it was the men who drove the camels who would spit in bad temper. Nevertheless, Shajara thought she saw in their haughty eyes a kind of contempt for people. She much preferred to walk.

In any case, there were no camels to ride, for each camel in the caravan would be burdened down with a huge package of Osman's goods. Osman and his caravan master would be the only riders, and his mount was not a camel but a piebald horse.

There were noises of angry men gruffly calling to each other, the snorting and grunting of the camels, the air pungent with strong smells. It was sheer chaos! Shajara caught sight of Osman talking with a burly heavily bearded man. He was the manager of the caravan, Osman's deputy and known to everyone as Mohammed Eye-for-Eye. All the men gave him great deference and Osman consulted him closely on all matters affecting the journey.

"Eye for Eye, please greet our most precious commodity, our gift to the Caliph, Shajara al Durr."

Mohamed Eye for Eye unused to dealing with young women offered her a quick *'Salam Alaykum'* and before Shajara could make the polite response, Eye for Eye barked out to a boy to come quickly.

"Faris! Come here!" A teenage boy raised his head from his task of winding thick rope around a large tether. Mohamed Eye for Eye took Shajara by her shoulder and pushed her towards the boy. "This is Shajara al Durr, keep her safe *and* out of trouble. She is the caravan's gift to the Caliph."

"Welcome, Shajara al Durr! I am happy to meet you. I'm Mohamed Eye for Eye's son." He looked straight at her when he spoke, and she couldn't help but smile when he smiled at her. She was a bit taken back upon hearing the connection to Mohamed Eye for Eye – as there couldn't be a more unlikely father and son combination. Mohamed was rough around the edges, but Faris was gentle. His face was also soft and hair free, quite the opposite to his father's long and heavy black beard. Faris was handsome with lovely large brown eyes shaded with long, black eyelashes. He was tall like his father, but much slimmer and hadn't the muscular strength of his father. The cloth that was wrapped around his head was a light blue, and Shajara presumed it was from the same cloth of his father's turban. At his waist was a small dagger, which Shajara noted must be very important to Faris as he rested his hand on it often and played around with it proudly.

Faris immediately started showing her around. "There will be several camel lines in the caravan, each with no more than 18 camels." He pointed to the camels that were already forming lines. "Osman Balabar has a mid-size caravan which is composed of almost 200 camels!" He walked on pointing to the men at the front of the lines. "Each of the lines will be led by a camel 'puller', and his job is to keep the first camel in the line moving at about the pace of a man walking, neither too quickly nor too slowly."

"In Osman's caravan, there are twelve pullers and each puller is an expert on camels, not only camels in general, but all the camels in his line. They all have names, and he looks after them." He pointed to a nearby puller who smiled at him and slapped Faris hard on the back. He teasingly nodded towards Shajara and then winked. Faris bashfully pretended not to notice the puller's jibe.

"This is Hussein, Shajara. Shajara al Durr is the gift to the caliph and Osman Balabar has put me in charge of looking after her." He puffed out his chest very slightly.

"Hello," Shajara greeted Hussein. "Can you tell me more about the camel line?"

Hussein was happy to oblige Shajara and was prone to a bit of showing off.

"Well, pretty girl, it's like this…we are the backbone of the caravan. We look after the camels, and if the camels get sick, or lame, or uncooperative, then everyone suffers and is at risk of losing money or investment. We know all the diseases from which a camel can suffer; the poisonous plants that must be avoided; where, when and for how long camels should be left to graze; when not to let a camel drink too much water and so forth. We also know the age and health, the problems and habits, even the personalities of each camel in our line. No one knows more about camels than we do." He winked again and gave her a toothless grin.

Shajara was fascinated. She could feel the energy pulsating as final preparations were made for setting out. There was so much shouting, and she made sure to stay very close to Faris. She was so eager to learn as much as she could. As Hussein started to fuss over the lead camel, Shajara asked him, "Excuse me, Hussein, what is his name?" Shajara indicated towards the camel.

"SHE," he corrected, "is called Halva, and she is my star girl." He gave her an affectionate rub on her neck. "Would you like to meet this pretty girl, Halva?" Shajara smiled at the camel's name. Halva was one of Shajara's favourite desserts, a simple dish made of sesame flour and honey sometimes with a sprinkle of pistachio.

"She is the same colour as halva" – Shajara noted – "but I hope you named her so because she is so sweet." Shajara was cautiously raising her hand to stroke Halva and turned to Faris. He showed her how Halva would welcome the affection. In fact, Halva moaned a low throaty groan, but did not show any physical objection. "Here," he said handing her a long, brown seedpod. "It's carob, and the camels love it!" Halva already having sniffed out the treat reached out to Shajara's hand. She stroked her neck like Faris did. As Shajara moved her hand over the surprisingly soft fur, she listened to Faris explain that not all the camels in the caravan were owned by Osman. He had rented some for the journey and some of the pullers owned some of the camels in the line they led: Osman would pay the puller for the use of the camel on the journey. Some of the pullers had negotiated with Osman to carry some of their own goods for sale as a fraction of a camel load. In addition, there were several 'walkers' who were joining the caravan for protection on the road to Baghdad and would pay for doing so.

Faris continued to take Shajara around and showed her all that he could. He was slightly taken back by how many questions she asked. He explained to her his duties and told her that he had been on every caravan his father Mohamed Eye for Eye had been on since he was six, which was when his mother had died.

"I am sorry to hear that, Faris," Shajara said. But Faris only shrugged. So, she asked, "Will this caravan travel through any of the Mongol territories?" At this, Faris lit up! It seemed he was not shy to speak of the problem of the Mongols at all. He was about to launch into a story, but was stopped when he realised, they were back to where Osman and Mohamed Eye for Eye were wrapping up last minute details. "I will tell you all I know later! They are the most violent warriors of all the world!!" Shajara was confused at Faris' obvious thrill when it came to the violent conquests of the Mongols.

"So, Shajara," boomed Mohammed Eye-for-Eye, "Don't try loading that pack of yours on any of our camels or it will be thrown off and left behind." Shajara knew that this was a man used to being obeyed, but also one who knew his business.

She asked Faris, "How much food do you need to take for the camels?"

Faris told her that every camel would carry around one-fifth of its pack weight in fodder. "So, as we get nearer to Baghdad, and as the camels have eaten their fodder, the pack gets lighter. And that is as it must be for the camel's tire at the end of a long journey."

"And how much food are we carrying for people?" Shajara enquired.

"Your questions are endless, Shajara!" said Faris smiling and explained. "We have bags of oats, some dried peas, barley and millet flour, together with animal fat. But we will get our meat along the way. We'll buy sheep and goats for roasting. We need to save weight wherever we can. Besides, at some of the roadside inns, which we call 'caravanserais', we can buy fresh bread and sometimes additional fodder for the camels."

The camel grumbled loudly as Faris put the first package on its back. The grumbling continued as he piled on further baggage. Then, suddenly, the camel was silent. "You see," said Faris, "the grumbling has stopped. That's when you know you should load on no more. The camel knows its own strength." Shajara saw this as further evidence that camels are contrary creatures, grumbling when they do not need to and not grumbling when you would expect it. Shajara asked, "Faris, how long will our journey take before we get to Baghdad?" He shrugged, "If we are lucky, 40 days and nights. But we need to return to Konya well before the winter snows. You know how cold it can be here in winter."

"Yes, I know, but" – Shajara stuttered – "I won't be coming back." She lowered her head. She had been using her questions as a way of not focusing on the terrible pain and betrayal she felt from her masters taking her away from her family, and now it was beginning to catch up to her.

Faris sensing her distress immediately put his hand on her shoulder, "Shajara, after seeing the magnificent city of Baghdad, you won't want to come back. Trust me." He winked and smiled at her. There was something about his smile Shajara thought. She found it impossible not to return his smile, even when she felt miserable.

Mohammed Eye-for-Eye shouted for the first line of camels to move out. The caravan was ready to go. Osman climbed onto his horse. Faris gave her another encouraging smile and she threw her pack on her shoulder. Shajara silently hoped her parents would not suffer missing her, and as she walked her first few steps, she could feel a lump in her throat grow. She had promised to write, and Abbas had agreed to read her letters to her parents whenever they wished. He also asked her to send them details of the city. He was very keen to see and know Baghdad, but too frightened of going on a caravan on his own.

Faris looked over at her for a few moments before he asked, "Are you missing someone Shajara…maybe someone you love?" She looked up to see his kind eyes looking worriedly into hers.

"Yes. I am." She wanted to say more but the lump in her throat seemed to be growing.

Faris's smile faded a little and murmured, "I thought so…"

"Hmm," said Faris. "I promise you this – I will help by keeping you company and telling you all my best stories and answering all your questions so you will not be lonely. Come! Walk with me. Have you heard, 'A journey of a thousand miles starts with just one step'?"

He looked at her as she smiled back at him. Quietly, she thanked God for Faris, for she was sure He had sent him to her on this long journey.

&♥

35

Chapter 8
Mongols

They left Konya and set out along the dusty road. An early chill was in the air. Shajara shivered and was glad of the shawl she wrapped around her shoulders. The camels, fresh from their summer grazing, kept up a good pace. Shajara knew some of the fields on the outskirts of Konya; but, soon, they came to places where she had never been, and she looked around with great curiosity.

At mid-day, the caravan halted and rested by the river. The sun was now high in the sky and both the camels and the walkers were feeling the heat. They rested only briefly and ate little, for they had to set out again if they were to reach the caravanserai before nightfall. Faris sat next to Shajara as they unrolled their packed lunch of cucumbers and bread. Shajara also had some tangerines, handed to her that morning by her father. She was happy to share one with Faris. They both laughed as he made a face at the tart juice in his mouth.

"What are you thinking about, Shajara?" Faris asked, "You wouldn't stop asking questions at the marketplace, now you are silent." Shajara smiled. "I'm trying very hard not to think of my parents." The sickening feeling, she had in her stomach when she had first learned of her future as the Caliph's gift came back again.

"Well, I was going to wait till tonight to tell you all I know about Genghis Khan and the Mongols! These stories are best told around a fire when it is dark and cold all around with no city within days travel. But I can tell them to you now, if you like…in order to distract you." Again, she felt warmed by his smile.

"I'm not sure about that," Shajara argued. "I might not be able to sleep if you tell stories about the Mongols."

"That's the point," Faris insisted, "it helps you sleep lightly so that you wake with every bump in the night."

* Surely he means 'heavily'?

"Why would I want to sleep lightly? I'll be exhausted after today's walk, and facing another long day walking tomorrow and every day after for a month or more, I hope I shall sleep very well indeed!" Shajara could not imagine why Faris would want to sleep lightly.

"But then, if we all slept lightly*, who will raise the alarm when bandits attack?" Faris was sorry he had said this so glibly as he saw the colour drain from Shajara's cheeks. He added quickly, "But not tonight as we will be staying at a caravanserai."

Shajara added sarcastically, "For tonight." She looked around them and saw the rising hills in the distance and wondered if there were bandits just waiting for a caravan like theirs to attack. She was beginning to wonder if it was a good idea to walk next to Faris for she remembered Jalal's words about worry and fear and was trying very hard not to waste time with them, but if Faris was going to tell her stories about the Mongols and bandits, ignoring fear was going to be very difficult. She would much rather focus on the beauty of the surroundings. But even she had to admit, that although the scenery was breath-taking, the fact that they were walking, meant the scenery was not changing rapidly. Shajara had exhausted all her questions about the caravan back at the market, and so she relented.

"Okay, then. I know I will regret this but tell me about the Mongols. But try not to make it too awful. Tonight, we have lodging so I would like to sleep well."

Faris laughed. He picked up his pack threw it over his shoulder and offered Shajara his hand to help her up, for his father had risen moments earlier and the caravan was starting to move again. Shajara accepted his hand and was gently pulled to her feet.

"Genghis Khan was the cruellest, bloodiest, cleverest warrior leader ever known, in all history!"

Shajara cut him off, "You sound like you admire him! He was a savage who worshipped animals. Even worse, he took delight in killing! How can you admire someone so truly awful?" Shajara was shocked. Faris seemed like such a kind soul. To admire a man who claimed to have killed 20 million people or more was unfathomable. Shajara thought back to Sabry, a boy with more than his fair share of bloodlust, but even he had the sense to admire men like Salah ad Din, a Muslim, and a kind man who offered his enemies generous terms to avoid further massacre.

37

"Well, yes, in some ways, I do admire him," Faris stated gravely. "In other ways, you are right, he found pleasure in killing, and that is unacceptable. But beside his ruthlessness, one has to admire the fact the he managed to build and expand the world's largest and most powerful empire during his own lifetime. He outsmarted many clever rulers and dynasties. He incorporated strategy in ways that have changed the future of warfare. If what people say is true, and that his successor will now look to take Baghdad, and the Sultanate of Rum, then we will have to defeat him, Shajara, and everyone knows that to defeat your enemy, you must *know* your enemy. Genghis Khan knew that. Before he tried to conquer a land, he sent spies in to learn everything they could about the people, the governing authority, the religion, the stratagem of their battle techniques. He also employed scholars to write down his conquests and spread the word of his greatness, and above all, his ruthlessness."

Shajara pondered these points. She had learned more than most servant girls about battle, war and strategy, from Abbas's teachings and Sabry's love of all fighting. She had understood the chess board as a military game and had learned to play it effectively. But she didn't understand why men and boys loved war so much, and she said so to Faris.

Faris's response was quick. "I don't know why either, Shajara. War affects women just as much as men. Women suffer and die, just like men do in war, often if they survive, they are left heartbroken for their sons or husbands who did not survive. Frankly, it surprises me that women don't take as much interest in it as they should."

This intrigued Shajara. She had been told tales about a woman's cunning or talent, but never when it came to war or the strategy of war. From what Shajara was able to ascertain from her sheltered life in Konya, women were thought to be the property of men, and with that came the acceptance that women's thoughts were not worthy. Many people believed that women were put on this earth to please men and to bear them children. Other than being a dutiful wife or daughter, their opinions on most matters were not given any weight. On a personal level, her own family worked quite differently. Also, within her religion, Shajara had been taught that the Prophet had brought rights to women which had not existed before – by instituting rights of property ownership, inheritance, education and divorce, trying to give women basic safeguards – but Shajara knew that many times, these were overlooked by men. Faris seemed to understand that a woman's true value was deeper than her physical external beauty, and Shajara was relieved. She did not know what to say, but of course, he was right. In fact, upon reflection, it was often that women suffered more than men. One more injustice in the world!

"You are right, Faris. Women do suffer, just as much as men. I think that war frightens me, and so I do not like to think of it. But perhaps if more women thought of war, and discussed it, then maybe it could be avoided."

"You should know, Shajara, that one of Genghis Khan's most trusted advisors was his own mother!" And so, Faris continued to tell Shajara all he knew about the fascinating Genghis Khan. Shajara listened attentively and was grateful that not too many violent details were discussed. Although she did think that Faris would have liked to add them, but for her sake, and that of a good night's sleep, he avoided them.

The sun was just tipping below the horizon as they came up to a large square building. The walls of the caravanserai were more than twice as tall as a man. A single gate, just wide enough to admit one heavily laden camel, led into a great courtyard open to the sky. The chief purpose of buildings such as this was to secure the caravan, both camels and people, from bandits. Neither the Sultan of Rum in Konya nor the Caliph of Baghdad had managed to put an end to the scourge of bandits; but caravanserais placed at regular distances along the main roads, provided protection for trade. This caravanserai had been built by the Sultan of Rum to encourage commerce in his realm, and traders like Osman Balabar took advantage of these safe havens.

Around the walls on three sides of the caravanserai were camel stalls. Along the fourth wall were chambers for the merchants and a shop that was selling bread together with cloth and ornaments. Some of the independent traders from the caravan approached the shopkeeper to see if they could sell them their wares. If they saw something they wanted in the shop, they would wait to buy it on the return journey.

Shajara offered to help the pullers unload the bales from each camel. They did so carefully, for the camels had molted over the summer and the skin was no longer protected by dense camel hair. It could be a disaster if a camel developed pack sores and could no longer carry its bale. Next, they helped the pullers lead the camels to be watered, watching carefully to see that the thirsty animals drank only the right amount. Only when the pullers had attended in these ways to the camels did they think of themselves.

The Cook was busy. First, he served Osman and Mohammed Eye-for-Eye. Then, the walkers who had paid to share in the costs of the caravan. Then, the pullers, beginning with those who owned their own lines, Faris and Shajara ate with the pullers. They sat by the fire at the centre of the courtyard. Mohammed Eye-for-Eye, although he had his own chamber, joined them for a while. After listening to everything they had to say, he turned to Shajara. "Master Osman tells me you can sing." He smirked. "So, let us be the judge if you sing as well as your master says!"

Shajara was nervous in front of them, but she saw Faris and his friendly smile and was encouraged by her friend to stand up. She was at a loss to think of a song that would suit the occasion. She looked up to the night sky where the moon was showing from behind a cloud. Her mind was suddenly made up: it would be one of her mother's favourites, a song that always brought tears to her father's eyes. The song told of a traveller, lost in a distant land, who looked to the stars for guidance and was led back to his home by the light of the moon. She put all her nervousness into the song itself and its tune carried away her fears.

The men listened quietly. She finished to applause and they demanded she sing it again. Then they wanted another song, but Mohamed Eye for Eye called an end to the entertainment. "You sing beautifully," he told her. "There are many nights on the road before we get to Baghdad, I expect you to sing for us again." With that, he strode away to his chamber. Shajara, now alone, headed to her appointed room wondering whether she would dream of brutal Mongols. She barely had enough energy to wash and was asleep before a single thought passed through her head.

෬

Chapter 9
An Eye for an Eye

Shajara woke the next morning with the call to prayer. It was rather a meagre call, and she presumed it was not from a professional caller. She knew there was a room in the Caravanserai used for prayer, but it was small and neglected. The caller was possibly also a stable boy, for he certainly had not boomed out his call to prayer like the callers in Konya. Moments later, her musings were confirmed as she heard jibes made about the caller. A rough voice called, "Are you calling men or sheep to prayer?" Laughter could be heard among the men.

Another man called out, "I think the sheep can do a better call to prayer than that!" Shajara could not help but giggle. She flung the thin, woollen blanket off her and started to move quickly – partly to shake off the dawn's cold, and the other to pray and be down to help, for she wanted to be helpful and earn the approval of Osman and Mohamed Eye for Eye. Not many people like to be told what to do, or how to behave, but for a slave, and particularly a slave born into slavery, it was all there was. But since the beginning of the caravan, every time she spotted Osman, she saw him scowling and worried, which was to be expected. There was a lot of risk with a caravan and tempers were high, so she planned to stay away from it, as much as possible.

As the caravan was starting to move, Shajara looked to find her companion. She was turning her head and searching as she walked. Perhaps Faris had already moved out with his father. Maybe he preferred the company of the men of the caravan. Shajara thought about the lonely hours that would pass walking on her own. The landscape ahead of her was littered with small stones and many smaller stones had not been cleared and she felt them under her tattered leather shoes. There were mountains in the far distance, and she wondered whether their long road ahead would lead them there. As she looked ahead, she spotted Faris, his hand resting on his dagger neatly tucked into the tie at his waist. He was grinning, his head cocked and his eyebrow raised above his kind, brown eyes. He walked towards her. "Were you looking for me?" His eyebrow teased her as it raised even higher. She blushed as she nodded her head.

"Good," he said, "I've been looking for you too! You will never guess what I saw this morning!" His eyes bulging with amazement. "My father woke me before sunrise to tell me there was something disturbing the camels. When we went to investigate, we found nothing, but I heard something from outside the walls. I went up the staircase to the top of the walls, where the lookout stands are, and pacing up and down outside the walls of the caravanserai was a leopard!"

Shajara gasped. "Tell me, what was it like?"

"He was wild, magnificent, angry, frustrated and hungry!" Faris laughed. "Leopards hunt at night, and perhaps the smell of the camels or sheep was driving it mad, for it was pacing up and down yowling. He was much larger than I have ever seen before!"

Surprised, Shajara asked, "You have seen more than one?"

"Oh sure," Faris shrugged, "but only when we have been sleeping outdoors and then I was only ever able to see its yellow eyes and a rough outline. This morning, the sun was just starting to rise, and I was able to see its colours and teeth when it snarled!"

Shajara made a mental note that she needed to add leopards to her list of things to be wary of when sleeping outside the safety of the caravanserais. Everywhere, Shajara turned seemed to be new and fantastic aspects of life *and death*. She thought back to the safety of her home and thought of her daily routine. She still missed her parents, but with every passing hour, she realised she was learning about life by living it. It was dangerous and frightening at times, but also thrilling. She began to understand what Jalal was trying to explain to her.

Faris continued with details of his morning sighting until Mohamed Eye for Eye's loud booming voice could be heard echoing over the long caravan. He was giving a puller a very hard time, and although Shajara could not hear the words exactly, everyone could understand that he was angry. Shajara said, "Your father is a hard man to please."

Faris gave a low throaty chuckle. "You don't know the half of it! He's a perfectionist and it really upsets him that few share his high standards. He also has only one way of doing things and that's *his* way. Any other way is the wrong way." Faris paused. "Mind you, he's usually right. He says my mother was the only person who understood him and could calm him down. Since she died, whenever he gets in a fury, he usually stays there for a while." Sorrow spread across his face. "I know you miss your parents, Shajara, and maybe there's even someone else you left behind?" His eyebrow raised with the insinuation.

"You are very wise, Faris, and nosy!" Faris looked bashful but she was not ashamed to answer him. "No, I have no one else besides my family and a few friends to miss, and I think that is painful enough. You realise I am a slave? I am not free like you. Even my heart cannot belong to another. I belong to Master Osman and it is his choosing to give me to someone else. It is unlikely I will ever be free."

The smile dropped from Faris's face and his fists clenched tight. A dry wind brought leaves swirling in front of them. She did not want his pity, nor did she want him to feel that she was unhappy. She was a slave, so why dream of freedom? It was unattainable and would only make her unhappy.

As the landscape started to change, she asked, "Can people survive the desert without the help of the caravan?"

Faris eyed her carefully. She continued, "I mean if someone was on their own? Got lost or thrown off? Could they survive?" Now Faris looked worried, "You aren't thinking of running away, are you?" His eyes scanned her face for clues. "Because if you are," he started, "I can tell you right now, you won't last more than a day or two once we get into the desert." Shajara opened her mouth to say that she had no such idea of leaving, but Faris continued, "Look, Shajara," he turned around to make sure no one could hear and spoke in a hushed tone. "I know that you must not like the idea of going into the Sultan's harem." His eyes met Shajara's. "I know you miss your parents, but it is possible you will have a good life there. But if you are set on leaving the caravan" – he paused and sighed – "then I will help you."

She was touched by Faris's obvious care. She knew the name Faris in Arabic meant valiant horseman – a man who showed courage, devotion and valour. But often names were given to those whose character was at odds with their meaning. Shajara knew of fools named Akeem (Arabic for wisdom) and the thief in Konya who lost his hand was named Abdul Muqsit (slave to the just) but Faris embodied the meaning of his name completely. Her second thought surprised her – she began to wonder whether in fact she *should* run away. She had never imagined it to be a possibility. But why not? She could find work as a servant. Or perhaps as a cook, a dancer…

Faris's hands were still holding her shoulders, and as the thoughts raced through her head, he gave her a little shake. She looked into his worried eyes and smiled. "Thank you, Faris." But she did not wish for him to get into trouble, and she could imagine what Osman and Mohamed Eye for Eye would think of his actions!

They started walking again. His brow furrowed as he spoke to her in a whisper. "I have some money saved up; I will give it to you. When we reach Damascus, I will give you a map which will take you to my aunt's house. If you explain to her that I sent you, she will help you. She is my mother's sister and has always told me she will help me however she can. She is married to a man who works for the city government; he is influential and can help you find work. I will come to you on the return from Baghdad."

Shajara tried to make sense of the new option open to her. Faris was offering her an escape and previously she thought only of duty and servitude, now she felt like throwing it all away and running away...with Faris. It was a dream, but deep down she knew it could not be. Shajara touched Faris's arm. "Thank you Faris, that really means a lot to me, but I am not going to run away. I will not let Master Osman down. If I did, it would be at the cost of my parent's happiness. They would be the ones to feel the wrath of Master Osman when he returned, and they would feel ashamed. And if I ran away, I would not be able to send them letters, as I promised I would. It is simply not an option for me. But I am truly grateful for your kind offer."

Faris's face strained with the effort not to look disappointed. "So you do not mind being given to the Caliph?" He flinched visibly, as the idea certainly bothered him.

"I am a little worried about what will be expected of me. I have heard stories about the women of the Harem and not all of it has been positive." Shajara felt uncomfortable discussing her feelings with Faris. She was a slave, what did her feelings matter? It was as Rehan said, she should count herself lucky. What right did she have to dream of a life where she could fall in love with a man, marry and have children? It was only a dream. That was her only right – to dream. But here was a kind boy willing to take her away from her slave status and help her build a free life. Did she deserve less? Although these thoughts danced in her head, she told Faris, "This could be a good opportunity for me too. I will put my trust in God and see what will happen."

For the next few hours, Faris and Shajara exchanged stories about what they had heard about the Sultan and the Harem. And several hours later, as they walked into their next caravanserai, they both felt as though the day had passed too quickly. They did not feel as the others did – dusty and exhausted, but quite ready to unpack and set up for the evening. That evening as all were resting around the fire, Shajara asked Faris, "Could you please tell me how your father came to be known as Eye for Eye. I have tried to look for clues, but it's clear that he sees very well out of both."

Some heads turned to Faris eager to hear more about the fearful man who ran the caravan. Faris knew the story by heart and, since some of the pullers were new, he told it to them all as the fire burned down. As he told the story, all could see the son's pride in his father.

"Many years ago, before my father was leader of a caravan, he went as a puller in a large caravan. He had worked very hard and over many years saved enough money to buy his own camel. The camel, though, was old and blind in one eye, as that was all he could afford. When it became lame, he had to leave the caravan and wait for its blisters to heal. There was no caravanserai and he had to stay by the side of the road on his own with his camel.

"That night, two soldiers of the Sultan came along in the dark. The soldiers were no better than bandits. They accused my father of stealing his camel and threatened to enforce the punishment for stealing there and then. 'An eye for an eye,' they told him.

"Under our law, as we all know, a thief is subject to the principle of an eye for an eye, and the thief's hand can be cut off as penalty for theft. What could my father do? He could only say, *La Hawla wa la quwwata illa Billah*, there is no power or strength except in Allah.

"My father persuaded them not to cut his hand and that they should take his camel but leave him to go on his way.

"The soldiers agreed. It was dark and they failed to see that his camel was lame and half-blind. As my father went off, the soldiers tethered their own camels next to his and lay down to sleep.

"My father, as you all know, is neither a fool nor a coward. He went only a little way before silently returning a few hours later. The soldiers were sleeping, as my father crept up. He quietly took one of their camels but left his own.

"The next day, to everyone's astonishment, he caught up with the caravan that had left him behind. By what magic, they wanted to know, had an old, lame, half-blind creature been changed into one that was young, fit and had both of its eyes?

"My father told them: 'It is simply a question of an eye for an eye'.

"And that is how he came to be known as Mohammed Eye-for-Eye."

෨

Chapter 10
Delays

The tenth day was one of troubles and a near disaster.

First, they were held up by an accident on the road. A camel lost its footing at the edge of the road, slipped and fell. Its puller had been injured as the camel fell. Mohamed Eye for Eye galloped on horseback to the accident. The camel had scraped its skin so badly on a jutted rock that the bone could be seen. The camel had awkwardly stood up again and remained standing. Blood was gushing from the wound, but already there was someone attending to the wound, applying a paste and bandaging the leg. The puller's injuries were not so apparent. He complained about his knee and said he was not sure if he could walk. Mohamed Eye for Eye told him to stand up and he obeyed. The puller managed a few steps, albeit with a look of suffering on his face. Mohamed Eye for Eye stared at the puller for a moment, and then said, "You have two options: you can walk with us or stay behind. The choice is yours. But make it quickly; we have wasted enough time on your idiocy."

The puller aghast, blurted "*My* idiocy? It was the camel that fell!" pointing lamely at the stoic camel who was standing with its enormous load and bandaged leg.

Mohamed Eye for Eye without a second's pause barked back, "Yes! And you are meant to lead him away from jagged rocks that are clearly in the path." He drew his sword, its blade glinting in the sun; there were a few sharp intakes of breath. Shajara held her breath as she saw the blade come swiftly down on its mark – the stone. The metallic twang was a relief to those who suspected the puller's head to be the mark. "This is on the path that over fifty camels and their pullers have already trodden and managed to avoid. It is an idiot that cannot see that great boulder! Now give me your answer quickly before I dock more of your wages!"

Shock and fear passed over the puller's face. He swallowed visibly, and mumbled, "I will walk."

Mohamed Eye for Eye looked at Faris and yelled, "Redistribute a few packs onto other camels for today. Be sure to check its wounds tonight." And with that, he kicked his heels into the sides of his horse and was off to give the news to Osman. That was one delay, and it cost them over an hour.

The next delay came about when they found an old woman sitting in distress by the road. She was saying over and over, "We are from God to whom we are returning." It was obvious that the woman had somewhat lost her mind and had wandered from her village. She was confused.

Osman leapt from his horse to tend to her. Osman told her, "We will take you to your home." The village was back on the road they had already travelled. Osman was a good and pious man and knew that his family, work and everything that had come to him deserved his gratitude to the Creator. He commanded that the caravan wait while Osman took the woman back to her village on horseback, and that he would return shortly. He kindly put the old woman on the back of his horse, and as he galloped past, she proudly waved.

For every minute that passed, Mohamed Eye for Eye became more agitated. He looked repeatedly into the sky to check where the sun was, and each time cursed more loudly. He rode up to Faris and Shajara and dismounted. His stallion looked as annoyed as he did and its powerful head moved forcibly up and down, its neck wet with sweat. Mohamed Eye for Eye pulled on his beard, "Osman is an idiot, and we will be lucky if we survive his...his *charity*." He wanted his distaste for Osman's actions to be as clear so to underscore his anger, he turned and spat. Shajara stared at Mohamed Eye for Eye not comprehending his anger. Her master was doing his duty as a good Muslim, and her ire grew when she saw that Faris, in complete agreement with his father, was shaking his head over Osman's actions.

"We are like a wounded animal standing here, and I won't let the falcons start to circle!" Thinking more clearly after offloading his frustration, Mohamed Eye for Eye remounted his stallion, shouted orders for the caravan to start moving without Osman and galloped away.

She turned to Faris. "What?! What was my Master supposed to do? Was he supposed to leave that poor old woman?" She did not wait for his answer. "It would be the death of her. Does your father agree to that?" There was only a moment's pause before she continued her harangue, "Where is his sense of obligation?"

Faris knew Shajara was upset. He was also upset with his father, but for quite a different reason. He knew his father to be a man who could not control his temper very well. He had come over to them to vent his frustrations. Faris moved closer to Shajara so he could explain. He knew he would have to tread carefully.

Faris had been aware of Shajara's beauty from the moment he laid eyes on her. But it was now, less than a fortnight later, that her external beauty paled against her other traits – honesty, intelligence, kindness and piety. But now, she looked fierce with outrage. She looked at him daring him to speak out in defence of his father. Her green eyes were dazzling like jewels in firelight, her nostrils slightly flared and her hands were on her hips. Faris felt he might be less threatened by a coiled snake ready to strike!

But he wanted to explain and to apologise for his father. "It's just that we are in a bad place in our journey. Today was the longest stretch to reach the caravanserai. We had easily 10 more kilometres to cover today than all our other days so far. That's why we started out before dawn. And now with these delays…"

"So we should just leave helpless women to die on the roadside so we can save ourselves from *delay*?" retorted Shajara.

Faris had plenty of patience, and that was what it would take to calm Shajara. "It's not quite so simple, Shajara. Because today we have the longest road to travel, so it's also the most dangerous. Bandits know that. They know that often caravans can't make it to the next caravanserai before dark and must camp on the side of the road. And now there's been reports of Mongol attacks. They are pushing further into the Sultanate. They are ruthless as you know, Shajara. My father's actions may seem cruel, but Osman was foolish. There were other options open to us – we could have taken that old woman to the caravanserai with us and asked or paid someone to take her back. But now we will probably have to camp under the stars tonight." Faris could feel the shift in Shajara's mood. He could see it in her eyes too. He had not wanted to frighten her, but he knew the risks of Osman's actions.

"I'm sorry, Shajara. I said too much. I did not want to frighten you. My father sees it as his obligation to keep all of us alive, and all our goods – our livelihood safe too. He was wrong to have come and called Osman an idiot, though." Faris cautioned a slow smile.

Shajara was embarrassed that she had allowed her anger to get the best of her. She had turned on Faris, her only true friend on this caravan and raised her voice to him. "No, Faris, it is I who am sorry. I judged your father and you too, without knowing all the facts. He is in charge of keeping us all safe, and that must be a huge responsibility."

And so they walked on, silently thinking to themselves what would become of them sleeping on the side of the road.

The result was that night fell before they could reach the next caravanserai. It was a dark night with only a sliver of the young moon showing. Master Osman had caught up with the caravan. He did not seem to notice that they had been moving. No angry words were spoken between Osman and Mohamed Eye for Eye, for they both seemed to understand why the other had done what he needed to do.

It was indeed the worst possible day to have been delayed. The moon was only a crescent, the clouds were heavy in the sky. The stars were invisible, making the road to the safety of their caravanserai ever more uncertain. There had been general agreement that the caravan would continue to move, no matter how slowly or how precarious the path was, as it would simply be more dangerous to camp.

Abdul Hamid was leader of the guard. He was a trusted man of Mohamed Eye for Eye and they had made many treks and caravans together. Abdul Hamid was from Nubia and had different methods and ideas, but over time, they had become very close friends. Abdul Hamid was black, tall and muscular. He didn't say much but when he did, his accent was thick and his voice deeper than any man's she had ever heard before. His dress was also different. Instead of wearing a tunic over baggy trousers, he wore what looked like a long dress. It was black, as was his turban which was wrapped in such a way that it not only covered his head, but had parts swinging low to cover his neck and chin. But the most impressive thing about Abdul Hamid's appearance was the sash around his waist which housed many daggers and swords, some of which were larger than Shajara's entire arm and some blades no bigger than her hand. All of them had impressive hilts and handles and all of them were sharp enough to split hairs. At night, Abdul Hamid did not sit around the fire with the others but sat far enough away to be just beyond the firelight. Faris explained that this was strategic placement for him and his handful of men. No one ever saw him, but everyone could hear what he was doing – long, slow rhythmic sounds of metal against stone could be heard in the night, the sound of blades being sharpened.

Abdul Hamid had scouts up in front and some trailing behind. The caravan was moving closer together for safety. Abdul Hamid had suggested some additional men be taken away from their normal duties and added to his pack of guards. Everyone was told to walk in silence. If all went well, the caravan would arrive at the caravanserai and safety just after midnight.

Just before dusk turned to night, Abdul Hamid came to Faris and Shajara. He pulled out a dagger from his side sash and handed it to Shajara. Its handle was slightly curved, made of bone and inlaid with copper. It was a small and beautiful knife. He held it out to her, motioning her to take it. Her hand moved apprehensively towards the knife. Faris noticing her apprehension tried to intervene, but Abdel Hamid interrupted.

"This is for the Caliph's gift. She must be able to protect herself tonight. I will be too busy if bandits strike." She took the knife. The handle was warm, and she felt a jolt of excitement. Faris again tried to interfere, "But *I* will look after Shajara. No one will hurt her! No one will come near her." Faris was puffed up like a cockerel, outraged that Abdul Hamid should suggest he would not be able to defend her.

Abdul Hamid looked Faris up and down. Faris looked so much smaller now he was standing next to the large Nubian man. He had nowhere near the older man's strength or power, nor skill and experience. And yet, he had so much courage, but Abdul Hamid spoke, calmly but firmly. "Where I come from, we allow our women to speak for themselves. I have seen this girl for many days, she looks agile and strong, she knows her own mind. Let us ask her if she will protect herself?"

They both turned to her. Was Shajara capable of killing a man in her defence? Faris laid his hand gently on her arm, "I will not let anything happen to you, Shajara." His eyes bore deeply into hers and she felt how much he cared for her.

"Yes, yes I will protect myself." The very words seemed to give her additional strength. She felt mighty holding the dagger in her hand.

"Good," Abdel Hamid said. "This was my mother's knife." Both Faris and Shajara took a renewed interest in the knife, wondering what Abdul Hamid's mother was like. "She was stubborn. And strong," he said as if he knew what they had been thinking. Then turned and started to walk away.

Shajara called after him, "It's beautiful. Thank you…is this camel bone?" Shajara ran her finger over the handle, tracing the copper lines.

Without turning around, Abdul Hamed said, "No, my mother told me it was the bone of a man she killed." And with that, Abdul Hamid disappeared into the night.

Faris and Shajara spent a moment straining their eyes to make out his black form in the night. Shajara felt the knife go cold in her hand, as if by magic he had warmed it with his presence and now it was just a cold blade with a dead man's bone lying cold in her hand. Shajara felt something warm in her other hand. It was Faris' hand. The pair looked at each other, eyes popping and mouths agape. Finally, Faris said, "I don't think he was serious, Shajara."

"Oh, I think he was!" and then she erupted into a fit of forbidden giggles. She was stifling them and covering her mouth and her shoulders shook. Faris joined her, tears running down his cheeks with the force of his suppressed laughter. And as they walked along the slow and silent caravan path, their bodies shaking with laughter, the fear of bandits dissipated.

৯৯

Chapter 11
Attacked

As the hours passed, Shajara was eager to feel relief from the constant worry. When would they see the lights of the caravanserai in the distance? Her mind imagined every sound was either butchering Mongols or soulless bandits. Then came the memory of Jalal's soft voice, 'safety never comes from seeking safety'. She took a deep breath and smiled inwardly, happy to remember her friend.

Faris plodded alongside her, walking closer than necessary, offering whispered words of encouragement, and helping her when she stumbled over the rocky path. She could sense the thoughts going through his head were not unlike her own. Mohamed Eye for Eye rode up beside them just before midnight and declared that the caravanserai was under a kilometre away and that he doubted very much whether they would be attacked so close to the caravanserai. Shajara felt hope wash over her.

It was just as Mohamed Eye for Eye said, for within minutes, a faint and distant glow could be seen ahead. Shajara felt the pace pick up. She wondered whether the camels could sense their relief, perhaps even sense the proximity of food, drink and rest, for even they seemed to have a renewed spirit.

The next day, Shajara woke feeling sore in every bone in her body. It was as though fear and worry had feasted on her muscles all through the night. After arriving at the caravanserai, the general agreement had been that sleep was preferred over dinner; and after the chores of unpacking and taking care of the camels, simple bread had been handed out. The camels needed rest, and so they would all sleep late. The night's long quiet walk had made Shajara think much of her parents – remembering the love and support they had given her, missing them more than words could say. She reached for the basin and jug filled with water for her morning's ablutions.

She tried to persuade herself that the morning's prayer would help her feel better, as it often had when she was feeling low. But as she closed her eyes to pray, her mind wandered back to how it had been back home, setting her prayer mat aside her mother's, hearing her father's hushed voice as he prayed.

Although the caravan would be setting out later in the morning, there was still much hustle and bustle down in the courtyard. Other caravans were making preparations to leave, and shop owners were cleaning the area in front of their stalls. There was the smell of baking bread in the air and Shajara felt her stomach awaken with it. As she headed down the stairs that led to the courtyard, she noticed a group of men had stopped talking and were watching her instead. She did not to look at them, as this was the advice given by her mother. It angered her that these types of men never dared to behave like that when there was a male present. They were cowards and bullies and it annoyed her that they were part of this caravan. Master Osman had made it very clear at the start that she was to be protected and respected for she would be the key to whether there might be future trade with the Caliph. As she reached the last step, she heard a vulgar comment.

Shajara felt the heat rise in her cheeks. She had been made to leave her home, her parents, her friends, her city. She had spent the last two weeks walking many kilometres a day. She had been under threat of Mongols and bandits. She had missed dinner the night before. She was emotionally and physically exhausted and the hissing and leering of these men was the last straw. She would not cower and run from these scoundrels today. Now, she turned on her heels to face the men. Her voice was high and shrill, her temper was hot, and her words were spoken with fury, "Do you have no shame? You cannot speak to me like this! Osman Balabar has proclaimed I shall be respected on this caravan. I am not here for your amusement. Men as faithless and feebleminded as you should not call themselves Muslim!"

To question someone's faith was truly a great insult, but Shajara was blinded with fury. In Islam, it was clearly stated that women were intellectual and spiritual equals to men. The Prophet Muhammed whilst giving his famous sermon on the Mount of Mercy in Arafat had reminded Muslim men to treat all women with kindness and respect. And yet, these men had the audacity to pick and choose which parts of their religion they would submit to. But as two of the men made their move towards her, Shajara was reminded that she was just one, and they were four. The look in their eyes was enough to make Shajara understand that her admonishment had only angered them.

Shajara's mind now raced through her options. What would she do now? Would she stand against these men? What would they do to her? She wanted very much to run, but her feet were planted firmly on the ground. She would not beg for mercy; she would not cower. The last thought that raced through her mind before she was struck, was why, if women are intellectually and spiritually equal to men, could they not also be physically equal?

Shajara did not know how much time had passed, but she woke with her face on the ground, and that there was dust in her nostrils, inching down her throat as she gasped for air. There was a strong smell of camel urine mixed with baking bread. And then she felt the pain in her face, her jaw and her neck. Realisation crept up on her. She had been struck by one of the men whom she had insulted, and with such force, that her body was thrown across the courtyard. If she had been hot with temper moments before, she was now feeling the heat of shame well up in her as she pulled herself into a sitting position. Her surroundings started to spin and she felt like she might be sick. A hand was thrust in front of her and she took it but could not bring herself to stand. She tried to follow the length of the arm to see to whom it belonged, but then everything went black.

She was being carried but could not tell by whom. All she yearned for was the comfortable oblivion from which she had awoken. She could feel a powerful heartbeat and strong arms enveloping her. She heard angry voices and loud noises coming from the courtyard but could not make out anything in particular. Ashamedly, she knew it was most likely a commotion which she was guilty of starting. She wondered whether Mohamed Eye for Eye was there and Master Osman and where was Faris?

Things were becoming clearer and she couldn't bear the consequences. What would be the results of her actions? She stirred and she moaned, "No! Oh no."

She heard a creaking door open and the person who had been carrying her laid her onto a bed. When she tried to open her eyes, she found that only one could open. The other eye was already swollen shut. It felt as if her skull was cracked too. Her one open eye saw that she was lying in her own room. Abdul Hamed was sitting on the edge of the cot. He was mixing something in a small copper bowl. Shajara tried to sit up, but one look from Abdul Hamed stopped her.

"Don't sit up and don't speak," he said. "I am making an Alum paste for your eye." Shajara gave him as questioning a look as she could manage with her one good eye. "Yes, alum can help. Yes, we are carrying it as part of the caravan and it normally sells for use with dyes, but it is also used as an astringent, to control bleeding and helps promote healing. Now sit back as I put this on."

His fingers were warm and strong, and she winced as he applied the silt-like paste to her eye. He applied it all around her eye and as far down as her neck. She watched his face while he applied the paste. He looked upset and Shajara could imagine she would be in a lot of trouble for her actions. She knew Master Osman was a kind man, but he took his caravans very seriously. There was a lot of investment riding in and on this caravan, and she was meant to be his prized gift. She had wanted to make him proud and instead she had brought shame to him. She could not imagine what she had been thinking this morning. Abdul Hamed stopped applying the paste.

"Am I hurting you?" he queried.

Shajara shook her head, which made tears run down her cheeks.

Abdul Hamed sighed heavily. He stopped applying the paste and sat back to look at her.

"You are young. You have a lot to learn yet, and a caravan is no place for a girl. It's important that this swelling and bruising is gone before you are presented to the Caliph."

Shajara had not even thought of that! She felt more miserable than ever. She had been so confident, so certain that her chastisement of the men would remind them of proper behaviour. She thought they might even feel sorry, that they would apologise! She was beginning to think she knew nothing of the world, and nothing of people, either.

A deep sound rumbled in Abdul Hamed's chest. Shajara looked at him with curiosity. How could he find her misery something to laugh about?

"Yes," he replied to her obvious question to his amusement. "You have got me into a lot of trouble! Osman will have my head for this! So just stay here and relax. And do not leave, I will come for you when the caravan starts, and you must draw your headscarf over your face so no one will see your bruising. Is that clear?"

"I have made trouble for *you*?" Shajara croaked guiltily.

"Yes. I am in charge of the safety and security of this entire caravan...*and* its prize gift to the Caliph. I have failed to keep you safe and the fault is mine." Abdul Hamed stood up after having admired his handiwork of Alum paste applied to Shajara's face and neck. "I heard you wake this morning at the call for prayer. I thought after last night, you would go back to sleep. I left your door to"

– he paused to find the words to explain his actions politely – "to relieve myself. I had no idea you would head down to the courtyard so early."

Shajara could not believe that Abdul Hamed slept outside her door all this time without her knowing.

"I am so sorry." Shajara was exhausted and sad.

Abdul Hamed looked at Shajara and shrugged. "I have dealt with worse." He stood up to leave. His large form towered over Shajara. He looked down at her and spoke, "You need to learn how to choose your battles. You never attack when outnumbered four to one." He walked to the door but stopped, turned and added, "But if you do, you need a plan, a strategy and a damn good one at that. Never engage in battle, yes, even a verbal battle, on a whim and without thought. You're hot-headed and courageous and a good warrior needs that, but you didn't take the time to know your enemy. Those men aren't pious, nor do they care to be. Even if they were, they certainly would not like to be scolded by a young girl. You're lucky you ended up with only a black eye."

Shajara thought back to the first day of the caravan and remembered Faris telling her about Genghis Khan and how he went to great lengths to 'know' his enemy. She had already forgotten that important lesson! As Abdul Hamid passed through the door, Shajara called out, "Wait! You think I am a warrior?"

Abdul Hamed laughed. "Life is a battle, Shajara. It is best to be a warrior if you plan to succeed." And he walked off.

Did she agree that life was a battle? Women were not made for battle, for they lacked the strength of men. Women were not warriors. But yet, it was as Faris had said, women should take more interest in war. Shajara was confused and her head hurt. Moments ago, she was berating herself for being so brazen and foolishly outspoken. Now she was proud that Abdul Hamed thought of her as a warrior. She rolled to her side in the small cot. Too tired to cry, she closed her eye and slept.

δ❧

Chapter 12
Abandoned

It seemed as though no time had passed at all, when Shajara heard a loud knock on her door. As Abdul Hamed walked through the door, she could see the strong sunlight pouring in behind his large frame. She was sure it had to be at least mid-morning. She was groggy. Abdul Hamed reminded her to cover her face and told her they would leave in five minutes. She grabbed her scarf and started to arrange it over her hair, and then over her face. Nearly every person she knew wore a head covering of some sort – Christian, Jew, Muslim or pagan…it helped keep hair clean. It kept the head warm in the cold months, and in the dusty and windy months, it was useful to drag part of the scarf across the face to keep the dust out of the eyes, it was simply practical. Additionally, the Prophet taught that Muslim women should promote virtue by dressing in a modest manner and women's hair was considered beautiful and at times provocative.

Shajara wondered how disfigured her face might be and wished she could peer into a mirror. She took a deep breath and quickly asked God to send her strength in order to deal with the day ahead. She would have to show Master Osman and Mohamed Eye for Eye that she was capable of managing, and that the morning's disaster would not interfere with the success of the caravan.

She wanted to look for Faris, but Abdul Hamed was in a hurry and Shajara raced to keep up. He led her to a kneeling camel. She looked it in the eye and the camel looked back with its huge eyes, shaded by long lashes. There was sweetness and patience in its look. Maybe, she was wrong to distrust camels.

Before she had time to object Abdul Hamed had whisked her off her feet and placed her on the back of the camel. He tapped the animal twice on the back and it lunged forward, forcing Shajara to grab hold of the horn which formed part of the saddle. The camel rose up as she had seen many times before, starting with its hind legs first. Then it straightened its front legs, sending Shajara reeling backwards with such force that she almost slipped from the mat placed on top of the saddle. The movement felt so unnatural. Looking down, she saw for the first time that both legs on the one side went together at once. No wonder they call camels ships of the desert, for the movement was almost that of a rolling boat.

The camel was carrying only a couple of bags, and Shajara wondered how this was possible as she knew every camel was carrying a full load. She knew, too, that every pack became slightly lighter as the days passed, but not so that a camel could carry less than half a load. She looked around her to assess the loads of other camels. It appeared that they were not carrying extra.

Shajara was dismayed that Faris was nowhere to be seen. She hoped that he would soon appear with his smile and encouraging words, but, the caravan was moving out and Mohamed Eye for Eye was bellowing orders as he rode forward. She was alone and felt disturbed and disconnected. She felt uncertain of who she was anymore and, just as worrying, of who and what she needed to be. She had never suffered much from self-doubt. Her footing had always been strong. How was she meant to survive the complexities of Harem life if she continuously made so many mistakes?

Jalal had told her if she knew who she was; she would be able to make the right choices. Know your soul, he had said to her. But she was not the same person she was before the caravan. She was no longer just a slave girl from Konya, content with her daily chores and lurking in the courtyard to learn lessons. Everything felt different. Her heart ached for her old life and the comfort of home and her parents. Yet at the same time, her heart leaped at the thought of all the new wonders she may behold as part of the royal harem. The priority of duty and piety seemed to fade when she imagined a different life of running off to be free and live in Damascus. She wished Faris were there with her. Where was he? Why hadn't he come to look for her?

She looked around at the surrounding terrain. It had been changing ever so slightly each day since the journey began, but it was different now to anything she had seen before. The rocky hills had given way to lush green meadows. To the west were hills and sheep wandered freely. There were fields in the distance and Shajara knew they were entering the area Faris had told her about. She had heard stories only of the desert and its cruel beauty, but Faris told her that just before the desert, there was an area with rich soil where anything grew. Shajara could smell something fresh and sweet in the air. She was glad of it and breathed in deeply. For although she had come to appreciate camels, no one could deny that their scent was pungent! There was enough breeze to carry the scent of pistachio blossoms over the entire caravan. "Truly, God is Great," Shajara murmured.

In Islam, prayer five times a day was one of the five pillars, but apart from that duty of prayer, there existed also Du'a, which was literally a calling to God – a small prayer, outside of prayer time. For Shajara knew that God had said to call on Him, and he would answer.

Shajara sat atop her camel, and put her hands shaped like a bowl in front of her face, and thanked God and prayed for guidance and strength. For everything was in God's hands.

Shajara looked up to the sky to see the position of the sun. She saw that there was little time before they would break to eat, and she would take that time to search for Faris. She had been upset about many things that morning, but for one thing she was very thankful that she was not alone, for she had her friend Faris, and that made all the difference in life.

The area where they stopped was beside a river. The sky was a vivid blue and there were only a few puffy white streaks of cloud. The river burbled slowly along, birds chirped, and the grass and flowers' scent filled the air. She waited patiently for someone to come help her down from her camel, but everyone seemed too busy. All the other camels were taking long slow sips of water from the river. Master Osman appeared from behind a cluster of trees. He tugged on the rope by the camel's mouth and without much persuading, the camel bent his front legs and then his back legs. Shajara gratefully took Master Osman's hand and felt the spongey grass underneath her feet.

"Show me your face, Shajara." His tone was calm, but direct. His reaction to her unveiling her face was impassive. "I see," he said. He stroked his beard and looked at her face some more. "All right. You had better put the veil back across your face now. Abdul Hamed tells me it will heal better out of the sun." Shajara sensed he was not as irate as she had feared. She delivered her apology quickly and with meaning. Master Osman did not smile exactly, but the corners of his mouth turned up very slightly.

"I'm glad you are all right." He turned to leave, but Shajara quickly cleared her throat and asked, "Master Osman, do you know where Mohamed Eye for Eye is?"

Osman turned his head back to eye Shajara with suspicion. "Why would you need to speak with Mohamed Eye for Eye? What is your business with him?"

Shajara stated her purpose, "I have been looking for Faris, his son, but cannot see where he is."

Osman inhaled deeply, his chest expanded and he crossed his arms on his chest. He did not seem eager to speak. Shajara waited, but saw concern spread over Master Osman's face and she could sense her own panic beginning to mount. He breathed in slowly and started to rub the back of his neck. She had seen him do this many times, usually when faced with telling his wife bad news. Shajara started to wring her hands.

"I had not realised that the two of you had grown so close so quickly. Perhaps it is for the best." He sighed again.

Shajara was screaming questions internally 'What are you talking about?' But instead, she cocked her head innocently. She was hugely grateful that the scarf covered her face, as she was certain it would have given away her true feelings.

"Faris" – Osman paused not knowing how to continue – "Faris has been left behind."

Shajara was stunned. "Why?" was all she was able to get out.

"After you were attacked this morning, Faris foolishly tried to take matters into his own hands. He overestimated his own strength and ability. He was" – Osman paused searching for the right words – "beaten quite badly. His injuries were significant enough for us to leave him behind."

Shajara felt the blood drain from her face. Her vision was blurred, and her swollen eye was throbbing. She opened her parched mouth to speak but could not find a single word to say.

Osman looked at her with concern. She wished she could ask how they could do such a thing. Especially when he was in need of medical attention, but she knew her place and kept quiet.

"I have paid for someone to look after him. I will see him on our return from Baghdad, if God wills it."

&❧

Chapter 13
The Fertile Crescent

The hours passed in a blur of anguish and frenzied doubt. At times, she almost made up her mind to steal away from the caravan and make her way back to the caravanserai to help Faris. But with every passing kilometre, she realised there was less and less chance to do so. She would have to escape and travel at night and might lose her way. She would have to take food and water from the caravan for her journey, but to do so would be theft. Besides, Master Osman would know where she had gone and would send someone to fetch her. Her disobedience and disappearance would disgrace her in his eyes. But how could she continue in the caravan? How could she leave Faris to suffer alone? It was, after all, her fault that her friend had been injured. She would never forgive herself.

She had been told by Master Osman that Mohamed Eye for Eye was in a rare temper. Understandably so, as he too must be worried sick about his son. Master Osman had given her the facts of the morning – Faris had seen the incident unfold but had not been able to reach Shajara before she was struck. He had stood in front of Shajara and told the four men they would have to go through him to reach her. The four men laughed and jumped on him. He had been badly beaten. As a result, the men had been punished by Mohamed Eye for Eye with the approval of Master Osman by eviction from the caravan. In Konya, the men had paid to join the caravan, for they had products to sell and wanted Master Osman's protection. They had no camels, and so Osman had provided one for them, at an additional cost. Osman and Mohamed Eye for Eye could dictate who would travel under their authority or not. The four men's involvement with Shajara and Faris had cost them their transport and protection.

The departure of the four men was the reason why Shajara now had an unburdened camel to ride. Osman had thought that Shajara would be relieved to hear that the men were no longer on the caravan. Instead, it worried her that Faris was alone in the caravanserai with those violent men, already enraged by their punishment. She prayed for his health and safety.

Shajara had known that while traveling in the agricultural area, it was considered safe to camp in the open, for there were few hiding places for bandits and there was little threat from sandstorms. Now, however, they had travelled beyond the borders of the Sultanate of Rum, and desert sands were stretching on either side of the road.

That evening as Abdul Hamed was helping Shajara erect the tent in which she would sleep, she begged him to tell her if he had seen Faris and how badly he had been hurt. She saw the worry in his eyes when he spoke and guessed that he was giving her the best possible version, but even that seemed bleak. His account was much like Master Osman's, except his version included the knife wound to Faris's shoulder. Shajara, more despondent than ever, understood that a quick and easy recovery was unlikely for her friend.

She fought to keep tears from forming in her eyes, "Is there nothing I can do? Please, Abdul Hamed…" She stopped, struggling with her emotions. "I must do something!" She searched his face to see if there was any hope.

"He will either live or he will die," Abdul Hamed said simply. He continued to tie a rope onto the ends of the tent and, after securing it with a large knot, he moved to the next corner of the tent. "You yourself can decide neither of these outcomes. But still, there are two things you can do." Shajara moved closer to him to listen to what he would say.

"You can continue your journey to Baghdad safely and you can pray. These are the things you can do. Nothing more."

The next two days and nights passed more slowly than Shajara could have imagined possible. In the evenings, instead of sitting with the others exchanging stories or singing, she stayed in her secluded tent. She preferred to be alone, for she was overwhelmed with guilt whenever she saw Mohamed Eye for Eye. Everyone looked tired, and it almost seemed that the spirit of the entire caravan had been depressed after leaving Faris behind.

&

Chapter 14
Visitors in the Night

On the fourth night after leaving Faris, Shajara suddenly awoke. She did not know what had wakened her. It was still very dark on this moonless night. The caravan was silent other than the occasional snort of a camel. Yet she felt an overpowering feeling that something was wrong. She sat up, her heart pounding in her chest. She started to pull the cover from her in order to wake Abdul Hamed outside her tent, but stopped, then pulled the cover back over her legs. She could not awaken Abdul Hamed from his badly needed rest to tell him only that she *felt* that something was wrong. He would scold her for being foolish.

However, Shajara knew that sleep was impossible. She was wide awake; her heart was racing, and she felt a heavy feeling in the very pit of her stomach. Wrapping a shawl around her head and shoulders, she pulled the tent flap aside. Cold night air greeted her. She could just dimly make out Abdul Hamed's large figure sleeping in front of the tent. She quietly stepped over him and barely able to see one step ahead of herself walked slowly towards the camel line.

Shajara had no idea what she was looking for, but after standing very still and listening, she heard something. It was only a very faint noise and she did not know what it was or where it was coming from. She strained her ears to hear it again. Something was moving in the sand somewhere up ahead.

She moved along the camel line using the camels' occasional snorts and snores as a guide. The sound was coming from the back of the camel line. She pulled out the sheathed dagger that Abdul Hamed had given her and which she kept tucked in the fabric sash around her waist at all times. Soundlessly, she drew the dagger from its leather sheath.

If the sound up ahead was bandits or Mongols, she had little hope with her small blade to do more than cause them a few seconds delay, but she could sound the alarm with a loud scream. She would try her best not to fail Master Osman this time. She remembered Jalal's words – cunning and courage.

Sometimes the noise sounded like stomping, other times tugging. Perhaps it was a sick camel, or one tangled up in its line. She started to breathe more easily. Inching her way steadily forward, she suddenly saw the dark outline of a huge beast. She heard the heave of its breath and the smell was very different than that of a camel. She stopped and then heard a very comforting sound – a horse's snorting.

Yet, there were only two horses on this caravan: Master Osman's, a white and brown piebald, and Mohamed Eye for Eye's jet-black stallion, and neither was ever tethered at the camel line. Even in the near total darkness, she could dimly see that this horse was a mottled grey.

As Shajara approached, the horse threw back its ears and she saw the whites of its eyes flash. The horse returned to determinedly pawing at the hay bales, which were covered and tied at the back of the camel lines. This is a lost horse in the desert she thought, and a hungry one at that!

"I see what you want!" she spoke quietly to the horse to reassure it. She bent down to untie the bales of hay as best she could in the darkness. The horse nudged her hand out of the way as soon as it sensed the hay was within its reach. She stroked its long neck. It was wet with sweat! This horse had been galloping hard and recently! How strange, but now she looked forward to going back to bed and having a few hours more sleep. First, she would wake Abdul Hamed to tell him about the horse, for he would want to tether it to the same post as the other horses.

As she turned to go back to her tent, she saw a dark shape lying on the ground. It was a sack, she thought, that might have fallen from the horse. Her eyes strained to see and then, in the same instant that she saw it was a human form, it moved ever so slightly. Her body shook with fear, her hands trembled and her mouth went dry. Was it a bandit or a Mongol? She decided not to find out for herself but called out at the top of her voice, "HELP! Abdul Hamed! Please come quick!" She stumbled away and saw a torch being lit from the camp's dying embers. Abdul Hamed was looking around, running swiftly his torch held high.

"I'm over here!" she called out. Within moments, he was near her and saw the horse. He grabbed her harshly by the arm and she felt his strength, "What are you doing out of the tent?" Even in the dark, she saw worry etched on his face. She could hear other sounds behind her. People were waking. She didn't say anything, just pointed at the body. He turned and as he did so the light from the torch showed the body lying on the ground.

This was no bandit nor a Mongol. It was the body of her friend Faris! They rushed towards him. Within seconds, Abdel Hamid had bent down to feel the pulse at his neck. He shouted for Mohamed Eye for Eye who, awakened by Shajara's first cry of alarm, was already on his way.

Shajara took hold of Faris' hand and gasped – it was clammy and cold. Mohamed Eye for Eye had come quickly and knelt down on the other side of Faris. He leaned forward and pressed his hand to his son's neck and heard his breathing. "He is still alive!" He shouted out with immense relief and then pulled his son's head onto his lap. Cradling his head, he whispered, "Faris! Faris my son! Can you hear me?"

There were more men standing with torches now and Faris' eyes fluttered open. Shajara thanked God. She was overwhelmed with worry, but her heart filled with gratitude to God for saving her friend. This was an answer to her prayers.

"Father." Faris could barely speak his voice raspy and no louder than a faint whisper. Mohamed Eye for Eye raised his head and bellowed for water to be brought. Faris coughed and it seemed to pain him. Mohamed Eye for Eye put the water to his son's lips and lifted his head. More people crowded around to see what the commotion was about. "They are coming," Faris managed to say. He swallowed hard and tried to wet his lips to speak more. His breathing was short and laboured. Mohamed Eye for Eye was reading his son's face for more clues, "Who is coming? Those four men we threw from the caravan. They are coming?"

Faris gave a very weak nod. He was looking into his father's eyes, but he gently squeezed Shajara's hand. Gratitude washed through her. God is merciful.

"What do they want?" Mohamed Eye for Eye growled. "Let them come! They are four. We are many. They cannot hurt us." Mohamed Eye for Eye scoffed. He stroked his son's head to help sooth him.

Faris shook his head ever so slightly, "They have joined with bandits." He struggled to say more but he was faint and drifting in and out of consciousness. By this time, there were two dozen people standing around with torches, listening and asking about what was going on. Mohamed Eye for Eye put the water flask to his son's lips again. He drank only the smallest sips and struggled with the next few words. "They will strike at dawn!" Faris' voice cracked. Abdul Hamed reacted instantly, barking out commands as he left. He was already preparing for the bandits. By now, the whole camp was awake, moving and preparing – there was no time to lose.

Everyone's eyes were now on the horizon, which was still dark, but it wouldn't be much longer before there was a delicate pink sunrise in the east. Master Osman was woken and told everything that had passed. Mohamed Eye for Eye was anxious and looked desperately at his son. Then he turned to Shajara.

"I need you to look after him. The bandits will be upon us soon and I have much to do. Will he be safe in your hands?"

Shajara met Mohamed Eye for Eye's gaze directly.

"I will look after him." Overwhelmed with happiness at her friend's return she was adamant she would not fail her friend again. "I will keep him safe." And she held up her sheathed dagger as testament to her conviction. Faris looked peaceful now that he had delivered his urgent message and was back with the caravan. His father stood up with Faris in his arms and walked towards Shajara's tent slowly.

"So, are you going to tell me how you came to discover my son wounded and unconscious at the end of the camel line in the middle of the night, Shajara?" Mohamed Eye for Eye asked gruffly. Shajara struggled to find the words to explain. He turned to her and raised an eyebrow reminding her of Faris' tendency to do the same. Faris moaned in his sleep, and Mohamed Eye for Eye looked worryingly down at his son, "Nevermind, you keep your secrets, Shajara. I'm just happy to have him back, and" – he hesitated for a moment – "I am grateful to you." Shajara winced at the words.

"Grateful?" she murmured. "This is all my fault!" She lowered her head. "Your son has been a good friend to me, and I…I let him down, I let the whole caravan down." Her cheeks burned with the shame and anguish she had been carrying with her since they left Faris behind. They entered the tent and Mohamed Eye for Eye carefully laid Faris down.

"Shajara, did you ever think that your actions which left Faris behind are the same actions that led him to warn us of the attack?" Again, an eyebrow lifted with his question. He pulled his son's robe slightly off his shoulder revealing a bloodied patch which was the stab wound.

"I will bring you something to clean this wound. You must watch for fever and keep him hydrated. Other than that, there is nothing we can do. He must rest. He is in God's hands."

"But," stammered Shajara, feeling she did not deserve his forgiveness.

"Your orders are to look after Faris, that is all. Don't worry about the bandits, Abdul Hamid can handle this and worse, and thanks to my son, we will not be caught unaware, we have the advantage, now."

He stood up and she saw his large leather booted feet approach her. "Look at me, Shajara." She raised her head slowly. "Yes, your actions were careless and naïve…and I don't have time for fools, but you are no fool. You are young and still have much to learn about people and life, but your heart is good. My son did what was right, and I am proud of him. He, too, has a good heart."

He left to go get the paste for Faris' wound. Shajara knelt down in front of Faris. His face was dark with dust from his night ride. She unwrapped the scarf that he wore around his head and his neck. It was filled with dust and splattered with blood. His brown curly hair fell around his face, and she glimpsed for a moment what he must have looked like as a child. His sleeping face serene and a faint smile danced on his lips. His long eyelashes no longer black but dust coloured splayed across his cheeks. She wet a cloth and applied it to clean his face. She felt his forehead and was relieved that he didn't have a fever.

A young man opened the tent flap. In his hand, he held what Shajara recognised as the same copper pot that Abdul Hamed had mixed the alum paste for her face. "Mohamed Eye for Eye has told me to give this to you." He handed it to her with instructions and clean bandages. Shajara took the copper pot. "I am just outside your tent if you need me. I am tying bells to the camel ropes…then if the bandits take any, we will be able to follow the sound." He winked and left.

The wound on Faris' shoulder had been stitched closed and the colour of the blood had already turned brown, there was no fresh red blood and she was relieved by this, but could not stop the tears that came with the shock of the deep gash on his shoulder. He may never be the same and he would never forgive her. She cleaned the area careful not to wake him. Then applied the alum paste.

She left his shirt open to help dry the paste quickly and looked at his heaving chest rising slowly with each breath. His skin shone in the candlelight and she saw the purple and red swollen bruising of his ribs and stomach. He had a lean and muscled torso but the wound on his shoulder would leave him scarred for life. She could now see a sliver of light filtering in through her tent and she knew the sun was rising.

Mohamed Eye for Eye pulled the tent flap open and she heard a whistle of wind. He bent down and looked at Faris' shoulder, the alum paste almost dry. "Ahh, now that looks a lot better." His face softened.

"You need to apply the paste to these too." Pointing out the bruises. "We do not know what damage has been done inside him. Those brutes kicked him. There may be bleeding inside…and that we cannot sew up."

"Oh Faris." She folded her hand over his, and stroked the curls away from his face with her other hand.

Mohamed Eye for Eye rolled back onto his heels. A low rumble of laughter filled with a hint of relief came from him. Shajara unable to see anything remotely comic asked, "What could you possibly be laughing about?"

He slapped his leg, smiled at her and started to get up. "Oh, my son will be sorry to hear he slept through that." Eyeing her hand which remained on his face. Shajara felt a blush rising in her cheeks and removed her hand.

"What about the bandits? Are we ready for them? What shall I do if they…if they come here?" She indicated the space around them in the tent. She needed the advice from a man like Mohamed Eye for Eye, a man so sure of his step and his thinking, she could not imagine he would ever second guess himself. When would she ever feel so confident?

"Didn't you show me a knife earlier?" His black eyes glinted with something resembling amusement. "Instead of admonishing them with religion and morals, use the blade instead." His large form filled the tent as he stood up. "But don't worry. The bandits will try to grab what they can and run. They will not come here." He turned to exit the tent hunching his back, but as he pulled the flap back, he stopped abruptly in his tracks.

"God help us." He stood frozen. Shajara saw the colour drain from Mohamed Eye for Eye's face. She looked down the path of his gaze and saw, silhouetted against the early dawn sky, a huge dark cloud.

"What is it? Are those the bandits?" she asked incredulously. The large, dark mass appeared to be moving towards them. "There are so many!"

"No. *That* is not the bandits. *That* is a sandstorm." And Mohamed Eye for Eye left and the flap of her tent swung closed behind him.

෴

Chapter 15
The Sandstorm

Shajara recalled a time years ago, back in Konya, when Master Osman told stories about his caravan treks. She loved those stories – so full of adventure and intrigue! He had said the sandstorms were far more dangerous than bandit attacks. Camels and people were eaten up by the sand, and the treasures they carried were lost. Tracks disappeared, scenery changed, the sky obscured and nothing was spared. Sand found its way into everything and the air became impossible to breathe. People could actually drown in the sand! And now here she was, standing amidst a caravan preparing for both a sandstorm and bandits! There was nothing to do but pray.

Shajara knew that the fate of the caravan was in God's hands, and it was Faris who needed her now. She looked at his sleeping face. He was very much paler than she thought was healthy, but she had seen sick people before and was pleased that he showed no signs of fever or infection. She sat close to him and reasoned that sleep was the best medicine for him at the moment, and the less he knew about their current situation, the better.

Outside the tent, she could hear the shouts of the men and general hustle and bustle. The wind was picking up and she could taste dust in the air. She heard Abdul Hamed shouting for his men to line up the camels to the leeward against the oncoming sand. The desert was the camels' natural habitat and they were adapted to survive the sand. The men would use them as a barrier and hide up against their sides. Abdul Hamed told them to link arms so they would not be torn away by forceful winds.

At each end of the camel lines would be Abdul Hamed's armed men. If the bandits were to attack, they would choose vulnerable camels at the ends of the line. Abdul Hamed and Mohamed Eye for Eye would stay in the centre to stave off a frontal attack. Tents were folded and all movable objects were collected and put by the camel line. The horses, of which there were now three, were whinnying, stamping and rearing with fear. Shajara's tent would remain intact and was sheltered behind a gigantic stone and deemed safe enough.

Abdul Hamed pulled open the tent flap and Shajara's nostrils immediately filled with a fine sandy silt. Her eyes watered. "You will remain in the tent with Faris, for it is the best chance he has of survival. It is unlikely the bandits will strike in this storm. But if they do, they will not waste time with your tent. Take your headscarf and dose it with water and cover your nose and mouth. Do the same for Faris." Abdul Hamed reached into his pocket and pulled out a small tin. He opened it to show her a white jelly. "Put this on your lips and in your ears and nose…it will help keep them moist." Shajara did as she was told. She could smell a strong animal scent and guessed that it was sheep fat. She reached in the tin for some for Faris. He looked at Faris lying blissfully unaware, gave Shajara an encouraging smile and left the tent.

Shajara returned to Faris's side and tried her best to push the jelly paste into his nostrils, ears and lips. It was an awkward task and she was pleased that Faris slept through it. She then reached for the scarf tied around his neck, gently removed it, and then used water from her flask to soak it liberally in water. Faris had told her about the trick in the first days when walking together. The idea being the fabric would filter out the sand.

Within moments of the wet cloth touching his face, Faris began to move. The noise outside the tent was ever louder. People were shouting to make themselves heard against the noise of the wind roaring overhead. The sides of Shajara's tent shook loudly and violently and the light was quickly dimming as the sand obscured the sun. The storm was upon them. "Don't worry, Faris." Shajara comforted. "I'm here. Just lie still and God willing, all will be well." She spoke the words for herself for her hands shook and she could feel the beating of her heart pounding hard against her chest.

Faris had not opened his eyes, but she knew he was conscious and could hear her. "There is a sandstorm coming, Faris. Abdul Hamid says he thinks it's unlikely that the bandits will attack in the midst of a storm, but I can hear that he is preparing his men just in case." Shajara tried her best to soothe him with her calm words, but her anxiety mounted as the sand thrust into the tent and swirled around them.

The wind gained in fury and sand surging into the tent was suddenly everywhere around them. The wind was now deafening and the sand was pouring into the tent as if there was nothing barring it. Every breath she took was filled with fine sand. She heard Faris coughing and peeped open one eye to see Faris was already covered with a thick layer of sand. She helped him sit up and wrapped her arms around him and his head lolled forward. She rested her forehead against his and hoped that together they could act as each other's barrier. She felt the abrasive sand whipping her back and heard the loud, frightened whinnying of the horses.

Shajara had heard that sand storms could last anywhere from a minute to an hour. Her throat and nose started to burn with each breath. Her eyes were closed but she could feel the sand forcing its way under her lashes. Her hot breath was drying the damp scarf and with each inhalation she tasted the fine sand dryer than the breath before. Her face so close to Faris' she could hear his shallow breathing and the occasional cough. Glad they were finally together again, she wondered if this would affect his already weakened body. She must be strong, for he would need her in the days to come, if they could just survive this storm. She silently prayed for strength, and for the health of her friend.

"Our Lord, let not our hearts deviate after you have guided us and grant us your mercy. Indeed, you are the bestower." Sura 3 Al Imran verse 8.

Time passed slowly, and Shajara began to overcome her initial shock. A sudden lessening of the wind led her to hope that their little encampment might be spared further fury. The wind was still gusting violently, but the roaring noise was less. She ventured to open her one eye again to check. She discovered as she looked around that the wind had completely blocked the side of her tent with sand and now the sand was blowing over the top of the tent. She released one of her hands from propping Faris in his sitting position and moved her scarf around her face to find more damp cloth to breathe through. She found her breath less scratchy and she adjusted Faris's scarf to do the same for him. She could hear his rasping breath, but it was slow and sure.

It was then that she saw the roof of her tent starting to buckle under the weight of the sand. They were going to be buried alive if she didn't act quickly. She looked around frantically wondering what she could do to keep the roof from caving in. Then she remembered her knife. If she were to slit open the fabric, the sand resting on it would pour down, but it might relieve the weight just enough to prevent the whole tent collapsing on top of them. She unsheathed her knife and grimacing with effort, Shajara made the cut. The sand and roof collapsed to the side as planned. She knelt down immediately and moved Faris away from the avalanche of sand pouring down. He was like a rag doll as she moved him, his scarf slipped from his face and his head rolled to the side. He gasped and spluttered, his eyes opened and then immediately shut against the swirling sand as he sheltered his mouth and nose with his forearm. Shajara gestured that they should tuck their heads between their upraised knees to further protect their breathing passages and again prayed for God to have mercy upon them. *Fel yarhumana Allah.*

At long last, after several long moments of quiet, Shajara began to believe that the sandstorm had passed. She raised her head and checked on Faris, who still had his head tightly tucked in between his knees. The air was thick, hot and filled with a cloud of sediment, but the wind was gone. She took a clean handkerchief from her pocket and used it to wipe her eyes, nose and mouth. Her eyes watered but she saw Faris wiping his face with his scarf. Then he tilted his head, and Shajara knew he had heard what she too had heard, a very faint scratchy voice raised. "God is great! God is great! God is great!" The storm was over.

Shajara decided that they must both try to stand at the same time but with as little disturbance as possible to the swelling dune outside that threatened to bury them. As they did so, the dune shifted heavily against the tent and sand poured in silently all around them.

Shajara, relived to be in the open air inhaled deeply but instead of finding relief, found her lungs were screaming, she bent over coughing and spluttering. She looked at Faris, now watching her with increasing concern. His dark-brown eyes were framed in red and were swollen, but they still managed to twinkle at her. He passed her the flask that she had refilled for him before the storm. She gratefully sipped from it, and slowly felt her airways clear from the sand.

As Shajara looked around, she could barely recognise their campsite. Even the sparse trees were painted with sand. Even the people were sand-coloured, their faces and clothing camouflaged in sand. Yet the sky was blue with no trace of clouds and Shajara looked up and thanked God for their safety.

Abdul Hamed came up to them and shared the news that everyone had survived and nothing was lost. He had already sent two men to higher ground to see if there was any sight of the bandits. They would not be dissuaded by the storm and having come this far, they would surely attempt a strike in the future.

"What about the horses? Did they survive?" Shajara remembered their terrified squeals.

"They are still weakened by the storm. Unlike the camels, their instinct is to run from the storm and, because we had them tied up, they fought and reared against the storm. Mohamed Eye for Eye's stallion is still unable to stand."

This news sparked Faris's interest. "The bandits travel by horse, not camel," he croaked. Abdul Hamed nodded and smiled. "That's good news. Let's hope they have suffered more setbacks than we did." A wave of relief flooded Shajara. She had survived the sandstorm and although her lungs still felt raw, she felt triumphant. She had not been cunning as Jalal had advised, but she did feel courageous.

᪥

Chapter 16
The Caravan Moves Again

It was several hours before the caravan was again on the move. Faris and Shajara rode the camel together this time. Faris slept but Shajara, knowing he must drink to heal, occasionally woke him to give him water. He refused all food.

However, by evening, Faris was a very different person. The colour had come back to his cheeks and now he told Shajara he was hungry. The caravan was again camping under the stars as they would for the next few days just before they entered Baghdad. More men had been given sentry duty by Abdul Hamed and more people were sleeping next to the camels, and all were armed. The caravan was so close to Baghdad, they must not lose anything now.

Shajara brought Faris his food that night – cold lamb and rice. "You're lucky, Osman said you should have your dinner with dates and honey! He said that the Prophet Mohamed prescribed honey for all ailments, and dates are prized for curative properties, the lamb will build your strength." Faris' eyes danced, and his smile widened. Clearly, he was feeling better. As she passed him his plate, he grasped her hand with his other hand. His hand was rough in hers and she felt the warmth from his skin. "Thank you, my dear friend," he said and gave her hand a squeeze. Shajara sighed with relief but still her mind tugged at her guilt. *It's your fault he nearly died.*

Later that evening, people came to congratulate him on saving them from bandits, there was a lot of back slapping and handshakes. Soon, without any firelight, under the light of the moon and stars, Faris was persuaded to tell the caravan his story of how he had come in the middle of the night on a horse with news of bandits. A hush came over the camp.

"Several days ago, when I stayed behind at the caravanserai, I was taken to a room above the baker's, but couldn't sleep. As I lay on the bed, I overheard fragments of a conversation from my window. There were men speaking behind the wall of the caravanserai. I immediately recognised the voices of the four scoundrels who attacked Shajara and wounded me." His face darkened as he recalled the event and Shajara shuddered at the memory. "They were scrounging for pieces of stale bread thrown out by the baker. When I heard the voice of a fifth man I decided to listen more closely and catch every word."

The caravan murmured approval at this. Faris was a natural storyteller and a leader! He met her gaze and the corners of his mouth turned up.

"The new man had also come to scout for stale bread. The five men began by arguing over mouldy bits of bread, but soon I heard their talk take an interesting turn. Why, the new man wanted to know, had the men not left with the caravan?" Faris paused and took a sip of water and everyone waited patiently. "They began their tale, angrily condemning my father and Osman for ousting them from the caravan. The newcomer laughed and told them that he and his friends planned to attack our caravan at dawn in two days' time." Gasps and curses erupted from Faris' keen audience. "He told them that if they shared information on the caravan's defences, they might be welcome to join his band, and share in the plunder, while seeking revenge on my father and Osman. A deal was struck, and they spoke immediately of Abdul Hamid and his strategies of protecting the caravan."

Faris continued, "Immediately, I climbed from my bed and went out into the dark night. Keeping a careful distance, I followed the five men as they returned to their bandit camp. There I was shocked to find no less than twenty men. It was a force big enough to overwhelm our caravan in a dawn raid without question." There was a grim realisation in the circle that this plan may have been successful had it not been for Faris' warning. Faris took another sip of water. "There were arguments and laughter as the deal was struck and then the camp grew quiet as the bandits slept. I knew then that it was my time to act." The men huddling round had eyes wide with amazement. "So, I crept quietly towards horses tied in a line behind the camp. I managed to take one from the line, lead it gently away and untie the others, when at a safe distance from the camp, I climbed on and began my long ride to find the caravan and warn you."

Now the men of the caravan heaped praises on Faris. Mohamed Eye for Eye stood leaning on a large boulder and beamed with pride.

"I rode the rest of the night and the following day. I had little water and a bit of dry bread, but I knew that to rest by the way would cost me my life. So, I just kept on going, getting weaker and weaker until I finally found the caravan. I remember hearing the camels and knowing I was close, but I must have fainted and fallen from the horse. The next thing I remember was Shajara screaming for help." He stopped speaking to give Shajara a warm smile and she felt a flush rise to her cheeks. "It's thanks to her that I am alive."

"You are truly the son of your father, Faris...stealing a horse from thieves who wish to do us wrong!" Whooped the men of the caravan. Again, Faris shrugged and stole a glance at Shajara, and she was able to make out a shadow of a proud smile.

Faris told his story with great modesty. Everyone was deeply impressed by the courage he had shown. Shajara wanted to tell him how sorry she was to have caused him all of this pain, but she didn't know how. How could she explain her intense shame and sorrow at the outcome of her thoughtless actions? She stood up to leave the warmth of the circle of the caravan.

The cooler night breeze brushed against her and she wrapped her shawl closer and peered up at the moon. She heard footsteps behind her and turned to see Faris. He came to stand by her and looked up at the sky, the moon illuminating his face. How could she tell him what was in her heart? They stood in silence for a moment and then Faris shifted his feet to face her and took a step towards her. The cool air suddenly warmed by his presence. "I want to thank you, Shajara." He bit his lip and his eyes searched hers. "I owe you my life."

"You are thanking me?" Shajara blurted out angrily. "Why? If it wasn't for me, you would never been hurt!" Her shame chilled her, and she shuddered.

"Faris, it is I who must beg *your* forgiveness. I was foolish and naïve to have said anything to those men. I got hurt, but worse, I got you hurt too." She saw his mouth tighten, and continued, "I was miserable and ashamed when I found out that you had been beaten because of me and then left behind to care for yourself."

She paused to clear her throat from emotion but could feel her eyes fill with tears. "I am so sorry. I hope you can forgive me!" She felt small and her ears were ringing with the desperation to be forgiven.

Faris turned his dark eyes to hers and searched them for a moment, "Shajara, there is nothing to forgive." He took his thumb and wiped the tear running down her cheek. She felt heat pass from his finger onto her cheek but felt cold inside. "I let *you* down, Shajara. I am ashamed that I was unable to defend you from those vile men. And worse, I wasn't even able to avenge you." His eyes flashed with anger. "I failed *you,* Shajara."

Faris lowered his head and in a low voice barely higher than a whisper said, "The thought of not being with you on the last few days of our journey to Baghdad was unbearable." Faris paused and then said, "Knowing I would see you again is what got me through everything."

She could see in his eyes that she had his forgiveness and she admired his valour and kindness. Faris smiled, but his eyes clouded with sadness and she knew why. The next few days of the journey would be the last days they would ever see each other, and the thought of this made her stomach ache – it was a feeling she knew. She had felt the same way when she had to leave her parents.

The next day, Shajara told Faris how glad she was he was back. "I have been riding this camel on my own for many days with no one to speak to, and I have so many questions!" At this, they both laughed. Faris had missed his inquisitive friend, and Shajara was now bursting with questions about Baghdad.

"What does the name Baghdad mean? Do people there speak our language?"

Laughing, Faris told her that Baghdad meant 'Gift of God' and that for five hundred years it had been the most important city in the whole world. It was by far the largest city in the world with a million inhabitants or more. The Great Mosque at its centre was the most beautiful ever built, and people came there from all over the world speaking many languages. Arabic was the language used, but in the market, you could find people speaking all the languages of the world.

Faris soon discovered that each of his answers would start even more questions. "Is the road we are on the only road to Baghdad?" Shajara asked. "There are many roads to Baghdad," replied Faris, "and the great rivers of the Tigris and the Euphrates are also routes by which people come. Traders like Osman, craftsmen, scholars and artists travel there from Armenia, China, Persia, India and Europe."

The next day, as Faris was helping water the camels, Shajara found a nice flat stone to rest on. She watched him as he patted each camel, cooing soothing words while giving them water, they blinked their long lashes and slowly dipped their long necks to refresh themselves before the afternoon's long walk. He isn't as tall as his father, Shajara mused but the outline of his strong arms and broad shoulders were traceable under his shirt and she suspected he would be as formidable as Mohamed Eye for Eye, but Faris, she smiled would be loved, not feared. He stood up and looked at Shajara warming her with his smile. He set down the water jug and walked towards her, his smile unwavering. He sat down close to her and she smelled traces of carob.

"What are you thinking Shajara?" He smirked at her, "I could feel your eyes on me."

Suddenly embarrassed, Shajara spluttered, "No I wasn't I mean I was, but it…"

"I'm only teasing you, Shajara," and he elbowed her in the ribs playfully.

"I was thinking if so many people live in Baghdad, how is it that they get all the water they need?" Shajara lied. Faris told her that there were canals and dykes that diverted river waters into the city, underground pipes, great cisterns for storing it and a huge irrigation system. He told her that Baghdad had beautiful gardens and they talked about the famous gardens of Babylon, an ancient city that had stood not far from Baghdad, and of which she had heard when Abbas was at lessons with the tutor.

"Master Osman told me that I would not be presented at court until several days after we arrive in Baghdad, do you think I could see some of the sights of the great city?"

Faris beamed, "I will show you as much as I can. You will be amazed by how its broad avenues all come from the centre, where the mosque is." His eyes were full of life and shone like bronze. "It's like the spokes of a wheel, Shajara, and all the streets lead to the city walls and then out of one of the city gates to the world beyond, which is why they call it the Round City. Today, the great city fills up all the space between the Tigris and the Euphrates and beyond."

Shajara felt her head swim with the picture Faris was painting of Baghdad as the centre of the world! It thrilled her and scared her at the same time. Would this be her home for the rest of her life?

"Soon Shajara you will know more about Baghdad than I do." And the spark that was in his eyes moments before was gone.

"The pilgrims on Hajj to holy Mecca, leave Baghdad from its famous Kufah Gate, and the Anbar Gate links the city with the bridges over the canals and the Euphrates River. There are more gates in use by the great private homes, shops and factories but all of them built to protect the city against all enemies. Yes, Shajara, even the Mongols will have a hard time to break through!" They both smiled at Shajara's relief.

"Well, at least that will be one less thing to worry about." Shajara joked.

Osman passed by Shajara and Faris's camel and stopped to inquire after Faris' health. After tales had circled of Faris' stealth, bravery, thievery and horsemanship, Osman was grateful that his caravan was blessed with such a young man. Mohamed Eye for Eye had proven to be capable at his job and was worth every penny that Osman paid him. But the son was a true rising talent and he must find a way to reward him.

☙

Chapter 17
Tale of Khoraysan

In the last evening before reaching Baghdad, everyone was relieved to see that a new caravanserai had been built on the road to Baghdad. Neither Osman nor Mohamed Eye for Eye had known of its existence, and the prospect of a night spent safely there brought a new calm to the caravan. For days, fear had ruled them and now, with Baghdad only a day away, it felt like a time to celebrate.

That evening while sitting around the fire in the central courtyard of the caravanserai, everyone was talking and laughing with relief. They were at ease as the firelight lit their faces and warmed them. Osman started to praise the wise Caliphs for regulating trade so that the markets were fair to all. He told them stories of the Khurusan Road, the pathway to the wealth of Persia. He told how Baghdad was first built at a crossing of the Road, thereby becoming the meeting place for caravan routes from every direction. The Khurusan Road led eastwards across Persia to Samarkand, where it forked: one branch led north to Tashkent and the other eastwards to China.

"In all the world," Osman assured them, "there is no better place for a trader to do business." His eyes were bright at the prospect of the deals he would do in Baghdad. He knew himself to be a great negotiator.

Osman turned to Shajara who was sitting close by. "And talking of trade, there's no more important door for a trader to open than the door to the Caliph's court. And that, Shajara, is where you come in."

"You owe us a song," Osman told her. "Let's hear the one you used to sing in Konya, the one Rehan taught you about journeying to distant lands." It was a song about the sadness of parting and the joys of meeting again. As she sang, the men around the fire grew silent, their expressions changing with the words of her song.

"You have a gift," said Osman as she finished. "A gift for song like that of the great Khayzuran herself. *Jazakallahu khayran*. May God reward you."

Shajara was quick to respond. "Master Osman, will you tell us the story of that great Khayzuran?"

Osman laughed and shook his head, yet he began the tale.

"The word '*khayzuran*' means 'bamboo'," he said. "It is a plant that is both beautiful and supple, slender but strong, which bends in the wind without breaking. Khayzuran was rightly named. The winds of destiny buffeted her mightily, but she remained strong and unbroken.

"She was a Yemeni girl brought by a Bedouin to Mecca to be sold as a slave. Her life as a young girl was very hard.

"Then she came as a slave to Baghdad to be sold again. From the slave market in the city, she was brought to the Golden Palace and then led before Caliph al-Mansur, the wise Commander of the Faithful, the founder of Baghdad.

"Mansur was wise not only about finding the best site for a city in all the world, but wise, also, about people. He saw that Khayzuran could become an ornament to his court and to the harem. Already skilled in song and dance, the girl soon made herself noticed. Her voice was as sweet as that of the nightingale.

"Khayzuran outshone all the other slave girls. She learned to play the lute and accompany herself. She chose songs carefully not only to add to the evening's entertainment but also to display her talent to best advantage. Because the Caliph and his courtiers loved poetry, she memorised a thousand verses and could recite them to suit the occasion. She learned to read fluently and would often be asked to read aloud in her melodious voice. She could match most men in her knowledge of arithmetic. It is even said that she had much more in the way of *fiqh* or religious knowledge than most of the courtiers, for she took religious instruction from one of the greatest teachers in Baghdad and never left any doubt as to her piety.

"As Khorayzan grew in these ways, she became ever more valuable in the eyes of the Caliph. She had been bought for 100 dinars, but now the Caliph would not sell her for 10,000 dinars. Her value as a beautiful slave girl was one-hundredth of her worth as the educated woman she had become.

"It was not long before Khayruzan became the favourite of Mansur's eldest son, Prince Ibrahim Ibn al-Mahdi. He loved to hear her sing; but he loved, as well, the fact that she could converse with him and with the most intelligent men around him. Soon, Khayruzan became more important in the life of the court than al-Mahdi's wife, the aristocratic Raya, a princess of royal descent.

"As Khorayzan's importance grew, she became the object of jealousy and the target of plots. Raya sought to have her banished. Each new slave girl brought into the harem competed to outdo her in song and to win al-Mahdi from her. Many of the courtiers feared her influence and gossiped maliciously about her.

"Yet, Khorayzan held onto al-Mahdi's trust. She continued to dazzle him with her talents in song and dance and, even more, with her new-found knowledge in subjects that fascinated him. He came to see that she possessed both intelligence and judgment.

"On the death of Mansur, al-Mahdi became the Caliph. Now, Khorayzan would really be put to the test. The resentment of her influence had been strong when the old Caliph was alive; now, it grew ever more intense and her enemies more numerous.

"It was clear to all that al-Mahdi trusted her, for he permitted her to hold audiences and to grant favours in his name. There was a constant flow of people through her door: she received gifts in return for her influence with the Caliph, she made promises of pardons and she arranged meetings with him. He made decisions only after talking with her. She was more powerful than any vizier.

"Her enemies soon learned who Khorayzan was. Not only did she push the aristocratic Raya to one side, but she pushed aside Raya's children, excluding them from the succession to the Caliphate, in favour of her own sons by al-Mahdi.

"It was Khorayzan's sons, not Raya's, who would inherit from al-Mahdi. Imagine that! A slave girl would be the mother of the new Caliph!

"Al-Mahdi officially named Khorayzan's older son, Musa al-Hadi, as his heir apparent.

"Khorayzan's next aim was to have her younger son, Harun al-Rashid, named as the next in line. Al-Mahdi loved all of Khorayzan's children, but he adored Harun al-Rashid and took him with him when he travelled or went abroad with his army. He named Harun as next in line to Musa al-Hadi without a moment's hesitation.

"When campaigning with Harun in Taburistan, al-Mahdi took ill and died. The heir apparent, Musa al-Hadi, was also many days travel away from Baghdad. But Khorayzan was there, at the very centre of events, and very much in control. Despite efforts by others to seize the throne, she made certain that her husband's will was enforced. By her quick and forceful action, she assured Musa al-Hadi's succession.

"Khorayzan was now the Queen Mother. Yet, she was much more than that, for she continued to hold audiences and to make promises in the name of her son, the new Caliph. After only a year, he died.

"Next on the throne was Khorayzan's younger son, the famous Harun al-Rashid, of whom many tales are told. None of those tales is more certain of truth than that this great Caliph loved and trusted his brilliant mother. She was his principal and closest adviser and remained so until her death.

"Memory treasures as one of its brightest jewels the loving partnership of that great Caliph and his formidable mother.

"Thus, Khorayzan made herself as powerful as three caliphs: her husband and her two sons. Once a slave girl, she became a great ruler."

Osman finished speaking. Shajara was quiet, but her green eyes were shining. Osman leaned towards her, "So, Shajara, I saw you listening intently: what did you learn from that story?"

"Few things are certain in this life, Master. But, God willing, many things are possible for a girl," Shajara replied.

᪥

Chapter 18
A Bad Beginning

The great city was still many kilometres away, but already they were meeting its citizens and already they were sharing a paved road with many other travellers. Soon they found themselves passing by shops, houses and buildings of many kinds. Clearly, the city had grown far beyond the design of Caliph Mansur, its founder. They were in the prosperous suburbs of Baghdad.

Then they saw the city's great outside wall, ringed by its wide moat, and beyond that an even higher wall with towers placed at intervals along its length. Mohammed Eye-for-Eye led the camel train to a station outside the walls and began to supervise the unloading of the camels. The baggage had to be guarded against thieves before being carried into a warehouse for safekeeping. From there it would be taken into the marketplace or sold in lots to merchants.

Osman, with Shajara following humbly behind, strode through an enormous gate, so wide that ten camels walking abreast could enter through it. They walked past a troop of the Caliph's soldiers and made their way towards the city centre.

Osman woke Shajara early that morning and told her to get ready and follow him into town. There were people everywhere, crowds of them, and they seemed to be talking or shouting all at once. The busiest streets of Konya were never half so busy as this. Shajara saw people in the finest clothes, others in rags. She heard different languages and Arabic spoken in many different accents. She realised that her own Anatolian speech made her a foreigner in this place.

There were people of many races of all parts of the Caliph's empire and from many other parts of the world. Many were dressed in fashions that she had never seen. Salesmen stood at every corner pressing their wares on passers-by. Beggars, blind or lame or grievously disfigured, recited their woes and pleaded for alms. Fine ladies, carefully veiled, were carried by in litters. Musicians sought payment for entertaining the crowd. A man with a dancing monkey was making children laugh. Street kitchens offered foods of many kinds. There were more new sights and sounds and smells than the mind could readily handle.

They were making their way through the crowds towards an inn not far from the Caliph's palace – the Inn of the Golden Tree. They went quickly on, jostling their way through the crowds. Osman had much business to conduct, other merchants to meet and many deals to make. He needed to leave Shajara in safekeeping with the innkeeper.

"This young woman is my gift for the Caliph," Osman told Abdulla the innkeeper. "Please ask your wife to keep a close eye on her, a lot rides on the success of my introduction to the Caliph." Osman greeted his old friend, Abdulla with a handshake and a hug. They were old friends and Osman always stayed at the Inn of the Golden Tree when he was in Baghdad.

Abdulla's wife proved to be a kind, plump woman with a Persian name, Soraya. Osman whispered instructions to her and went off to his business.

"So, you are the gift," Soraya said to Shajara. "You are the lucky one!" Shajara bristled, for these were the same thoughtless words used by Serine and Rehan. What was so very lucky about being taken away from the parents she loved and the place she knew?

"Where I come from, it is the one who *receives* the gift that is thought lucky." As soon as the words were out, Shajara realised how rude she had been and murmured an apology.

Soraya eyed Shajara intensely but did not rebuke her. She would learn soon enough, she thought. Soraya continued, "Your master has given me money to buy you a beautiful new dress and get you ready to go to your new home in just a few short days, so we don't have much time. Now remove your headscarf, I want to look at you." Shajara did not understand "But I cannot stay here! The caravan is camped by the city walls. I must return to them this evening!" Shajara could not understand, had master Osman taken her out of the caravan without a chance to say goodbye? He had been in such a hurry! Would she see Faris again?

Soraya stood before Shajara reading her panic. "Your new life begins now Shajara. The caravan is not your home, just your transport. You will not go home, and it is best if you do not waste time and grief over it." She crossed her arms indicating that her understanding ended there. Shajara obeyed and removed her headscarf and allowed Soraya to look her over. She hovered over Shajara's eye which was almost completely healed but had just a shadow of a bruise left. She felt her hair and asked Shajara to open her mouth and then smile.

"Well, you need a good scrubbing. But otherwise, you look fine. We will head to the hammam after the dressmakers. They will only need to take your measurements, so it won't take long. Then tonight we can review the songs you will sing and the dance you have prepared. We have much work to do to get you ready!"

Shajara's heart sank. She was not prepared for this part of her journey. When Osman had come to collect her early that morning, she had not realised she would not return. The last days were spent with Faris dreaming of all the places they would go and the sights they would see. More unrealistic dreams for a slave. Faris was free, and she was not – but what a foolish but beautiful dream. *Would she not be able to say thank you to Abdul Hamed and Mohamed Eye for Eye?*

They arrived at a large two-storied house some streets away from the Inn of the Golden Tree, where a score of dressmakers plied their needles and thread. They climbed the stairs to the second story to discuss their needs with a dressmaker Soraya said was the dressmaker to the ladies of the palace.

"We need to be rid of this," Soraya said, plucking at the rough travel-worn and stained dress that Shajara had worn all the way from Konya. "First, you need some clothes to wear day to day in the harem," she said, "then, we'll take our time to find you a fine dress that will highlight your best attributes and match those bright green eyes – the dress you will wear when you are presented to the Caliph."

In all her life, Shajara had worn only dresses made by her mother, always of the same rough, un-dyed cloth. Now, even her day-to-day clothes were to be made of smooth, dyed and coloured cloth. The dressmaker promised to have them ready in just a couple of days and they turned to discuss the best dress.

The dressmaker had many fabrics brought out. Soraya would feel each between her fingers, glancing as she did so at Shajara's figure and face wondering aloud which would best draw attention to Shajara's most attractive attributes. Shajara drew a quick breath when one of the bolts of cloth was brought out. "Oh no, my dear," said Soraya, "we can find something better than that." And so they did. Both women knew as the dressmaker brought out the material – dark green with embroidered gold florals – that this was exactly what they had been looking for.

As Soraya settled down with the dressmaker to decide the price and collection day, Shajara wandered across the floor to see other dressmakers at work with the many different fabrics.

At the far end of the shop, a young woman was looking in a metal mirror as she tried on a new dress. Shajara thought her the most beautiful woman she had ever seen. She wandered closer, fascinated by the older woman, by her beauty, by her stunning dress, by her mysterious foreign accent. She could not take her eyes away.

Suddenly, the woman who had seen her in the mirror rounded on her. "Who do you think you are staring at?" the beautiful woman demanded. Shajara, bewildered, looked around: was it she who had offended? "Yes you, the one with those disgusting, dirty peasant clothes." Her eyes flashed with contempt as she spat her insult at Shajara.

Shajara felt heat rise in her heart and, before she could catch herself, she retorted angrily, "Soon these rags will be exchanged for something more beautiful, but your ugly manners cannot be hidden by your dress."

Soraya pulled Shajara quickly away before anything further might be said. Hustling her out of the dressmakers', she uttered the words, "*Nowtthuballah*, God provide refuge to us."

In the street, she pulled Shajara harshly around to face her and shook her shoulders. "There, that's done it! You've made an enemy of Hababa, the Caliph's favourite singer. I should have told you back at the Inn when you made that insolent comment to me, that you should learn to hold your tongue. You may be beautiful and clever, Shajara, but do not think for one moment it will be enough to save you from the manipulative, back-stabbing women in the Harem, for they are as beautiful and as clever, but with more status, friends and experience than you. If you are talented enough to pass the tests to remain as an entertainer, then that will be good, but do not be so foolish as to think that will keep you safe."

They walked in silence for some time. Shajara's mind was in turmoil. How could she have made such a wrong move, again? When would she learn? What would Master Osman say? Her thoughts turned to Faris. She remembered the damage she had caused them both by her angry remarks back on the caravan. What would the ramifications of these remarks be? Thoughts of Faris brought her even closer to tears.

She turned to Soraya as they came to the Hammam. "I have disgraced Master Osman," she moaned. "Hababa will not forget. Now, the Caliph will not want me as a gift. Now, Master Osman will have no goods to take back to Konya. And it's all my fault!" She could no longer hold back the tears.

"Let's not bother Master Osman with this." Soraya comforted Shajara. "He has business enough on his mind without thinking of our little problems. Secondly, it is true you have much to learn, and that is why Osman has brought you to me! I will tell you all I know, and hopefully you will learn to bite your tongue!

"Now I will take you to my local hammam. It is not as exquisite as the ones you will see at the Palace, but it will be sufficient for our needs today. Baghdad is said to have more hammams than any other city in the world! One man wrote that there are 60,000! This particular hammam is open to women during the day, and to men at night."

Upon entering the hammam, Shajara felt like she was entering a palace, for although the exterior had been somewhat plain, the inside had decorative tiles and heated marble floors. The air was perfumed with orange blossom. The towels were thick and embroidered. The rooms had brick domes with only a bit of glass at the top to let in some light. First, Shajara was stripped down and rinsed off. Then they moved to the steam room, which would open their pores to the hot steam and then to a warm room to wash. They sat in a quiet corner to get away from the other ladies laughing and gossiping. Soraya told Shajara that by the time they were finished with her, Hababa would not recognise her! She told Shajara many helpful hints to avoid future problems with other dancers, and even the Caliph's family.

Soraya and Shajara then moved to the washing room, where Soraya brought out a brush, slathered it with an olive oil and lye soap, told Shajara to lie down on the bench and started to scrub! Shajara thought that she would scrub the skin clean off, but at last came the room for massaging oils and perfumes while sipping tea and chatting with neighbours. Finally, Soraya oiled and combed Shajara's long, black hair.

Out on the street where the sun was shining brightly, Soraya appraised Shajara again, and told her, "You see, I have done a good job!"

&

Chapter 19
Soraya's Story

"Let's go home now, and after our evening meal, I'll tell you of my life. Did I tell you that many years ago, I was a dancer for the Caliph's grandfather, the Caliph Al Nasir?" Shajara hid her surprise and shook her head. It was difficult to imagine the very large Soraya as a dancing girl. *Indeed, it must have been many years ago,* Shajara thought.

The bread at the evening meal was very different from the Konya bread, the sauces for the meats were strange and she had never tasted cakes so delicious. Yet, it was a fine meal and Shajara was able to forget for a while her awful exchange with Hababa. "Please, Soraya, tell me about dancing for the Caliph."

Soraya began ominously, "What I will tell you of life in the old Caliph's harem must never leave your lips. It is dangerous to share Palace secrets, even after so many years. Nor should you think I would tell you all I know. I will tell you just enough to help you find your way in the Palace maze. For that is what it is: a place where you must watch your every step, where danger lurks in corners, but where there are many good things that come to those who walk prudently."

Soraya told first of her young life, how she had been born a slave to parents who themselves had been slaves. Shajara interrupted to ask how it was that, if Soraya had been born a slave, she was now free. "Any slave who bears a child to a free man becomes free herself," explained Soraya. "And now I have five sons and three daughters with my good husband. So, I am free, indeed." Shajara stored this interesting fact in her memory.

"Yes, like you I was a slave. Unlike you, I was brought to the Slave Market just streets from here. There, I was lucky enough to catch the attention of the Caliph's scouts. Perhaps I was not so beautiful like you, but well worth the gold dinars paid for me."

Soraya described her first day in the Palace. She had been taken before the dancing master and made to dance a few steps. "I knew the dances only of my own people, country dances, nothing like those that entertained the Caliph and his court. But I was graceful then and I passed the test. Then they had me sing, but I had no gift for it. I failed the test. I was not to be one of the most favoured girls, those who could both dance and sing." As she heard the note of sadness in Soraya's voice, her disappointment remembered from years ago, Shajara nursed a hope that she might pass both tests.

Next, Soraya spoke of the Harem itself. She remembered it as a comfortable home, where some hundreds of women lived carefully ordered lives, out of sight of the men of the court. "There were rules that could not be broken," she said, "and I learned them quickly and well. We heard old stories of disobedient girls who had been taken to the river and drowned. Whether true or not, I learned to speak only when spoken to. I had to be careful even in front of the older dancing girls, for they were quick to find punishments for new girls who spoke out of turn." Soraya described how she was taught to cast her eyes downward in the presence of the Caliph's mother, wives and daughters.

Soraya told Shajara about the vizier, a man she had never met, but whose reputation was of kindly wisdom. She told of the Eunuch Master, whom she feared more than anyone, for he came often to the dancing girls' quarters and frightened them with his angry face and harsh words. She told, also, of the intrigues and plots in the harem: Caliph's wife against Caliph's wife, the wives of the Caliph's sons against one another in bitter competition. Shajara made a mental note of everything Soraya told her, knowing that somehow or someday she might need this knowledge.

Soraya's memories were mostly good ones. "Our lives were not hard, we were well fed and we enjoyed our lessons in the dance. When our training was done and we were ready to dance before the Caliph, we were thrilled to be part of the evening entertainment, wearing our most beautiful dresses." Soraya's face lit up at the memory. Rising to her feet, she demonstrated an intricate little dance. Her agility astonished Shajara. "You see, my dear, this old body has not forgotten the steps it practiced so long ago."

Tired by her exertions, Soraya sank back onto the cushions where Shajara was ready with a hundred questions. She wanted to know about the Caliph himself, but Soraya had only seen him out of the corner of her eye as she concentrated on her steps at the dance. Her memory was of a man with a beard dyed jet black, his clothes shining with silver embroidery, and more often than not with his face turned away from the dancers to speak with the vizier or other great men of the court.

"Did you ever see any sultans or princes come from abroad?" Shajara wanted to know. "No, I have never seen the Sultan of Rum, nor any ambassadors of the Byzantines or Franks. Remember, my dear, I was there to dance not to gape at the audience."

"What about the splendours of the Golden Palace?" Shajara pressed, eager to know so that she would be able to tell Faris one day, if God willed. "No, I have never been in any of the Caliph's rooms. I have never seen the famous collection of diamonds and rubies in the Jewel House, nor climbed the staircase made of alabaster and gold, nor gazed through windows of pure crystal. All these fine things were described to me by others." She sighed happily. "Nor did I ever see the Golden Tree. But I know that it is, indeed, one of the greatest wonders of Baghdad, and God has given me my own Golden tree."

Shajara's eyes grew wide with amazement and knew she was about to hear the story behind the name of the Inn.

"The Golden Tree was made by the greatest goldsmith in all the world. It stands on a huge block of agate, into which are set its golden roots. The Tree itself rises higher than a man, its trunk and branches are made of solid gold, its fruit balls of purple chalcedony inset with diamonds. Most astonishing of all, there are birds of silver that, as they move among its branches, sing like nightingales!" Shajara let out a small gasp of excitement, and Soraya took her hand in hers as if she was about to share a valuable secret.

"When I heard of this tree, I thought it the most wonderful thing in the world, more beautiful and valuable than any other thing made by man. I knew that it could never be mine, but its name lived on in my mind." She paused to look into Shajara's eyes. "What could be more desirable, Shajara? But in fact, I have learned that there is something. In my heart, there was something I yearned for even more than a wondrous golden tree – freedom, a home of our own and a family."

Soraya let go of Shajara's hand, stretched and yawned. "So, now you know why we called this house the Inn of the Golden Tree. *Subhanallah.* Glory to God. But of course, you probably already guessed that, no?"

"How could I know that?" Shajara asked her.

"Your parents are slaves but were allowed to raise their child in the home of their owner, no? Of course, I presume that is why they named you tree of pearls – more precious than any jewel." At the mention of her parents, Shajara's smile grew and then faded from her lips.

"It is time you were in bed and asleep. Tomorrow we have much work to prepare for your big day at the Palace."

Before Shajara went to sleep, she got out her paper and pen and wrote to her parents. She was too tired to tell them of all she had seen and learned that day, but instead she decided to write to them about the Golden Tree, both the one in the palace, and the Golden Tree Inn, Soraya and her family. She signed it 'your tree of pearls'.

ॐ

Chapter 20
The Slave Market

The next morning, Osman came from the street into the inn. His brow was furrowed with worry and he cast a dark look towards Shajara that frightened her. Had Soraya told him after all about her clash with Hababa?

Abdullah greeted his friend and brought him into the front room. He asked Shajara to bring tea, but as she ran off to get it, she saw the serving boy already with a tray of steaming tea and she took it from him. Osman and Abdullah were seated on cushions around a low table and Shajara set down the tray. She would've liked to stay and hear what it was that so obviously upset her master, but Abdullah waved for her to leave. As she left, she heard Abdullah, "What is it, my friend? How can I help?" Abdulla's soft voice encouraged Osman to speak.

"Oh my friend, it is bad as can be!" Osman lamented.

Shajara, now just outside their sight, but still within hearing stopped abruptly. She knew that eavesdropping was wrong, but she suspected it might concern her, so she silently moved to a dimly lit spot in the room next door.

"My security man, Abdul Hamed, has heard rumours in the bazaar that the Mongols, those fearsome, pagan horsemen, are threatening Anatolia! They are trying to invade the Sultanate of Rum, and if they succeed, they will head straight to the capital – Konya!" There was a heavy silence, and the men sipped their tea.

"I pray that the rumours are false, Abdullah, but I fear for Serine and my children. You have surely heard of the Mongols' ruthlessness." He sighed heavily. Shajara was equally distressed by the rumours.

"Oh my friend, all we can do is pray." Abdullah offered soothingly to Osman. A long silence passed as they all thought of their loved ones back in Konya and what would become of them?

"Ahhh, but that is not all I am worried about." Osman continued, "My other great worry is for the Baghdad-Konya trade. I need the Caliph's endorsement if the Baghdad merchants are to trust me. I cannot begin to buy without it. Yet, the Caliph's man, Rasheed, has not come, and he has known of our arrival since setting foot in the caravanserai *outside* Baghdad – I sent word so I could start buying as soon as possible."

"What can be the delay? Has he changed his mind? Perhaps he has received the goods from another trader? Why else would he wait so long to send word to me?"

"It is possible that the delay is due to some very important matters keeping Rasheed busy. Don't fret my friend, it will work out. The rumours of Mongols are probably just that – rumours. I will not let you spend your time in Baghdad with all this worry!" The two old friends sipped their tea thoughtfully.

"Listen to me, Osman, in the worst-case scenario, and the Caliph's man does not show up, all is not lost. You will easily be able to sell your goods in the marketplace; you will be able to buy through trusted sellers I know. And to recoup some of what you might have lost by doing business with the Caliph himself, you can sell Shajara, she's worth no less than gold 200 dinars in the slave market," Abdulla assured him.

Osman's face was set in a scowl, but his mind turned to the alternative. Perhaps he could sell Shajara. A sum of 200 gold dinars would help to make up for any lost trade.

It was at this point that Shajara, whose mind was racing, heard Soraya ask the serving boy where she was. She did not want to be caught eavesdropping and so silently made her way to the kitchen. Yet she was filled with fear and worry.

"Come! Shajara! Where have you been? It is time to try on your dresses." Soraya bustled Shajara out of the house and into the street.

They walked down narrow and dark streets which had houses on either side and were three stories high. "This is the Street of the Merchants," Soraya explained. "Some of Master Osman's friends live here," Soraya said gesturing to the houses they were passing. "Up there" – she pointed at the top story – "is where their wives and daughters watch as the people walk past. We can't see them behind the window screens, but they can see us!" She winked at Shajara, but her good mood was unable to shake the dread that Shajara felt.

"You might think, 'Why would they live on such a dark street? If I were a rich merchant, I would not live here'. Ahhh, but you would be wrong, my dear," said Soraya. "Gloomy the street may be, but behind some of those high gates are fine gardens, beautiful fountains, reflecting pools and arbores covered with flowering vines and roses. The merchants of Baghdad live well."

Shajara did not hear a word of what Soraya was saying, she thought only how Faris had offered to take her away from all of this weeks ago, but she had declined, and now she would be sold.

They emerged from the Street of the Merchants into a square almost empty of people. In the middle was a platform. Steps led up to it and there were rails at its sides. Soraya stopped, "This is the place where thirty years ago I was brought to be sold," Soraya said in a quiet voice.

Shajara felt a lump form in her throat.

"Sold to whomever would bid the highest price. I was so frightened. They put a cotton rope around my neck, and I stood there trembling, sick with fear." Shajara looked at Soraya with horror and could see that she was reliving that moment and was sick with fear herself. Why had Soraya brought her here? Was this to be her fate? Just sold to whomever had the dinars to buy her. Soraya turned to her and said, "And now you know why people say you are the lucky one – lucky to have avoided this place! You don't know the stories I have heard! They still give me nightmares, and the faces of the girls sold and dragged off by cruel masters still haunt me to this day."

An old woman, a dark shawl draped around her thin, bowed body, approached them. Dark eyes were set deep in her wrinkled, weathered face. Her bony arms were raised towards them and Soraya pressed a small copper coin into her hand. The old woman murmured a thank you and then looked steadily at Shajara, "You will bring a pretty penny at the market."

Shajara backed quickly away. "I will never again set foot here," she yelled. She ran ahead of Soraya, anxious to put the horrid place behind her. She could feel all her muscles tense with the imagery of shackles, neckties and servitude. She would race to find Faris and escape this nightmare. They would run away together to Damascus as they had planned in their dreams. As she ran, she tried to calculate how she would find him; it was after all the largest inhabited city in the world. She knew only that it was near a warehouse near the main gate. Up ahead, she saw a man wearing a uniform walking down the street. She stopped, tried to regain her breath. The man was quite clearly sizing her up, and Shajara knew within a moment what he must be thinking – a foreigner, ragged clothing, running desperately from the slave square. This realisation prompted action from both of them and as the man raised his voice for her to stop, Shajara turned back and ran to look for Soraya. She found a breathless Soraya not far from where she had left her. She wanted to apologise and explain, but instead fell to her knees and put her tear-stained face in her hands.

"I have upset you, Shajara." Soraya bent down and took her hand and patted it reassuringly. "That was not my intention. I like to come here to remind myself how fortunate I am. Things could have been worse for me but look at me now – I have my Golden Tree."

"I may not be the *lucky* one after all," Shajara blurted. "Master Osman is thinking to sell me." The story tumbled out and when Shajara came to a halt and looked to Soraya, she saw only a smile.

"That will not happen, Shajara. My husband is only giving your master some assurances, but the Caliph and his advisors work on their own schedule. They have not forgotten about your master; they will come when they are ready. Trust me, I have seen many dealings like this before. There is much fuss and drama, but in the end, it all works out. Come" – she helped Shajara to her feet – "when you see your new dress, all this worry will be forgotten, you'll see."

On the way to the House of the Dressmakers Shajara remembered Jalal's words on the first day at his house – 'safety never comes from seeking safety.' She wiped her tears dry and followed Soraya.

What Soraya had described as 'day to day clothes' seemed magnificent to Shajara. She felt the smooth, soft fabric and marvelled at the bright colours, fine embroidered detail and how they fit her perfectly. They were a very different fashion from Anatolian costume, but she couldn't imagine anything finer. Next was the best dress, the one she would wear when she was presented to the Caliph. When the dressmaker brought it out, Shajara fell silent. It was far too beautiful for her! Her tears had long dried up and now she felt the glow of pride that she should be the owner of such an extraordinarily beautiful dress. She stared at the golden stitches and saw the skill and quality of the work.

"Come on," urged Soraya, "it's the material we chose together. Don't you like it?" Words still failed Shajara. She stared for a few moments more before exclaiming, "I have never seen anything more beautiful."

"It's made for you, Shajara al Durr" – using her full name – "Tree of Pearls," Soraya tried to reassure her. "Try it on and then let's see how you perform in it. Give us one of your Anatolian dances. I want to see the Caliph's gift dance."

Shajara knew that Soraya's expert eyes were on her. She put the dress on carefully, cautiously, wondering as she did so at the glistening material. She looked for approval to Soraya and the dressmaker, twirled around to see the skirt move and glitter. She danced, slowly at first and then, in sheer delight, she threw herself into her favourite dance.

Soraya and the dressmaker were impressed. "Yes, the Caliph will be pleased with his gift. He may even think himself lucky to have such a graceful, young woman at his court. Now, let's return to the inn."

క

Chapter 21
Good-byes

As Soraya and Shajara came up to the inn they heard a man asking for Master Osman. Abdullah ran for Osman who embraced the man and greeted him warmly. "Rasheed, my friend, I have been so worried. How glad I am to see you!" Turning to Soraya and Abdullah, Osman told them, "This is the Caliph's man in charge of all the imports from around the world! The man who will take me to court."

Rasheed said, "Prepare yourself, Osman Balabar, because this week, we will go to court together." Soraya eyed Shajara and winked.

"I told you so," she whispered in her ear. Shajara was flooded with relief.

The next day, just before noon, Rasheed came into the inn to meet Osman. "Let's go to the warehouse, my friend. I want to see all the merchandise you have brought from Konya. Then, if there is time, we will go to my own warehouse where I will show you the fine things that have just arrived from China. You will see silks so rich and bright that when you touch them, they flash with light. There is porcelain more delicate and subtly coloured than is made in any part of the Caliph's empire. There are sables, furs of the marten, bowls of ebony inlaid with metal, and much more."

Shajara's eyes widened at the description and although she would have liked to have seen these things, she was thinking of her friend, Faris, who she hoped would be near the warehouse. Sensing that Osman was in a good mood, she said boldly to him, "Master, I could come with you and carry that heavy book you have under your arm, if you so wish." Osman agreed with a smile, handed her the book, which was indeed heavy, and she followed the two men out into the street. She hoped that Faris would be nearby and an opportunity to excuse herself would arise.

Walking along the busy thoroughfare, they passed by the food stalls selling lemon chicken and lamb roasted with cardamom. They passed the public baths which were much more impressive than the one Shajara had visited and came to the Street of the Booksellers and the men went into one of the bookshops where Osman purchased another, even larger book, its leather cover emblazoned with gold lettering. "This book is the work of a great scholar, dead many years ago, but whose wisdom is un-faded by the passage of time. Carry it carefully, Shajara, for did not the Prophet, peace be upon him, say that the ink of the scholar is as sacred as the blood of martyrs! Great scholars have their place in Paradise. Our Caliph, the Commander of the Faithful, Al Mustansir, is himself a scholarly man."

On the left bank of the Tigris River, they could see the University of Al Mustansir. This was a large and beautiful place recently built by the Caliph around a great central courtyard. The university housed a library, dormitories for students, a kitchen and baths. Already, Rasheed told them, the university had attracted scholars from all around the world.

Now, Shajara had a book under each arm as she followed the men down long streets to Osman's warehouse. His merchandise seemed dull compared with Rasheed's description of the Chinese wares. Here were bags of dried apricots, and sacks of refined sugar. There were Anatolian rugs of the kind that lay on the floors of Osman's house, soft kilims and bolts of a kind of cloth coloured in the Persian fashion that she knew from Konya. There were copper wares made by Konya's coppersmiths, dishes of many sizes made of Anatolian silver, enamelled pottery and many rolls of mohair.

Rasheed was enthusiastic. "I see pottery shining with a lustre finish such as we see only in Syrian ware. Your mohair will sell quickly for use in the best winter clothes. It is as cold here in Baghdad as in the Sultanate of Rum, and we love warm, soft clothes in winter. And look at all the alum," he exclaimed. "That will sell overnight to the cloth factories. They never have enough for dying their multi-coloured fabrics."

The men went from bale to bale. Occasionally, Osman would tell Shajara to bring him the book she had carried from the inn, for it recorded details of the prices he had paid in Konya for the many different goods.

After both men were satisfied, Rasheed suggested to walk to the river where the covered shops on the embankment might be displaying goods that could be of interest to Osman. It was finally the moment for Shajara to ask permission to leave to see Faris.

Osman stroked his beard. "Now we are so close to meeting the Caliph, I would hate for anything to happen. I'd like to keep an eye on you, just in case…Baghdad can be a dangerous city at times." Shajara's heart sank, but as they left the warehouse, Faris bounded up with his father, and told her they had been waiting for her. She already felt that so much had happened in her life, there would not be time enough to tell him. In fact, she knew that she had a very short time to spend with him and seeing the sights of Baghdad would be impossible.

Faris unable to contain his good news, told Shajara he was the proud owner of a camel! Osman had gifted him one of his own camels for the service he provided the caravan by risking his life to save it from bandits.

"You see, Shajara! If you hadn't insulted those men, I wouldn't have been able to warn Osman about the bandits. Now I have a camel! And it is all because of you."

She laughed at Faris' incongruous logic but was very happy for him. Together they followed Osman, Rasheed and Mohamed Eye for Eye as they strolled the broad avenue that led to the river. At last, the river came into sight. Before they reached it, they came up to a mosque, its minaret built in the Persian style. The roof was covered in metal, its dome in glazed tile glinting in the sun. At the embankment there were stalls set out with oranges, cucumbers and melons, all piled high in pyramids on stands. In front of the stands were trays of black raisins and grapes, and most enticing of all, display after display of honeyed rolls and candied fruit.

As they walked, Shajara yearned to tell Faris about her scare with the Slave Market. She wanted to tell him that she cared deeply for him and wanted to run away from all these horrid pitfalls that awaited her in the Harem. Let them run away and live their lives in Damascus…but she hadn't the chance because Faris was telling her excitedly how he intended to earn enough money with his camel to make some investments in goods to sell! Faris was too proud of his newfound status as 'hero' and camel owner, and Shajara could see he had made new dreams and she could not ruin his plans.

"My father was much older when he came by his own camel. Between the two of us, we will make our fortune! And I will come to Baghdad a wealthy trader like Osman Balabar and I will see you in the palace and wink at you!" She did her best to smile so he could not see her anxiety about the coming days ahead of her.

"What's wrong, Shajara? I can see you are not yourself. No questions? No commentary at all? Please tell me." His expression changed to worry, and he stopped and placed his hands on her shoulders.

And so Shajara decided to tell him about her interaction with Hababa, and her beautiful dresses.

"Stay out of her way, Shajara, she will forget soon enough. But if you have problems…" The sun was low and Mohamed Eye for Eye, who had been tolerant enough following them through the city, now approached and finished his son's sentence.

"She will not have problems, for she is a young woman with courage and intellect. Shajara you will succeed, of this we are all certain." Faris glared at his father and Mohamed Eye for Eye's face softened. "There is nothing any of us can do to help her now, Faris. Not even Osman. Once she enters the Harem, she will be out of our reach." Mohamed Eye for Eye approached Shajara. "It has been a pleasure travelling with you Shajara al Durr. We will not forget you, but we must say goodbye." The word goodbye immediately changed the feeling of reunion to one of sadness and finality.

"Thank you, Mohamed Eye for Eye. I have learned much from you."

Shajara knew she would regret not telling Faris how much she had appreciated his companionship and so embarrassed as she was, she stated, "Faris, you have been the best friend I have ever had. I will miss you and I shall never forget you."

Faris looked into Shajara's eyes and nodded. He reached into the folds of his tunic sash and brought out a carved wooden camel and presented it to her. As it lay in her hands, he pointed to the eyes of the camel and remarked, "Look, the eyes are made from chips of real tiger's eye stone, and here, look! The saddle is painted with such ornamental colours. I bought it for you at the market. I thought it might remind you of me." Shajara was filled with emotion. What a kind, caring person Faris was, and how awful it felt to have to say goodbye. She squinted her eyes desperate for the tears not to form, but it was too late. One solitary tear slowly made its way down her cheek and died on her lips.

He turned his head round at the sound of Osman and Rasheed's voice. He took Shajara's hand and squeezed it hard. "Goodbye, my friend!"

She tried hard to compose herself before Osman and Rasheed took notice of her inconsolable countenance.

That night lying in her bed, unable to sleep, she cursed the buzzing mosquitoes and the oppressive heat, but in her heart, she knew that she could not sleep because she thought of Faris. She had tied his camel charm to a thread which she attached to her wrist. She thought of his smile, the way he raised his one eyebrow at her, and his patience and good humour. She was sorry that she would not see him again. She prayed for his safe return and his future happiness, and thanked God for sending him to her to guide her through the long lonely days of the caravan. But she was sure the pain in her heart would not leave her for the rest of her life.

෪

Chapter 22
A Gift is Given

Soraya and Shajara were up at dawn to fashion Shajara's hair. It was not to be in the best Anatolian style, in which the hair hung loose around the shoulders with ribbons to hold it. Instead, Soraya carefully braided it, securing the hair with strands of green silk and setting small pieces of silver along each braid, before coiling it around the head.

When Shajara examined herself in the metal mirror, however, she was dismayed that this was the self-same coiffure of the haughty Hababa, and for a moment, she was tempted to undo it all. Her hair was then perfumed with rose water. Standing in front of the mirror, she never felt herself more beautiful, but the ache of yesterday's goodbye to Faris did not allow her to smile.

Soraya looked concerned at Shajara's dismay and so she put on her best smile, and said, "*Baraka Alluhu fika*, may God bestow blessings upon you. You were right, I am the lucky one and it's because I have you as my guide." Soraya took Shajara into a brief hug.

Soon, it was time to join the men. Osman was pacing up and down, his hands tightly held behind his back, his face showing worry about the day ahead. Rasheed, however, was calm and full of encouraging praise for Shajara. "Our Caliph, Al-Mustansir, will be enchanted." Carrying her best dress carefully packaged under her arm, Shajara went with the two men along the busy streets towards the palace. Her heart was beating hard, her mouth a little dry, but her eyes were bright, and excitement was quickly overcoming her fears.

From outside, the Palace loomed huge and forbidding, battlements set along the top of its high walls, its massive egg-shaped dome standing threateningly above. Uniformed men of the Caliph's guard, tall, bearded and grim looking, with scimitars gleaming at their sides, stood blocking the way through the great gate. Shajara knew these men were slaves, captured like her parents, but trained as warriors, not servants. The Caliphs had long used *Mamluks,* which meant 'owned', as their personal army. Trained from early childhood for military life, the *Mamluks* were proud of being slaves and Shajara knew that their foremost men were the Caliph's favoured generals.

Rasheed was known to the *Mamluk* guards and they were quickly allowed into the courtyard. Shajara could not believe the size of the courtyard. There were at least a dozen fountains, each set in a huge tiled pool from which water flowed along tiled channels to other pools and fountains. The sound of water, splashing and tinkling, filled the air. Flowering bushes were planted in raised beds. Trellises and pergolas were covered in brightly flowering vines.

They did not climb the great steps to the main door of the Palace and Rasheed led them to a side door. "This is where we will find my friend Hadi, the chief servant to the vizier. He is the one who will tell us what to do and when we can be received by the Caliph."

They found him in an antechamber to the vizier's offices. The room was grander by far than any that Shajara had ever entered. Hadi's clothes were finer by far than those in which Master Osman was dressed and those were the finest her master had ever worn. If these are the clothes of the vizier's servant, she wondered how splendidly must the vizier himself be dressed!

But as the vizier came bustling into the antechamber, she noted that he was dressed all in black save for a grey turban. He was in a great hurry and did not stop even to greet them properly. "This is a day of terrible troubles and tedious tasks," he called to them as he went out.

"Not an auspicious beginning," murmured Rasheed to Hadi, who merely smiled. "All days are like this," Hadi replied. "The tasks of Ali Izz al-Din, our great vizier, are never done. His service to our great Caliph, Al-Mustansir, is never ending. We will find him more at peace when he returns to eat. But now," looking at Shajara, "what shall we do with you? I don't think you will be seeing the Caliph today. Or perhaps for many a long day to come."

Osman looked downcast, but Shajara who had been dreading her inspection by the mighty ruler, felt relief. "These gentlemen have an audience in two hours' time, but you will be called only if the Caliph expresses a wish to see you." Hadi called a page dressed in the caliph's colours of blue and green. "Take this slave girl to see Wafik, the chief assistant to the Master Eunuch."

Immediately, Soraya's description of the fearsome Master Eunuch of years ago flooded into Shajara's mind. Clutching the package of her best dress, Shajara followed the pageboy. They went down steep stairs into a long basement corridor, dark except for daylight dimly showing through gratings.

They climbed stairs at the far end of the corridor. "The Harem!" the page told her as they came up to a sentry. Tall and bald, dressed in a flowing robe, a scimitar held across his chest, the sentry stood unmoving in their way. "Hadi sent her for Wafik," the page said before bolting back along the corridor.

The sentry silently inspected Shajara and then called for another page. Even younger than the other page, but dressed more finely in clothes of red silk, the boy silently motioned to Shajara to follow him and he ran ahead.

They went quickly through room after room, each grander than the last. Shajara had time only to glance at the gilt furniture, the satin hangings and the wall tapestries. The boy was almost running across the marble floors. What is the great hurry, Shajara wondered, or do pageboys always run?

The boy took her up to a closed door, tapped gently on it, and then ran off. Shajara wished these page boys were more informative as the door had not opened and she was afraid to knock. Minutes passed. Plucking up her courage, she knocked. Still there was no answer. Perhaps there was no one in this room! The door was suddenly pulled open. "What an impatient slave!" Wafik addressed Shajara as he took her by the arm and led her into the room. He looked her up and down. "Pretty enough," he murmured to himself. "But we have pretty ones enough. Tell me, why should we make room for you? What can you do? Can you dance? Can you sing?"

The words came quickly to Shajara's lips. "I can do both, Master Wafik." Had not Soraya told her that the most favoured girls would pass both tests? But the story of Khoraysan told by Master Osman came to her mind, her ability to read and learn led her to become a favourite, and so she added, "I can also read and memorise poetry and Quran."

Wafik grinned. "Well, we'll see about that! But I can tell that you do not lack for boldness. So, to begin, let's see you dance." Shajara looked questioningly at the man, but he seemed friendly and she began the Anatolian dance favoured by Rehan. Take it slowly, she told herself, but her pace quickened to the remembered rhythm and she threw herself into the final steps.

"A little too wild for our court," Wafik admonished her, "but I see you have grace and rhythm. You have natural poise. And I can see that, unaccompanied by an instrument, you are able to listen to an inner music. That is the gift that cannot be taught. I think it's just possible that we can make a dancer of you."

Shajara felt his approval, even though he had hedged it with criticisms.

"You will need much further training before you can pass the test and be permitted to dance before the Caliph." Shajara felt a flash of disappointment. It seemed that the dancing test still lay far ahead.

"Now, I want to hear your voice. I know all you Anatolian girls are taught sorrowful songs, of sad partings and long-lost love. But I need you to brighten my day. Have you something happy to sing?"

Shajara thought immediately of the song that Master Osman liked to hear during Ramadan. The song told of the happy day of feasting after Ramadan and of the joy of living in God's good world.

"Well, I couldn't make out all those strange Anatolian words," said Wafik, "I think we may make you into a passable singer. Yes, with effort, you may be able to pass the singing test. Now, I'm going to bring you before the Master Eunuch, who will himself decide whether or not you are worth our time."

Shajara's satisfaction with her performance collapsed. She was to be taken before the dread Master Eunuch!

Wafik led her into the great chamber next to his own. The Master Eunuch was a very heavy man. His red, silken robe stretched tight across his body. His beardless face was wreathed in folds of flesh. But he was smiling, and it gave Shajara hope that he would be kind. "What have we here?" he demanded of Wafik, who bowed before him. Shajara bowed very low, hardly daring to look at this powerful being. "I see she has a pretty face and a fine figure. But can she dance? Can she sing? We already have enough pretty faces in the Harem."

Wafik's response was cautious. "She has adequate talent for a beginner, but she needs training in both. Her Arabic is poor and I'm sure she will need a year of training to make her presentable, but she says she can read and has a good memory, that may be good for poetry reciting." A whole year! Shajara wondered silently what on earth could take so long.

As the Master Eunuch laughed, his huge body wobbled. It was a true belly laugh! But, thank heavens, he was a jolly man, far different from the Master Eunuch of Soraya's time. Shajara's fears began to fade. "Well," he boomed, "Wafik is the best teacher of dancing and singing that our court has ever known. Count yourself lucky, he will be your tutor. Now, I hear there's some talk of this girl appearing before the Caliph. So, Wafik, take her to the dresser who will find something suitable for her to wear." Shajara quickly pointed to her package and said, "I have my own dress." She realised immediately that she had been too bold, and she tacked on the words, "O Master," and bowed low.

The Master Eunuch laughed. "So, we have a brave one here!"

෫

Chapter 23
An Audience with the Caliph

Osman and Rasheed were pacing nervously up and down in Hadi's chamber. Suddenly, the vizier burst in and almost before they could reply to his courteous salutation, he was bustling them towards the great Hall of State. The heavy damask curtains were drawn across its tall windows and little was visible of its famous opulence. Standing out in the dim light was the Caliph Al-Mustansir's golden throne set on a platform covered in green satin with a blue and gold awning overhead. "Here is where our Caliph greets sultans, princes and ambassadors from foreign lands."

"Not so long ago," the vizier said glancing towards Osman, "the ambassador of the Sultan of Rum was here. *Alhamdulillah,* Praise be to God, all is well for the moment between our Caliph and the Sultan. The Mongols threaten us both. We seek a stronger alliance with your Sultan." The vizier looked keenly at Osman. "More trade between our lands could help build that alliance."

"I am a simple trader," he told him. "I know nothing of such affairs of state." The vizier ignored him and continued, "Now tell me of your business and your hopes from us." The vizier paused while Osman gave a hesitant account of his hopes for the Baghdad-Konya trade. He ended by declaring the thought that had come into his mind.

"I am a trader not a politician." The vizier smiled.

"I suppose traders don't negotiate their deals?" he said sarcastically. "Politics, like trade, is about successful negotiation. And traders who keep their eyes open on their long journeys come to know many things that we who stay at home can only guess at. You have journeyed to Christian lands and you have been beyond the Black Sea where the Mongols are gathering. What you learn on the road, what you see and hear," said the vizier as he turned towards the door, "could be quite useful to us. Now, we will meet the Commander of the Faithful."

As the vizier's light touched the golden door, huge and heavy as it was, swung easily and silently open. They were in the Caliph Al-Mustansir's personal chambers. On a table covered in shining white linen were gold and silver bowls filled with fruit and dates and candied deserts. No one was in the room, neither courtiers nor servants. There was no sign of the Caliph himself.

Into the room, shuffling rather than walking, came a small man, simply dressed in grey, carefully carrying a pot with a flowering plant in each hand.

The vizier bowed low. "O Great Commander of the Faithful," he addressed the small man, "may I present to you Rasheed el-Haki of Baghdad and Osman Balabar, merchant of Konya in the Sultanate of Rum!" The Caliph's greeting was simple. "*Assalamu 'alaykum,* Peace be upon you," he murmured. The three men bowed low before him. "*Wa 'alaykum assalam*, my Caliph."

"My vizier tells me that you have journeyed from Konya in Rum. He tells me, also, that you might make that journey often if…" The Caliph paused. "If only the Baghdad bankers knew that you had our favour." The Caliph smiled. "You tell us all that you learn on the road and you may use my name with the bankers. Is that a fair exchange?" Osman was quick to give assent. There was nothing to negotiate. The Caliph's endorsement was better than gold.

"Now tell us of events in Konya, of what you saw and what you heard as you went through the lands of the Seljuks and then of your journey through our own lands."

The Caliph and his vizier listened intently as Osman told of changes in Konya, and of how Jalal, his mother Mumima and other refugees had come long distances to escape the Mongols. They even wanted to know about rumours in the streets of Konya, for whether or not they were true, they could shape people's actions. They were especially interested to know that the Sultan had stationed additional troops in Konya to build up the city's defences. It was information that spoke clearly to their fears of a rapidly growing Mongol threat. Genghis Khan, the great Khan of the Mongols, had been dead for a decade, but there were worrying rumours that his sons and grandsons were mobilising in the east.

The Caliph wanted a report on the condition of the caravanserais in the Sultan's lands and in his own and to hear of threats to trade from bandits. Osman described the attempted attack by bandits on his caravan and, because he thought it might amuse the Caliph, he told of Shajara's role in how they came to learn of the attack. He ended the story by describing her beauty and her piety.

"We must see this slave girl! Beauty, courage and piety are a formidable combination. And you say her people are originally from the nomadic Qipchak Turks? Yes, I know of them – their men are who form most of my army – Mamluks. I am interested to see this Mamlukah."

The vizier had already risen to summon the Master Eunuch to bring Shajara before the Caliph.

The Caliph was still quizzing Osman when the Master Eunuch lumbered into the room. Bowing low, he greeted the ruler. He bowed towards Osman and Rasheed. "*As salamu alaikum wa rahmatullah wa barakatuhu.* May the mercy, peace and blessings of Allah be upon you, my masters."

"Ali Alumaki, my Master Eunuch, carries the weight of the Harem on his shoulders," the Caliph told Osman and Rasheed. "And, as you can see, the weight is not only on his shoulders!" The joke made Ali smile and pat his belly lovingly.

"O Commander of the Faithful, you wish to see your new slave girl," said Ali and motioned towards a doorway where Shajara stood just out of sight. Nodding courteously towards Osman, he continued, "She is a pretty one, indeed. But she is untrained in either dance or song. It will be long before she can take the tests and I hesitate to bring her before you."

"Do not hesitate! Bring her before me!" commanded the Caliph.

Shajara came in, her eyes carefully downcast as the Master Eunuch had told her told was the proper etiquette. She bowed low before the Caliph. "The Master Eunuch thinks you can neither dance nor sing," he said. "What do you have to say for yourself?" Words failed her. She dared not repeat the boast that she could do both very well. She must be prudent! "Osman Balabar said you were bolder than this." Shajara was still bowing low.

"Stand up! Let's see whether you can answer a few questions. What do you like the least and what do you like the most about our city of Baghdad?"

Shajara thought only for a brief moment before responding, "O Commander of the Faithful, I like least the fact that Baghdad is not Konya where I lived happily in Master Osman's house. I like best the fact that Baghdad is the greatest city in all the world, and now my home."

The Caliph's eyes lit up and he took a much closer look at Shajara. "Shrewdly answered! At once, you please both your old and your new masters. Perhaps you are a well-trained diplomat?" He teased as he looked at a very uneasy Osman.

The Caliph moved closer towards Shajara, lifting her chin, so that he looked directly in her eyes. "Which is better to be rich or poor?" Shajara knew the answer. "Better to be rich, my Caliph, and to have the happiness of giving to the poor." The Caliph murmured approval.

"Well, here's a harder one. Which of these two is the better? Power or wisdom?" Shajara pondered a bold response but decided on prudence instead. "Only the Commander of the Faithful, who is both powerful and wise beyond all other men, can answer such a question."

"Yes, well evaded with a pretty compliment. Now, answer the question!" Shajara replied, "Only Allah, the Most Merciful and Compassionate, combines true power and wisdom, O' Caliph."

"A pious girl, indeed, but one who dances around the question without answering it." Shajara sensed his displeasure, and the bold response she had first thought of now tumbled from her lips. "O Caliph, he who has power without wisdom will lose his power and only he who is wise uses his power in good deeds."

"Interesting!" said the Caliph. "My dear Osman, you have brought us a very fine gift. Even were she to fail both the Master Eunuch's singing and dancing tests, she would still be an ornament to our court. Nature has given her beauty and intelligence. She has been brought up to be pious and I can see she has a good heart."

"What is more, I think I see in her a capacity for true learning. And at my court we treasure true learning." Turning to the Master Eunuch, the Caliph said, "This girl is to go to our palace school. Teach her to dance, teach her to sing. But have her go as well to school. If she excels in her Quranic studies, let her be taught by the poetry tutor, then have her taught mathematics and her mind tested with astronomy."

"Shajara, you will come back here in two years' time," said the Caliph. "I am sure you will bring us delight with your dances and songs. What I hope for, as well, is that you can bring us delight in learned conversation. There is no delight that can compare with the pleasures of the mind."

The audience was over. They bowed low and, then, with the Master Eunuch taking her by the arm, they walked backwards to the door where, once again, they bowed. Shajara glanced a last time at the Caliph and saw that he was looking gravely at her.

§

Chapter 24
The Fate of Hababa

Months passed and Shajara had not made many friends in the Harem, she kept to herself, stayed out of trouble with the other women but was often lonely. She studied hard and at night read the Quran, mostly as it brought solace to her lonely heart which found it painful to think of Faris or her parents. She sailed through her dancing and singing tests, winning the highest praise from the Master Eunuch. "You are our new Hababa," he told her, "and I had never thought to see her equal." He promised Shajara a starring role in the upcoming Eid entertainment, the role Hababa had long held before her exile.

Hababa's mysterious disappearance from court was a subject of never-ending Harem gossip. Some said that she had been exiled for impiety, others that it was because she was rude to everyone and brazen in her behaviour.

Shajara knew the true cause, as did the pupils of the Palace school. Often as she left the palace school, Hababa would be standing by its door, her lip curling scornfully as Shajara passed. She had never spoken to Shajara, but that is because she saw herself as Shajara's superior and Shajara came to believe that she didn't recognise her from the Dressmakers – just as Soraya had said.

Hababa stood there, Shajara knew, waiting for Sahl, one of the Caliph's sons. The boy had come under Hababa's spell. He had fallen so hopelessly in love that he had told his father that nothing would stop him marrying her. The Caliph, who set a high value on piety, courtesy and self-restraint, would not permit such a foredoomed union.

The Caliph ended the romance by sending Hababa back to the slave market. It seemed a cruel thing to do, but the Caliph was not only offended by her impiety but convinced that Hababa had set out to entrap Sahl by her wiles. Older women in the Harem whispered that in the days of the Caliph's grandfather, the Caliph Al Nasir, the Master Eunuch would have drowned Hababa in the river.

As it was, Hababa was sold from the market to a Yemeni prince, so the court gossip went, and hence her fate was not of a maid, but starting life again as a dancer in another royal court. A memory of walking with Soraya through the slave market came to her mind. She imagined Hababa standing on the slave platform, her hands tied and a rope around her neck, waiting fearfully to see who would bid for her. In her heart, she felt sudden compassion for the poor woman. I hope I never meet such a fate. *Tawakkalna ala Allah*, I place complete trust in God.

Although dancing and singing came easily to Shajara and always lifted her spirits, the tutorials in the Palace school were made difficult by her fellow pupils. She was the only one who was not born as a noble. In fact, she was the only slave. Of course, the fellow students dared not question the caliph's decision, but they were not inclined to welcome her. They were quick to roll their eyes and sigh heavily when she made the slightest error. When the tutor was out of the room, they would mock her openly with crude jests about her parents or her likely fate in the slave market. The Caliph's older son, Al Musta'sim was already out of the Palace school and training with the vizier and his father to become the next Caliph. But Sahl, the younger brother often attended the same classes as she did. She made certain that whenever he looked in her direction, she cast her eyes down, for she had seen that he often looked at her.

In the evenings, Shajara would practice the day's lessons, and rising early each morning, she would memorise *sura* after *sura* from the Quran. She had heard of the Hafez – a man who memorised the Quran. And it soon became her ambition to do the same.

There was also a sophisticated postal system which had been established in the Abbasid Caliphate to enhance communications within the large empire, and Shajara was glad of it, as she would write her parents every month. She explained to them everything good that was happening in her life. She wrote to her mother in detail of the special dishes that were served. To her father, she described the flowers and the garden landscape. She even attempted some drawings so he could see the flowers and the design in colours as well as words. In return, she was given short letters dictated to Abbas by her parents. He had kept his promise and wrote often. The letters often told of the life of Osman and his family – Abbas' marriage and their children. Shajara tried not to become jealous of her mother's obvious affection for the new babies in the house. Occasionally, there was mention of her father's failing health or her mother's problematic arthritis.

Dutifully, Shajara would make a special request to the Harem's doctor, for advice, as he was claimed to be one of the best in the world.

She also continued to write Faris. His father and he had continued to do well as caravan masters, as well as small business with their camels. The exchange between the two friends remained as light-hearted and close as if they had not been parted for long. Of course, his letters came sporadically due to his work, but Shajara read them over and over and took pleasure in writing him about everything she learned. Shajara often thought of him in the evening, after the day's work and training had been completed.

In her letters, she told him about new innovations or buildings in Baghdad like the water clock which had been built and installed in the entry way of the Al Mustansir university. The clock was called a clepsydra which in ancient Greek meant water thief, and as she had learned in class, it was because a Greek man named Archimedes had written how to construct such a device a thousand years before! It was a monumental hydraulic machine which also had alarm bells installed to ring out five times during the day for prayer. It also traced the movement of the moon and was one of the most fascinating water clocks of all time. Faris wrote back with news of Konya and his caravan excursions.

Daily life in the Harem was busy for Shajara. She enjoyed her academic lessons and Quran studies, but also enjoyed her singing and dancing lessons. Poetry had become a highly prized art form and the Caliph sent poetry to the tutors for the singers to memorise. Shajara found that she had an excellent memory for recitation and enjoyed putting them to music with the accompaniment of the lute.

Later that evening while in her room quietly reading, a young domestic girl brought a letter to Shajara. Shajara delighted to have news finally from home, gave the girl praise and filled her pockets with the peaches that she had been eyeing.

She had not had news for several months and was anxious to hear from them. Unfortunately, she read that her father was dead. Her mother relayed that he died happy knowing his daughter Shajara was living in the most renowned Harem in the world.

Shajara felt lonelier than ever and cried for her father. That night, she dreamt of him, he was in the Harem's garden and calling to her window. He was trimming the hedges, and she, delighted to know he was alive and well, ran down the numerous stairs, but by the time she arrived, he was gone, and the garden path was writhing with snakes.

The next day, Shajara did not attend the lessons and instead decided to stay in her room and read the Quran. She felt a sadness which she felt she could not overcome in order to listen to her tutors. That afternoon, Sahl showed up looking for her.

"What are you doing here?" She was too shocked to use the correct title for the prince, but he didn't seem to notice.

"I am the Caliph's son; I can enter the women quarters as I please." He smiled, but seeing her face marked by the passage of her numerous tears, he softened and asked. "This is the first day you have not attended lessons, the tutor was worried." He sat down next to her on the sofa and waited. She saw little use in hiding her sadness and told him about her father and her awful dream.

"Indeed, *Anaalallah wa ennalahu rageoon*, to Allah we belong and to Him we shall return. Truly, I am so sorry to hear of your loss." Sahl put his hand on her hand.

"Thank you, Sahl, I appreciate your concern. How were today's lessons?" Shajara inched further away from Sahl and carefully removed her hand.

Sahl rolled his eyes. "The same boring classes day after day. Why don't you come with me and I will try to cheer you up?" He stood up and reached for her hand. Shajara knew that this would not escape the notice of the women in the harem and it would just fuel gossip, and so she politely declined by saying she must write a letter to her mother instead.

"I can show you some of the rooms in the Palace you have never seen before…there are some of the world's greatest treasures in them. You can write your mother later." He tried to persuade her, but again she refused. "There are no treasures in this world which could alleviate my sadness, but I am grateful for your efforts."

"All right, maybe another time." Giving her a wink as he left.

Shajara wished she could have a friend again like Faris – a friend to laugh out loud and to share secrets, and most importantly someone she could trust. She knew Sahl was not this person, for over the time she had spent in the palace school she knew they were very different people whose interests were completely at odds with each other. He showed little interest in his studies and instead spoke only of hunting and riding.

116

As the days passed, an upsetting development began to unfold. Shajara realised that in the case of Sahl, he found little excuses to meet her as if by accident. A special look came into his eyes whenever she looked towards him. She tried her best to avoid him. Yet, there he always was, standing behind a corner, and accompanying her to other lessons.

Sahl was, nevertheless, the second of the Caliph's sons, his heir apparent if anything should happen to Al-Musta'sim, and he demanded deference from all others. Shajara had to face the awful truth. Sahl was in love again. This time, it was she who was the object of his romantic affections!

Shajara began to imagine a dreadful fate. *"La hawla wala qawatu ila bi Allah*. There is no power but from God." And now, for the second time in her life she wondered if she faced the threat of the slave market.

৪৶

Chapter 25
The Final Test

Each night as Shajara sought sleep, she would murmur, *Bismikah Allahumma amutu wa ahyaa*, Oh God, in your name, I live and die. She prayed hard that she would not be blamed for Sahl's foolish obsession with her. She was worried, too, that her resistance to Sahl's loving looks were giving place to offence and angry threats.

It was the day of Eid Al Fitr, the feast after Ramadan, when Shajara would star in the evening entertainment. She was preparing to practice her dance one final time when the Master Eunuch came bustling towards her. "You know that dance perfectly well," he told her sharply. "Go to the dresser for clothes suitable to an audience. The Caliph himself wishes to see you, and I will not hide this from you, Shajara, he does not seem pleased!" There was no hearty laughter, not even a smile. Her heart sank. This would be her last dance in the Palace, and soon she would face the slave market. She had been lucky to escape it once before, how could she hope to be so lucky again?

Still unsmiling, the Master Eunuch led her to the Caliph's chambers. There, standing at the doorway, he gently pushed her forward. "Good luck," he whispered.

It was almost two years since she had stood before the Caliph. She saw his grave eyes as he beckoned her forward. It was all she could do to control the trembling in her limbs. "So, here you are again," he said. "Your tutor has told us of your progress. I understand from him that you have the whole Quran, every verse, in your memory and that you have perfected its recitation in excellent Arabic. He has shown me your writing, your lessons in geometry and he has told me that you have surpassed my son, Sahl in philosophy." Shajara trembled.

"If you were to find yourself at a foreign court, its ruler would be impressed by you. A wise prince would be less delighted by your singing and dancing, excellent as it is, than by what you have learned in my school. He would find pleasure in conversation with such a learned, young woman. In all ways, I am pleased with you. I am confident you would reflect well on us, uphold our honour and our reputation and be able to do so in even the greatest of foreign courts."

Shajara felt a glow of satisfaction. She had earned the Caliph's approval. But why had the Master Eunuch warned her? And what was this about foreign courts?

"So, as I thought," he told her, "you have proved yourself. But I have learned more about you than I think you know." Shajara's satisfaction gave way to foreboding.

The Caliph paced silently. Shajara dreaded what was to come.

"It pains me to say that I have a silly son," the Caliph said sighing. "Perhaps the only good judgment Sahl has ever exercised is to fall in love with you. Most girls in the Harem would have encouraged his affections. By spurning them, you show both intelligence and virtue, and you have earned my personal gratitude. But, you are earning Sahl's enmity. The boy is spoiled and vain. He is unused to being refused and he is as reckless in anger as he is in love. I will speak with you after the entertainment to speak about this further."

Shajara gave a quick nod and curtsey and left his rooms. The evening entertainment was held in the Great Hall where the caliph sat enthroned and surrounded by courtiers. The entertainment began with a happy serenade and joyful dance of twenty finely dressed harem girls. As they left, Shajara emerged onto the floor, more finely dressed than any of the others, bowed low before the caliph, and then stood for a moment in silence before beginning her song. It was far different from a typical Eid song for it told the tragedy of two lovers, their sorrow at parting, their joy when briefly reunited and then, in the final verses, the untimely deaths of both. She felt the emotions of those she sang about, losing for a moment herself in their story. Her song drew tears and then great applause.

Again, Shajara bowed low. Her poised figure stood motionless for a long moment before she began a slow dance, her face filled with expression her arms gracefully conveying sorrowful yearning. Then, as her tempo increased, the final movements of the dance and her smiling face told of the joys of life. Shajara left the floor to great applause, led by the Caliph himself. The thunderous applause seemed to end the evening and Shajara was about to leave the Great Hall when the vizier took her by the arm. "Come with me to the Caliph's quarters."

They entered the Caliph's chamber together. "You can stay here while I talk with the vizier," the Caliph told her. "Listen closely, for what we have to say may be useful to you in the future." Shajara knew that she was being accorded a great honour and, although she kept her eyes downcast, she listened to and remembered every word.

The talk was of the threat from the Christian crusaders. The Caliph and his vizier were speaking of a ruler who was in some way related to Saladin, one of the great heroes of Islam. Shajara even knew that hero's full name, Ṣalāḥ ad-Dīn Yūsuf ibn Ayyūb. Famed for his chivalrous behaviour to all, Saladin had reconquered Yemen, most of Syria, defeated the Crusaders at the great Battle of Hattin and seized Palestine from Crusader rule. Before Saladin died in Damascus, he had given much of his great wealth to his subjects. Shajara thought of him as a model ruler, at once brave in battle, wise in statesmanship and generous to his people. He had been dead for thirty years, but his fame would never die.

The Caliph was recalling that Saladin's nephew, Al-Kamil, had been Sultan of Egypt at the time of a great Crusader offensive and had only saved Cairo by breaching the dams and flooding the Nile. The Caliph had heard that Al-Kamil had died and, now, news was reaching Baghdad of a war between his two sons, Adil and Salih. Which should the Caliph support? The question was urgent, for there was news of a further crusade in the west at the self-same time that the Mongol horde was again massing in the east. The Caliph needed allies. Adil held Egypt, which he ruled from Cairo. Salih was at Damascus and held lands in the Jazira region, the lands of the Khwarezmians, once ravaged by Genghis Khan.

On the table before the Caliph were spread gifts from Adil. The vizier had made a careful account of them. "Here are 20 pieces of the finest silk cloth and 100 pieces of silk brocade of the highest quality," he told the Caliph. "It is a splendid gift with a value of something like 5,000 gold dinars. It is more valuable by far than these books that are sent to you by Salih."

"You speak of value as they do in the market," the Caliph said, "but the books are of more interest to me than silk and brocade. They are the more thoughtful gift. He knows that I have founded a university in my name."

The Caliph let his fingers run over the rich brocade. "Does such a valuable gift show that Adil is strong or weak?" Al Mustansir murmured. "He controls Egypt now, but for how long?"

The vizier replied, "They say that Salih is a determined young man, and they also say that Adil is too interested in the pleasures of Cairo. Yet, it is Adil who has more *Mamluk* soldiers and who controls more resources and it is Salih who is in uncertain control of Damascus and the poverty-stricken Jazirah. One thing of interest to remember about Salih is that he was given by his father as a hostage to the Crusaders in return for one of their own princes."

"So, living with them, Salih must have learned much about the Crusaders, their strengths and weaknesses. An interesting fact, indeed. In any event, one of Al-Kamil's sons will come out on top," said the Caliph, "and since we do not yet know which, I shall send a gift to each. I have two gifts in mind, each of a value greater than 5,000 golden dinars. The first gift is this scimitar." Shajara watched as the Caliph withdrew the sharp steel from a jewelled scabbard. "Either of Al-Kamil's sons would be proud to bear such a handsome scimitar at his side in court. In battle, because its blade is made from hardened Damascene steel, it would be a fearsome weapon."

"My second gift, is more valuable still." Turning to Shajara, he said gravely, "You, Shajara, are a clever, talented and beautiful slave, you are my other gift! Tell me, to which of Al-Kamil's sons should I send you?"

Some inkling that this might be her fate had been growing in Shajara's mind, triggered first by the Caliph's mention of foreign courts in the morning and then by his strange demand that she listen to his conversation with the vizier. Even so, his words shocked her.

"I know nothing of either of these two men, my Caliph." She struggled with his question as she mastered her feelings. "I know them only by their gifts."

"So, then, you must reason from what you know," the Caliph told her.

"My Caliph, Adil's gift shows he can call on the riches of Cairo. There is certainly much wealth, military and comfort there. And I dare say that there are also ladies in his harem who can sing and dance like me."

"Interesting. What of Salih's gift?"

"It is a clever gift that he sends you books says that he knows of your love of learning and of your great university. Perhaps he believes you will receive more pleasure from reading these books than a gift of wealth, it also may mean that Salih himself is a learned man."

"That is exactly my thought," said the Caliph. Turning to the vizier, he said, "This is what we will do. Send the captain of our guard to be the bearer of the scimitar to Adil in Cairo. Tell the captain of the guard to take Sahl with him and to put Sahl to the test on the long journey. Sahl is to walk every other day, not ride. It will teach him something of hardship for a change."

"The more eloquent gift, we shall send to Salih in Damascus. Yes, Shajara you are a gift who can speak for us. Tell Salih about us, of Baghdad, of our court, of the strength of our army, and of our determination to keep Islamic lands free of both Mongols and Crusaders."

Turning again to the vizier, the Caliph said, "Tell the Master Eunuch that it is my command that Wafik take Shajara to Salih in Damascus, where he must stay for three months. And Shajara, keep your eyes and ears open in the court of Salih, tell what you learn to Wafik, and he will come back with the information. Do what you must in your new position in his court to gain his trust but keep us informed!"

Shajara went back to the harem with her mind in turmoil. She was once again to be sent as a gift to a foreign land. She had spent the last two years being a student – learning to use her mind and her body. What would she need to learn that would interest Salih? Salih would not be so careless as to tell secrets of his intentions to her, would he? And if she was found to be collecting information and sending it back, what would be her fate then?

෫

Chapter 26
The Journey to Damascus

The Master Eunuch was bustling around the great courtyard of the Palace in his red silk robe, busily overseeing preparations for Shajara's journey to Damascus. He had last-minute instructions for Wafik, his assistant, and carefully counted out dinars for expenses on the journey. He also had a stern warning for Qipchuk, the man who was to lead Shajara's guard of ten *Mamluks*. "You and your men must guard the Caliph's gift with your life," he warned him.

The *Mamluks* were mounted warriors, skilled horsemen, who had lived all their lives in the Palace garrison. Shajara knew that, from youth, they had been trained for war. She knew, too, that they gave absolute loyalty to the Caliph and his commands. She had seen them by the banks of the Tigris practicing cavalry tactics and archery. She had seen them, too, playing polo and had marvelled at their control of their horses in the game, their tight turns and, then, their sudden bursts of speed. Sometimes, she had watched their competitions in mounted archery and their horseback acrobatics. What better preparation for battle against Mongols or Crusaders? Indeed, what better men to guard her on the way to Damascus.

Qipchuk and the guardsmen were *Mamluks*. Mamluk in Arabic means 'owned', and the name was given to all slaves taken in service of the Caliphs or other rulers of the Caliphate. She supposed that she too was a sort of Mamluk. Musa, her father had been brought from the same territories. Shajara was comforted by their presence, for these men were her people and spoke her own native tongue. They were an impressive force – their armour, their weapons, their horses and their training were immediately recognisable. No bandit troupe would dare come near them. She felt comforted by this as she had never forgotten the fear that had travelled with her on her first caravan from Konya. That fear had never entirely left her. Now she was preparing for another journey – far from the home she had made in Baghdad.

Shajara and Wafik, like the guardsmen, rode on horseback. Servants led two mules, one laden with Shajara's wardrobe of new dresses and her tent, but also carrying brocades for Salih. These fine brocades, the Master Eunuch told her, had been selected by the Caliph himself, so that Shajara could give her own gift to her new master. She immediately recognised the brocades as those that had been the gift from Adil, Salih's own brother. She smiled at the Caliph's private joke and knew that he favoured Salih. The other mule bore provisions and supplies for the journey to Damascus.

Wafik, whom Shajara had come to know and like over her two years in the harem, was a little ill at ease with the *Mamluks* and even more so with their horses. Like Shajara, he was to ride, but unlike Shajara, who quickly mastered her horse, he remained very uncertain in his saddle. He glowered at Shajara when she mocked his unease. He shrieked when she playfully slapped the rump of his horse and sent him galloping. He grew angry when Shajara and the guardsmen laughed as he clung desperately to his horse's mane. It took some time before he forgave them. But it was these fun and games that eased the tedious riding and long days on horseback.

Yet, Wafik was a good companion on the journey and helpful with advice and information for Shajara. Although he had never visited Damascus, Wafik knew that it had been the capital of the whole Caliphate before Baghdad. "The Romans built its walls," he told Shajara, "and also its seven great gates. Everyone knows it is the City of Jasmine and, outside its walls, in a place called Salihiye, there are the finest of gardens and great orchards." He told her how the Barada River flows by its walls so that the city has water enough to withstand long siege. "Its Grand Mosque has stood for 500 years and its Hammam Ammounah, the great public baths, are said to make the citizens of Damascus the cleanest of all good Muslims. Commerce comes to the city from both Byzantium and China, and Damascene silks are famous throughout the world. There are famous *madrasas* or schools and *maristas* or hospitals within the city walls." He told her, "Shajara, you are lucky to live in a city of such splendour and honour."

She flashed him a smile and thought back to the time, now years ago, when her mother and Serine had called her lucky to go live in Baghdad. Now, it would appear she was to be lucky again to live in Damascus. She had sent letters to both her mother and Faris telling them of the Caliph's plan for her. She told them to not write her until she could send word where she could be reached. There was a part of her that was excited and anxious to know what would await her. But she could not deny that there was also fear. She had tried to live her life without fear, as Jalal and Mumima advised a life lived in fear is no life at all. She depended on her own abilities to keep her safe, it wasn't all about luck. But the fact remained that she was still a slave, albeit to the Caliph, and so living in a beautiful palace, but still subject to the wishes of someone other than herself. But Shajara had found freedom in her life – the freedom of spirit through song and dance and the freedom of her mind through education. She had come to learn that the best way to keep herself safe was to know as much as she could about the situation she was in and using her knowledge and talents to create a situation which she could control.

Shajara knew that the great Saladin had captured Damascus fifty years before. It was because he had made himself the Conquerer of Damascus as well as of Cairo that Saladin had been able to declare himself Sultan of Syria and Egypt. To hold Damascus, the ancient capital of the Caliphate, was important not only strategically but symbolically.

On the second day of their journey, Qipchuk rode alongside Shajara and asked her if all was well. She felt this was an invitation for her to speak freely and so as she was full of questions of how life was for the Mamluks, she launched an inquisition upon Qipchuk, and much to her delight, he spoke to her freely and happily. He told her of the *Furusiyya*, the code of *Mamluk* warriors taught in the Palace garrison. "You see, it is a word that combines three basic parts of every Mamluk horseman's life: its *'ulum* or science, its *funun* or art and its *adab* or the written teachings of cavalry skill and strategy." He looked over to see if she was following, and she nodded for him to continue. "Basic to the *Furusiya* is the management, training and care of the horses that carry us in to battle and in our sport of polo. Basic, too, are cavalry tactics, riding techniques for different situations, mounted archery, and the making and use of armour and of bows."

Shajara admitted to him that she had come to love the horse provided for her. "Ahh Zolan is one of my favourites too. We call him the gentle giant, as he is the largest of all our horses, but also the sweetest in temper." Shajara leaned forward to pat Zolan. She told Qipchuk about riding the camel during the caravan and he laughed at her description of awkwardness of being on top of a camel.

During the days of riding amiably together, they would share stories of their early lives before coming to Baghdad. Qipchuk told her of his education in military tactics and was flattered by her intelligent interest in the subject. He spoke as well of the *Mamluks'* education in the military virtues of chivalry and courage. Shajara felt very safe with Qipchuk and his troop of guards.

She went over in her mind Qipchuk's account of military strategy and tactics. War, she knew, was a terrible curse. Yet, to know how to win in battle was a very interesting and important subject, and one she thought well worth her further attention. In the evenings, she did entertain them with songs of their shared homeland, and some new ones with which she had sung at the Caliph's court. Occasionally, she performed a dance. Wafik had advised her against both at the start, as it was deemed inappropriate and the Mamluks were not worthy of her talents, but as the days passed, they all grew weary of riding, and looked forward to some form of entertainment in the evenings, and even Wafik hadn't the heart to forbid her. However, for Shajara, she was entertained and fascinated by the stories they told her – stories of battles and war; of treachery and military escapades. She was no longer the young girl frightened by the Mongol stories Faris used to tell.

As they came towards the end of their journey, Wafik told Shajara some of the facts of her new master and his life. "His full name," he told her, "is Al-Malik Salih Najm al-din Ayyub. He is the eldest son of Al-Kamil, and the blood of the great Saladin flows through his veins." Shajara immediately wanted to know why, if he was the eldest son, Salih did not rule in both Damascus and Cairo, as his father had done before him. Wafik knew only that Salih had quarrelled with his father and that there were stories that Salih had been suspected of organising *Mamluk* troops to seize power in Egypt. Wafik had heard stories, too, of how Salih's uncle, as-Salih Ismail, was even now plotting against Salih. Only time would tell who would finally emerge as the paramount ruler of the Ayyubids, the descendants of Saladin. *What a quarrelsome family,* Shajara thought to herself. However, if there was one thing she had learned in the Harem, it was that the lure of power often outweighed the loyalty of blood. The more she saw examples of this, the stronger her faith grew. She never wanted to lose sight of what was truly important.

Shajara was fascinated to know more about Salih's years as hostage with the Christians, what he had learned about them, what he had thought of their ways of life.

"Well, I don't know everything about it, and you can bore him with all your questions," he mocked, "but what I have heard is that Salih returned an even more committed Muslim. He is known as a truly pious man," Wafik assured her.

"Hmm," Shajara shrugged.

"Surely, that must reassure you, Shajara!"

"I suppose it does, but I have heard many claims of their devout beliefs, and it is often the ones who boast the loudest, who have darkness in their hearts."

On the last night of their journey, Shajara decided that she would provide a special evening of entertainment. Selecting her best dress, the one she planned for her presentation at court the next day, she emerged singing and dancing in her old Anatolian style. As she finished, Wafik praised her saying, "You are more beautiful than ever! Assuredly, you will earn favour from Salih." Shajara bowed at the compliment, but she told herself that they were no more than Harem words. It was to the *Mamluks* that she sang her last song of the evening, a song of their lost homeland. It was their applause and approval that she relished. It was Qipchuk who came to her, he bowed and pressed his hand to his heart. "You hold us in your power. We will arrive Damascus tomorrow. We will do as you tell us. You are one of us." Wafik had overheard and Shajara saw his open mouth and understood the compliment Qipchuk gave her.

She retired to her tent and settled down to sleep. "*Bismika Allahumma amutu wa ahyaa*," she murmured the comforting words, "Oh God in your name I live and die." She smiled sleepily, happily. She was ready for Damascus.

֍

Chapter 27
Banuqa

Shajara's party entered Damascus at midmorning. Unlike Baghdad, there were no sprawling suburbs around the city, the gate through which they entered was guarded by a solitary soldier and, as they went further into the city, all in the group were struck that the streets were much less busy than at home. Great this city may be, but not half so great as Baghdad, Shajara felt.

The palace of Salih was an old one, built by the Ummayad sultans five centuries ago. As Shajara rode close to Qipchuk, he pointed out to her that its walls and main gate bore scars from some recent fighting. As they came into the courtyard, they saw *Mamluk* soldiers and Qipchuk instantly recognised their captain as a friend from years before. While Shajara and Wafik organised the unloading of their baggage, Qipchuk and the *Mamluk* captain were in deep conversation. Shajara looked over at the Mamluk captain who was one of the tallest men she had ever seen with his long blonde hair tied and hanging down his back.

Wafik turned to Shajara and told her of his plan. "I want to find a way to take you quickly into the harem. You should refresh yourself after the long journey today and put on your best dress. I will present you to Salih at an appropriate time." He continued that his plan was to use that time to learn as much as he could of court gossip about Salih: what kind of man he was, his attitudes to the harem, who were his chief advisers, and who his favourite courtiers. "I have learned after years in the service of the Caliph that knowledge is power. I think you have discovered this too; otherwise, you would not be so relentless with your questions! I do not like walking into a situation unarmed, so we will arm ourselves with knowledge!" Shajara smiled, yes, she knew this too.

But before they had finished unloading their mules, a large man dressed in military garb strode purposefully up to their group. He ignored Wafik, failed even to notice Shajara, and spoke directly to Qipchuk. "Have you and this troop come from the palace in Baghdad?" he said, pointing to Shajara's guards. "I am very glad to see you. I had heard that Caliph Mustansir was sending a gift and I can think of no better gift than these fine *Mamluk* warriors."

Who is this man? thought Shajara. Did he not realise that the men were not the gift? It was her! He was likely the head of the military stationed in the palace. She would have liked to set him straight on this point, but experience and maturity told her that this would not be wise. Instead, she waited for Wafik to explain. She looked to him, but Wafik hardly knew what to do. He began to speak, but the man waved him away in irritation, concentrating his remarks on Qipchuk. "We may have some fighting to do before long," he said. Pointing to his *Mamluk* captain, he went on, "Rukn here, whom it seems you know, has fewer than 100 men under his command and I would like you to…"

Qipchuk cut him off. "With the greatest respect, I must stop you there. I am the leader of this troop of men, it is true, and we have indeed come from the Palace in Baghdad. But I take orders from only one person here."

The man had his back to Shajara and she could not see his face, but she saw him put his hands on his hips and one of his hands on his sword. "And WHO may I ask gives you your orders here?" There was no mistake by the tone of his voice that he was angry.

"I do." Shajara stepped forward to make her way to face this man and clear up the misunderstanding. She pulled her shoulders back and tried to stand as tall as she could. She sensed his anger and strength all at once but refused to be intimidated. "These men are under *my* orders. May we enquire who you are?" Shajara asked politely.

"*You* want to know who *I* am?" aghast the man was clearly struggling with controlling his temper, but Shajara tried to ignore the fact that he was well armed and angry and just held her head high, and simply replied, "I do."

The man took a very long and deep breath, his huge chest heaving. "All right then, I will tell you who I am. I am Al-Malik Salih Najm al-din Ayyub, ruler of Damascus and the lands of the Jezirah, son of al-Malik al-Kamil Naser ad-Din Abu al-Ma'ali Muhammad fourth Ayyubid Sultan of Egypt. And now you know who I am, please do me the honour of telling me who you think you are!" Shajara's eyes grew wide and horror began to spread across her face. He made eye contact with her and she felt some of her confidence drain away. She could see from the corner of her eyes that Wafik and Qipchuk, and she assumed the rest of his men, were bowing low. It took her a moment to pull herself together and then lowered her head and made a bow.

What impossible luck, she thought to herself. Why would he walk around dressed like a soldier if he were in fact the ruler of these lands? This was most definitely an unfortunate introduction.

"I am Shajarat al Durr and *I* am your gift from our Caliph Mustansir. These Mamluks have been sent with me for my protection. They will stay with me for the first few months, as long as…until you are certain I will be a welcome addition to your Harem." She halted fearful of saying anything more. She heard no response from him and raised her head to look to his face. She saw him assessing her, but his face betrayed no trace of a reaction.

There was no welcome, nor was there recognition of her. Instead, he turned his head to Qipchuk and continued his previous conversation.

"Much of my army was bribed into deserting. Now we are hard pressed to defend even this palace, never mind the city. My cousin, al-Nasir Daud has allied with my brother Adil and at some point, I think he will be marching from his fortress at Al Karak towards Damascus." Still addressing Qipchuk, "In these dire times, I have a hard time believing that Caliph Mustansir thinks I have more use for a beautiful woman than ten armed and trained Mamluk soldiers." He turned and strode back into the palace.

Qipchuk moved uncomfortably in place waiting orders, and Shajara knew what needed to be done. "It seems that we have arrived at a very bad time indeed! Of course, Qipchuk what we must do is to offer help where it is needed while collecting as much information as possible about the situation here, and of course Salih's intentions. Meanwhile, Wafik and I will smooth things over with Salih."

Qipcuk and Rukn led their *Mamluks* away to care for their horses at the stables. The servants had finished unloading the mules. Wafik stared at Shajara uncertain what to do, wringing his hands and his eyes filled with anxiety.

"I'll find the women's quarters and you can come after," Shajara told Wafik. "Unpack the brocades now to bring them with you and then have one of the servants fetch my baggage while the other holds the mules." Her crisp instructions had elicited a bow from Wafik, the first he had ever given her. When men are uncertain of what to do, she thought to herself, they will obey someone – even a woman – who has a clear plan of action.

She looked up to the Palace and thought she caught a glimpse of Salih's shoulder armour glinting in the open windows of the Palace. So, he was watching her give orders. She had managed to anger the man she was intended to please, and now she would have to find a way to put everything right.

Shajara entered the palace by what she guessed to be the door to the Harem. The corridor was dark, the walls cracked with age, the furniture old and the hangings in need of repair. Nothing in the place was of the standard to which she had grown accustomed in Baghdad. The Harem itself seemed small and cramped. No uniformed guard stood at its entry. There was no Master Eunuch. Were there even any women?

The question was immediately answered. A very young woman stood before her, smiling a greeting. Shajara bowed so soon as she heard the name, Banuqa, for she knew that this was the younger sister of Salih. She shared her brother's features, like him her eyes were very dark, her hair black with tight curls and both were well above average height. Unlike him, she showed an air of uncertainty and sadness.

Wafik came up bearing the fine silk brocades, which Shajara immediately took from him. Turning to Banuqa, she said, "I am Shajara al Durr, I am a gift to your brother from Caliph Mustansir. This is my gift to you, Amira Banuqa. I am sure that you can put these brocades to use." She was careful not to look at Wafik, but she could imagine his shocked expression. She knew immediately that if she was to gain insight to Salih and his character it would be through his sister. And what need did Salih have of fine brocades in this time of a possible impending attack? Better to have an ally in his sister, as she had made such a poor first impression with Salih.

Banuqa was clearly impressed. "A gift bearing a gift," she exclaimed, "and both of great beauty!" She took Shajara by the arm. Before long, Shajara and Banuqa were talking happily together. At first their discussion centred on the brocades, which Banuqa fingered lovingly. "If we knew for sure that we would stay here in Damascus," she said, "I would have a thousand uses for them. But our future is so uncertain that I think it safer to put them with my other few treasures."

Banuqa's treasure chest was far from full, a fact that she explained by their sudden departure from Cairo. "It was my fate to be forced to choose between my brothers. I chose my eldest brother who is both more learned and more pious than Adil. Now, our hateful cousin, al-Nasir Daud, has allied with Adil and we fear that their combined forces will march against us in the next year. We may have to leave Damascus as suddenly as we left Cairo." Shajara could see that this fact weighed heavily on Banuqa and she saw the heavy dark circles under her eyes. Shajara felt a pang of pity for this young girl, who couldn't be older than she was when she first left Konya.

Shajara, always full of questions and taking in everything around her, quickly understood that Banuqa had been given an excellent education. Her room was full of books including several that Shajara recognised from her own studies. Shajara questioned Banuqa about Damascus and her daily life but tried also to gain insight to Salih without directly asking her.

"It seems I have arrived at a very inopportune moment. I fear I have already managed to upset your brother, and the best possibility I have to correct this, is to stay out of his way and put my Mamluks to his use."

Banuqa gave Shajara a friendly smile.

"The first thing to know about my brother," Banuqa told her, "is that his faith, always strong, was made stronger still by his years as a hostage with the Crusaders. Although they made every effort to convert him, he refused, and it seems to have strengthened not only his faith but his stubbornness too."

"I found during my time in Baghdad that nothing brought me solace and calm more than reading the Quran," Shajara said.

This shocked Banuqa. "You were unhappy in Baghdad? Were you treated poorly?"

"Not at all, I was very well treated in Baghdad and was given many opportunities to improve myself, and was even educated there, but I missed my friends and family from Konya, and did not make many close friends in the Harem. There was no one who shared the same interests as me." She laughed. "But seemingly within hours of arriving in Damascus I have a friend!"

Banuqa smiled. "I am so genuinely glad you are here. I have been so lonely since leaving Cairo!" She squeezed Shajara's hand. "But if it is faith and learning which interests you, then nothing could find you more favour in my brother's eyes." She paused but then with a hint of a blush said, "And although he says that it is what is in our souls which makes us beautiful, I cannot help but think he will find you a great beauty."

"I would like to be useful while I am here. If it cannot be through the art of dance, then perhaps I can find another purpose," Shajara told Banuqa.

Banuqa quickly responded, "Perhaps to be my companion and friend in these very troubling and lonely times. And in return, maybe I can show you around the palace. Salih does not think it safe for me to go into Damascus, but I can tell you all I know about Cairo!"

"That is more than a fair exchange, Banuqa, and I thank you for your generous offer and your warm welcome."

They spent hours chatting away like sisters, and found they had similar beliefs about life. Nothing, the two women agreed, is dearer to a true believer than faith. They who gain the sweetness of faith are those who accept God as Lord, Islam as religion, and Mohammed as his Prophet, peace be upon him.

෬

Chapter 28
Strategy in Damascus

It was nearing the end of her third day in Damascus and still Shajara had not been presented to Salih. Accompanied by Rukn, he had been busy at all hours inspecting and improving the city's defences.

Yet, the time went quickly and Banuqa was happy to answer all of Shajara's questions. They talked of Cairo in the days of Al-Kamil and of the old sultan's death, which brought Banuqa to tears. Shajara whispered the words appropriate to someone's departure from this life. "May God's mercy be upon him and the forgiveness of God grant him entry to his garden of heaven."

Banuqa described the bitter rivalry of the brothers and the treachery of Al-Nasir Daud, their cousin. She told not only of the man's impiety, but of his murderous ways, his slaughter of fellow Muslims, and his use of poison to rid himself of powerful rivals.

Shajara saw confusion and anger in the young girl's face and tried to bring her relief by quoting the Dawn Sura.

In the name of God, the Most Compassionate, the Merciful, by the growing brightness of the morning, and by the darkness of night when it covers, Your Lord has not forsaken you, nor does he hate you. The afterlife is better for you than the preceding life. Soon your Lord shall give you so much that you shall be satisfied. Did He not find you an orphan, then give you shelter? And He found you drown in His Love, therefore gave way unto Him. And He found you needy, so He enriched you. So, put not pressure on orphans. And chide not the beggar. Publicise well the favours of your Lord.

"I don't know much about life, Banuqa. I am still young and inexperienced. I often feel lost and confused why God has put certain obstacles in my path, but I know that I trust Him and wait to see His wisdom reveal itself."

After much conversation Banuqa was summoned by her brother. It was an hour before she returned. "My brother will see you now but do not bother to wear any of the beautiful dancing dresses you have brought from Baghdad," she told Shajara. "My brother has little interest in dance or song at this time." Timidly she tried to explain, "His mind is very much focused on the future, and it seems any suggestion of song or dance will only anger him" – here she paused before she added – "in fact, Shajara, he has strictly forbidden it." Shajara's heart sank. *If he cannot find any delight in the arts of song and dance, what can I do?* she wondered.

Banuqa led the way to Salih's chambers where they found him alone except for Rukn. She bowed low and awaited her new master's command.

Salih addressed her. "Welcome, Shajara, my sister has praised you highly. I am afraid you find me at a time where I do not think song and dance can be much use to me, but at this time every day, I like to sit with my sister, and talk quietly. You are welcome to join us for today."

Shajara understood that if he was not pleased, then she might not be welcome in the future. She had gained some insight into his character through Banuqa, but her mission by the Caliph was to report back, and that would prove difficult if she had no access to Salih. In her heart, she felt the Caliph wished Salih to be Sultan of Egypt, this of course was her wish too, but how could she be of any help to him?

She sat down next to Banuqa and looked into Salih's face. His eyes were dark brown almost black from where she sat. His hair too was black and curly and he wore it loose. There was a scar that cut through one of his eyebrows, and she could see some faint lines impressed upon his tanned forehead, but he was still young, strong and very handsome. Shajara saw there was kindness in his face, much like that which existed in Banuqa, and she smiled at him, waiting for him to speak. Instead, he stood up quite abruptly and turned his back to her. She could see him rubbing the beard which was cut short on his angular jaw.

"Tell me, Shajara, did the Caliph give you any indication of the situation to which he was sending you?" He paused and turned to face her, his intense stare unsteadied her. "Did he tell you of my circumstances?" He did not wait for an answer. "I thought I had the support of the Caliph, I thought I was the favoured brother. Do you know the gift which was sent to Adil?" His voice started to grow louder and Shajara was very tense. "I knew he would send gifts to both of us, but he knows of my appreciation of knowledge. He knows my army is under

135

manned. He is aware that it is *my indulgent brother* whose weakness lies with beautiful dancing girls." His voice was loud and strong and Shajara was afraid. He continued, "I am at a loss to why he has sent you to me… Or perhaps he has sent you here as punishment!" He laughed maniacally.

It was Banuqa who spoke, gently and with some hesitation. "Brother, Shajara is a dancing girl from the great palace of the Caliph Mustansir. She was not likely to sit with him every evening like we do, speaking of the intentions behind his every action! You were the one who told me that the Caliph would send you and Adil gifts that would show his intentions. Let us sit with Shajara and see what she can tell us, but if we are unable to see his intention, or if it becomes apparent that he has chosen to favour Adil, there is little we can do. It is not the fault of Shajara, we must do all we can to make her feel welcome." She placed a hand on Shajara's hand and smiled.

Salih sat down again, "As usual, my sister, you are right." His agitation diminished.

They both turned to Shajara and waited for her to speak. She was still quite shaken by Salih's temper. She had seen it flare up twice since her arrival, but she had also seen Banuqa quell it by talking rationally and quietly. She had been formulating a plan, and she hoped it would work. Now was the time to impress. "I understand that you have no desire to hear me sing or dance. May I suggest something else which might put your mind at ease?" Salih didn't look happy but did not refuse either, Banuqa nodded.

Shajara knew from experience that the Quran is the ultimate source of guidance and so she decided to recite the first two suras from the Quran. Her religious tutor had informed her that often one could find the answers sought in the Quran's divine knowledge. She started with the Sura Fatiha – the opening chapter and continued through the Sura al Baqara. She dared not make eye contact with either Salih or Banuqa, as she felt nervous and did not want to make errors. The beautiful Arabic words poured from her lips as she brought out their poetry. She knew their holy music, and she knew the words spoke to the soul.

At the last paragraph, Salih interrupted her and to her surprise, he joined in the recitation himself.

"Allah burdens not a person beyond his scope. He gets reward for that which he has earned, and he is punished for that which he has earned. "Our Lord! Punish us not if we forget or fall into error, our Lord! Lay not on us a burden like that which You did lay on those before us, our Lord! Put not on us a burden greater than we have strength to bear. Pardon us and grant us forgiveness. Have mercy on us. You are our protector and give us victory over the disbelieving people."

Salih leaned back, his hands resting in his lap, his legs outstretched and on his face was an air of serenity. When Shajara turned to Banuqa, her new friend leaned forward and whispered, "Thank you."

Shajara moved from her kneeling position and smoothed down her creased silk skirts. Shajara remembered that Caliph Mustansir had told her to tell Salih of Baghdad. His words had been 'you are a gift who can speak for us. Tell Salih about us, of Baghdad, of our court, of the strength of our army and of our determination to keep Islamic lands free of both Mongols and Crusaders'. After some while, she spoke. "Shall I tell you of Baghdad? Have you been? It is truly a wondrous city." The evening passed with Salih quizzing her closely, interrupting her answers with yet other questions, he asked many things of Baghdad which she was proud to answer. Throughout the evening, he drew out some of her beliefs and opinions as well. He asked her what books she had read, what she thought of them, and which books she hoped to read. Shajara recalled the Caliph's last instruction to her and spoke glowingly of her education in Baghdad. "The Caliph believed that it is the duty of every Muslim, even of a slave, to seek knowledge and he gave me every opportunity and encouragement to do so. My master, you have a wise friend in our Caliph Mustansir, the Commander of the Faithful."

It was getting late and Rukn who had spent the evening standing in the corner of the room moved and whispered to Salih.

"Much though I would like to continue this conversation with you and my sister, I need to discuss the larger problem of our military strategy before the end of the evening. And that, I am sure, is one subject they did not teach in the Palace school at Baghdad!" And he smiled at Shajara and much to her surprise, she was filled with delight that she had gained his approval and sorry that the evening with him had come to an end.

As they headed to the door, Salih turned and said, "I look forward to speaking with you again tomorrow evening Shajara al Durr. Please let me know if there is anything I can do to make your life here in the Palace more comfortable."

The audience was over and as Banuqa and Shajara made their way back to their rooms, Shajara's head swam. What did she think of Salih? Clearly, he was intelligent, principled, strong and perhaps even wise, but it was the smile he had given her when she left that had her head spinning.

The next morning, she decided she must talk further with Qipchuk and learn more of military affairs. It annoyed her when he had suggested she knew little of military affairs and had been correct! Her own personal strategy with Salih would be to learn about military strategy. She would read and study as much as she could to learn more.

Her days in Damascus fell into a routine. In the daytime, she would talk with Banuqa, who had quickly become her good friend. Often, they would walk around the quiet Palace garden, never as grand as the garden in Baghdad, and now poorly cared for, but pleasantly cool in the heat of summer. Most days, they would go to the great field outside the city walls where the *Mamluks* would train and play polo matches. Here Shajara would question the Mamluks who had brought her to Damascus.

Sometimes, but only when Salih and Rukn were not present, Shajara would persuade Qipchuk to let her try her hand with bow and arrow. "Archery is a skill learned only over many years," he told her. Yet, it was not long before she made herself skilled with the bow and was drawing applause from the *Mamluk* troops.

Sometimes, Qipchuk would order his own *Mamluks* into mock battles with an equal number of Rukn's *Mamluks*. Shajara recognised that their polo games had trained them for the tight turns and bursts of speed that such mock battles required. She listened closely as Qipchuk explained *Mamluk* cavalry tactics and described the use of different manoeuvres against their enemies. I will master military strategy, she told herself.

On the way back to the palace from the field, Shajara would pepper Qipchuk with more and more questions. Why is a cavalry force superior to infantry? Because it has greater strength of weaponry, greater speed and greater striking power. Are there other reasons? Well, yes, it is better in pursuit and it is very much better in feigned retreat. Why is feigned retreat so important? Because it can lead the enemy into a trap when they mistake the retreat for flight. Why do some of your *Mamluks* carry hollow quivers for their arrows? When placed on the ground at night, such quivers can be used to hear the sound of horses' hooves long before they come into earshot. Why do your *Mamluks* carry iron shields while Rukn's carry leather shields? Leather shields are more easily pierced by lance or sword and our Caliph wants the best for us. What are the greatest keys to victory? Training and discipline before battle, discipline in battle, and a wise general. Shajara kept Qipchuk's every answer well in her mind. And like all she had studied before, she placed everything carefully in her memory, ready for use in the future, and remembered the old tutor's advice – knowledge is power.

She wrote often to her mother telling her of her new life in Damascus. She did not receive many letters in return, but of the few she did receive, the news was often the same, the same life she had led since Shajara was there. She often wrote of Master Osman's grandchildren, as if they were her own. The letters never divulged anything of her mother's life.

Every evening, Shajara would go with Banuqa to Salih's chamber. There in ever-longer conversations, she would express her opinions, and the three of them were able to laugh and tease comfortably with each other. She never sang, and never danced, but often she would recite the Quran, and knew the appreciation was more than she could have achieved with dancing or singing.

One evening, passing to collect Banuqa for their evening with Salih, she found her friend in her bed, pale and sipping tea. Shajara rushed to her friend to enquire about her health.

"I am well, Shajara, do not look so worried. I have eaten something that has given me some stomach pain, but I will very happily sleep after drinking this tea. Please do not worry about me. Go and tell my brother there is nothing to fear."

Shajara had been looking forward to seeing Salih. She had tried to hide the fact that as the days passed, she spent more and more time thinking about him. Thinking of his handsome face, his kind voice, his strong hands, and the way he looked at her made her forget all else in her life. Her favourite time of the day was evening when she knew she would be near him, listening to him, and conversing about all topics important to him. She kept repeating to herself over and over, that she could not, and would not fall in love. She kept thinking of the story Osman Balabar had told her of Khorasan, the Yemeni slave who rose up to become mother to a caliph, more powerful than one could have imagined. Could she allow herself to dream? No, Salih would need a woman of noble birth, or a woman who had a powerful or rich family. She must try her best to avoid these feelings, and so as she walked to his chamber with the unfortunate news of his sister, she resolved to abandon these feelings entirely before a disastrous ending like that of Hababa befell her.

But as she approached his chambers, she saw Salih hurrying down the hall.

"Shajara!" he startled. "I was on my way to enquire after my sister. How is she?" Salih's strong affection for his sister moved Shajara, and though this family was certainly torn, brother and cousin against sister and brother, there was goodness and caring in Salih.

"She has sent me to tell you that there is little to worry about. She is being looked after by her maid, and I will spend the evening by her bedside to make sure she wants for nothing." Shajara wanted so much to soothe Salih, his furrowed brow and his intense worry brought out a feeling in her which she had never felt before.

"Walk with me, Shajara. We will go to her chambers together."

They walked for a few minutes in silence before Salih said, "You care for Banuqa. I am glad you have made friends. She has had a difficult time since my father died. I have not done much to provide stability for her. She chose to come with me, but she misses her friends and her home in Cairo."

"She misses your father too," Shajara added.

Salih sighed heavily. "We all do." Just before they reached Banuqa's door, Salih turned to Shajara and said, "There is something I have been wondering about you." Shajara tilted her head questioningly, he cleared his throat, "Will you tell me why you are called Shajara al Durr?"

Shajara had always felt a certain embarrassment about her name. Often, she had been teased for her fancy name. But she explained a little about her parents likening her worth to fine jewels. Her thoughts went back to her parents and to Soraya's story of the Golden Tree. She sensed attention and felt the heat rise in her cheeks.

Salih looked into her eyes and she back into his for just a moment before looking away.

"I have wondered that since meeting you. I thought, 'who is this Tree of Pearls who gives orders to Mamluks and recites Quran and there is not a pearl in sight'!" Salih taunted.

Shajara's throat dried up, she felt ridiculous, and for the first time since meeting him, she had nothing to say. She smiled awkwardly back at him.

"And so," Salih continued, "I thought I could possibly remedy that." He reached into his pocket and brought out a tangle of pearls. Looking at her and waiting for her reaction. Shajara, stunned, just looked at the perfectly rounded gleaming pearl after pearl. Salih untangled the three strands of pearls. The clasp was a large golden pendant dotted with smaller seed pearls.

"It is a thank you gift from Banuqa and me. You have brought us friendship and happiness during these hard times. You have entertained us in the evenings with your presence." Salih brought the string of pearls forward intimating to place them around her neck, and then whispered in his deep voice, "May I?"

Shajara nodded and overwhelmed with emotion could feel her heart pounding as she stared up into his face. His hand brushed her hair gently to the side and fastened the necklace. She could feel the warmth from his hand on her skin and then the cold pearls circling her neck.

"There," he said smiling down at her, "now you are truly Shajara al Durr, the most beautiful tree of pearls." He stood close to her and Shajara looked into his smiling eyes, unable to speak and barely able to breathe. They stood for only a moment more and then the door to Banuqa's chambers opened and the maid came out. "Mistress Banuqa needs more tea," and she rushed past. Salih gave her another warm smile and then walked into his sister's room. Shajara still overwhelmed with emotion followed him in a daze stroking the pearls which now adorned her neck.

"Ahhh I am so glad to see you both!" beamed Banuqa. "I am feeling so much better! Stay with me for a while. Oh!" Banuqa exclaimed as she caught sight of the pearls glimmering against Shajara's skin. "So, my brother has given you our aunt's pearls! What do you think? Do you like them?"

"What a silly question!" Shajara stammered as she approached her friend and leaned over to kiss Banuqa's cheek. "I am overwhelmed by your generosity." Her heart was still pounding, and her mind raced to make sense of the situation.

"Salih, talk with me for a while before I sleep. I am quite fed up of being in bed."

Salih pushed the divan closer to Banuqa's bed and offered the seat for Shajara to sit, and then to her surprise sat down next to her. Salih made general enquiries after his sister and Shajara sat quietly and contentedly next to him. When the conversation turned to the military situation facing them in Damascus, Shajara asked Salih about the tactics of Crusader cavalry. She wanted to know how they compared with those of the *Mamluks*.

Salih laughingly told her, "The *Mamluk*s are much superior!" She heard condescension in his voice and pressed the issue, "in what ways? and why? Do you have actual examples?" And then, "Is it true that Crusaders' lances are longer than those of *Mamluks? And what does that mean in battle?" Soon, she was repeating the knowledge learned from Qipchuk as her own. Banuqa lay in shocked silence. Salih, however, laughed and smiled at her, the same charming smile that quite unsettled her.

"At first, I thought Caliph Mustansir had sent me a beautiful, dancing girl. Then I discovered in fact she is a pious educated woman. Now, I discover that she is a military strategist! Yes, my sister, the Caliph's intentions are finally becoming clear. His gift is truly magnificent."

Salih's praise was music to her ears.

ૐ

Chapter 29
Shajara's Deceptions

Nearly three months had passed, and it was time for Wafik, Qipchuk and the *Mamluks* to return to Baghdad. Wafik had discreetly questioned all the palace servants, seeking information for his report to the Caliph. There was very little to tell, no scandals, no court gossip. Salih's household prayed five times a day, no exceptions. On Fridays, the *khutbah* or sermon was always said with the proper mention of the Caliph Mustansir. Drunkenness was unknown. Other than Shajara, there were no dancing girls, and even she never danced. Salih himself seemed to spend all his days with Rukn and the *Mamluks*. Shajara had learned nothing of interest to add to what Wafik feared would be a very dull report. But that was not all Wafik would report, Shajara would not shirk her duties. The Caliph had requested her to report back, and so she would. She had spent much of the evening writing to the Caliph. She wrote that it was clear that Salih was the more knowledgeable, capable and honest man. She told of Banuqa's fears that Adil, a hopelessly disorganised man who only sought riches and pleasures, would bring ruin to Egypt. She underlined how desperately trained men were needed and hoped he understood that this was a plea to send Mamluks to Damascus. Of course, she knew that Wafik's report and Qipchuk's were the ones the Caliph would be most interested in, but she couldn't help but hope he would read hers too.

It was time to say sad farewells, for they realised the likelihood was that they would never see one another again. Laughingly, Shajara told Qipchuk that she planned to practice mounted archery. "Watch out," she said, "one of these days you'll see me riding into battle!"

At last, in a serious tone, as they were about to mount their horses, Shajara handed the letter she had written. "You must take Qipchuk to the Caliph immediately, and you Qipchuk, tell the Caliph that we expect attack from Al-Nasir in the new year."

Qipchuk said, "We know the situation well, Shajara. We will not leave you here to face this alone. We hope to convince the Caliph to send back up. We will try our best." There was little left to do but smile, wish them a safe journey and wave goodbye. Shajara was amused to see that both men bowed to her.

That evening, Shajara and Banuqa went to Salih's chamber. They sat like they did every evening, around a round, silver table etched with geographic designs. Salih sat across from Shajara and Banuqa to their side. Tonight, a tray of pastries drizzled with honey and sprinkled with crushed pistachio sat on a tray in front of them. They still talked a little of theology and philosophy, but increasingly their conversation turned to the military threat.

"So, you said goodbye to your Baghdadi friends Qipchuk and Wafik. I am already missing Qipchuk. No one could see a military situation and its implications better than he could. Rukn and I hardly know what we will do without him."

"Ah, but perhaps he will be back, and God willing with reinforcements." Shajara replied, soothed by the thought. This took Salih by surprise. "Why do you say that? What do you know?"

"Only that I sent a report back with Wafik and Qipchuk to underline how crucial it would be to have more men sent if you were to have any hope of defeating Adil," Shajara, noting his rising temper, calmly replied.

Salih stood up, he was visibly agitated. "*You* sent a report? Surely, that was Wafik and Qipchuk's report? Why would *you* send a report?"

Shajara was hurt and offended. Shajara had seen men all her life that treated women second to men, and who believed women had nothing more to offer than their beauty and children. There were so few who understood that women could be more than just a comfort to men. Women could challenge men in many ways, if they were allowed, and she had believed Salih to be a man who appreciated her for her abilities. Had this all been a guise? Had he treated her this way for some other, less admirable reason?

"Well, Shajara, I am waiting. Tell me this minute why you wrote a report and what was in it."

She looked him in his eyes but could not see anything but anger in them. She lowered her eyes. There was already a lump forming in her throat.

"I wrote the Caliph because he asked it of me. I wrote that you needed more men and that we expected attack from Adil in the new year. That is all." She stood up to leave but did not have a chance.

"Sit down! I'm not finished! Why didn't you tell me you were a spy sending reports? What else was in the report?"

Banuqa tried to reach out to her brother. "Salih…" she started.

"NO!" he bellowed. "Don't you realise, your friend has been spying on us. She has been sent here to spy and send back news. Of course, that is why he sent his most beautiful and clever slave. She was no gift; she was a spy." He laughed but it was not the laugh she had known; it was cruel and angry.

"No," Shajara protested, "it was not like that at all!"

"No? Then tell me what was it like, Shajara?" He practically spat her name.

But she could not deny it. It had been what was asked of her. She had been told to collect information and send back a report. Salih was angry because he believed her to have betrayed him. How could she tell him that she had fallen in love with him instead? The report begging for more men had been to save him, not save herself! She thought he would've been happy to know she had sent a request for help.

"No answer? I thought not. Well, I tell you what happens to spies here in Damascus…"

Banuqa stood up and came to Shajara to hold her hand. "No, brother, you will not hurt her!"

"No, but I can send her back." His voice was unwavering in its control and anger. "Her duty is finished here, and I never wanted a dancing slave well versed in manipulation and deceit. One of Rukn's men will set out at dawn and they will be with Qipchuk and Wafik the following day."

He spun around and was gone. Shajara fell to the ground, Banuqa rushed to hold her, and she cried.

"Don't cry, Shajara. Don't cry, you will not go, I promise. He won't send you away. I promise I will try my best. I cannot let you go, Shajara. You are too important to me."

Shajara looked at Banuqa, who also had tears running down her cheeks. Banuqa had been a true friend to Shajara; she deserved an explanation.

"Banuqa, I had to leave Baghdad. I had to leave my education. The Caliph's son had fallen in love with me." Banuqa's eyes grew wide. "The Caliph was kind to me, he could've had me drowned in the river, but instead he sent me here. If I

145

am sent back, it will be to the slave market." She sobbed, but continued, "The Caliph knows Salih is the better man, but he did ask me to report what I knew. But I promise you Banuqa, I did not tell him anything he didn't already know! I just asked him to send reinforcements. I never wanted to betray you or Salih." Nothing made sense anymore to Shajara. She cried. "I don't want to leave you, Banuqa, you have been the dearest of friends. I didn't mean to deceive him! I didn't mean to…to…"

Banuqa finished her sentence. "To fall in love with him."

Not more than an hour had passed when Salih returned to his chambers. His sister and Banuqa had already left. The cold night air had helped cool him down. Now he knew he would have to find Shajara and tell her he did not intend to send her away. The fact was he had overreacted. He knew it and hated it. His temper had often misled him. As he walked to the women's quarters, he wondered about Shajara's report. No piece of information that had been given was damning to their situation. The fact was he had nothing to hide from the Caliph. He had nothing to hide from Shajara. She had been nothing but helpful since she had arrived. His mind turned to his sister who had been in deep depression before Shajara had arrived. She now spent her days arm in arm with Shajara and it was clear to anyone that the two had developed a deep bond. He did not doubt her feelings for Banuqa. Why had he turned on her so – threatened her to be sent back!

His mind turned to Qur'an, 3:134 'Those who control their anger and are forgiving towards people, God loves the good'.

His own mother, who had died before Salih was a man often would tell Adil and him when they were fighting that whoever apologises first is the strongest and the bravest. He shuddered to think how she would feel if she knew the situation which stood between the two brothers now. *Yes, the world needs more women*, he thought.

It was Banuqa who answered the door. Her face was full of disappointment with him. Shajara sat on the floor cross-legged in front of a tray with steaming mint tea. Her eyes were red and swollen. His heart sank, it had been he who had caused all this misery and he meant to fix it.

"Good evening, ladies, I am sorry. I lost my temper." He continued, "Of course there is no excuse, but even a hint of a spy under my roof, was enough to confuse my rational sense." He had not finished his speech, he was about to ask their forgiveness, but before he could get the words out, Shajara was in front of him kissing his hand, and Banuqa had thrown her arms around his neck, and kissed his cheek. There was nothing to do but laugh. It seems they had accepted his apology.

Banuqa, who was now privy to all Shajara's secrets, spent her mornings with Shajara counting how long it might be before they could expect the Caliph's reinforcements, for they prayed he would send them. Shajara was certain that Qipchuk would relay a convincing appeal. They added the days it would take Wafik and Qipchuk and his men to return to Baghdad, speak with the Caliph, for the Caliph to make up his mind and the days to travel back to Damascus. They wondered how many men he would send. It was a fun game and often let their imaginations run wild, especially the wonderfully naïve Banuqa who was resolved to expect no less than a thousand men on horseback.

Several evenings later when Salih brought out maps, he was amused to see how quickly Shajara took them from his hands, spread them on the carpet, knelt down and began to estimate distances. "Look," she said, "this is the way I came from Baghdad in 40 nights by horse. Cairo must be 30 nights away from Damascus by camel. Al-Karak may only be eight nights away. If Al-Nasir had enough troops, he would have been at the gates of Damascus long ago."

Salih went on his knees to look at the maps. "I congratulate you on your reading of the maps and your calculations. You think like a man!" Shajara could not suppress her irritation.

"Both men and women have minds to think. Some women, as some men, think well. And there are as many foolish men as there are foolish women."

There was a muffled giggle from Banuqa, and it made Salih smile.

"All right. I agree. Now that you have estimated the distances correctly, and you are right that Al-Nasir would have long since been in Damascus if he had enough troops. But what do you reason from that?"

Shajara replied, "Again, it is obvious. Al-Nasir is waiting for Adil to bring enough troops so that they can march together on Damascus. And that, I fear, must be only a matter of time." Salih nodded grimly.

"Yes, that is our situation and there is little we can do to change it."

Shajara now added a thought that caught Salih by surprise. "You mean, my master, we cannot change the distances from Cairo to Al-Karak and from Al-Karak to Damascus. True enough! But that does not mean we are unable to change the military situation."

Salih looked sharply at her. "You suggest we flee?" he said angrily.

"I suggested no such thing," Shajara calmly responded. "First, I would say there is advantage in discovering when Adil is to leave Cairo for Al-Karak. That would be very useful intelligence." Salih looked at her gravely.

"I should have said you think like Rukn, my great *Mamluk* captain, for he has already set about getting such intelligence. He has sent one of his best men, riding one of my best horses, to Cairo. When he sees Adil's troops mustering for their long journey, he will ride quickly here to let us know."

"That is well done, but it means only that we will be better able to count the days before they are in front of Damascus. It does not change the situation; it merely forewarns us."

"So, Shajara, how do you suggest we change our situation?" The tone was sarcastic. "You said you had a second idea. What is it?" Shajara recognised that she had irritated him, but went on, reminding him of something Jalal had told her years before, "Courage and cunning can conquer every foe. You need to deceive Adil *and* Al-Nasir. You need not flee, but you can gain the advantages of flight." Salih was puzzled. "And how, exactly, would I do that?"

"If Adil and Al-Nasir can be led to believe that you have left Damascus, they may never march on us here." Before replying, Salih waited a moment as if he was remembering some lesson on strategy.

"Deception is a good tactic, best deployed before battle," he said. "But how would you deceive these two cunning men?"

"Merchants travel often from Damascus," she told him. "They carry not only goods but news. If they learn here in the bazaars and markets that you are planning flight, they will carry the news with them to Al-Karak and to Cairo. The first task must be to make the merchants truly believe that you plan to flee. Look at the map, master and find a place to which everyone might think you might retreat."

Salih bent to examine the map. He pointed his finger at Al Bukamal. "Here on the Euphrates is a city that my father ruled, held by one of his favourite men and one who should be loyal to me. Neither Al-Nasir nor Adil has power in Al Bukamal, and Adil might well think I would go there."

"How many nights is it from Damascus?" Shajara asked.

"Perhaps eight or nine. From Al Karak, it may be as much as 20 nights away. From Cairo not less than 40. Yes, I think my enemies could believe that, if I were desperate, I might go there. And it would certainly lead them well away from Damascus. But how do we deceive the merchants?"

Shajara told of her experiences with Osman Balabar, and of how he would talk with the merchants of Baghdad to select goods for his return journey to Konya. "We must find merchants who will go to Cairo and Al-Karak, from Damascus. Then, we need to find the traders here in Damascus with whom those foreign merchants deal."

Salih was listening carefully and nodded in agreement. "I am already thinking of the man I could use to begin…"

"No," she interrupted, startling Salih with her insistent denial. "*I* know the best man for this job. I will send for him and his father immediately. They will come and help us." She stood up and bade Banuqa and Salih a good night and told them she would write straight away to her friend in Konya, her mind reeling with delight at the thought of seeing Faris again.

Banuqa and Salih sat quietly together for a moment before Salih fell back in his chair and exclaimed, "What an unusual mind is at work behind those extraordinary green eyes!"

Banuqa smiled. "Yes, brother, there certainly is."

გა

Chapter 30
A Moonlit Ride

The next morning, Shajara went to find Salih and show him the letter she had written to Faris asking him and his father to come with the approval of Salih to bring goods, and trade in Damascus. She wrote nothing that would betray their plan, for Shajara knew letters that went to and from any palace were often read many times over before they reached their destination. She found Salih in his official study – a place where he met with many who wished to speak with him. She had always met him with Banuqa in his private living quarters and although he had seemed pleased to see her when she arrived, now that he had read the letter and approved it to be sent, his demeanour was gruff and annoyed. "Now," she said gaily, "all we need to do is wait." But still she could see Salih was displeased. Shajara felt uncomfortable and so she bade him a quick goodbye and turned to leave. Perhaps it was wrong coming to his official room – a place where he met men with official business.

"Who is this man? This Faris?" Salih bellowed after her. She turned around to face him and explain, but his reddened face was filled with hatred. "Why should I trust him? Why should I take your word? I think it better to use the man I had intended to use."

What had happened? Shajara wondered, why was Salih in this angry mood all of a sudden? How had she offended him?

"I think it would lessen the credibility of the lie," she explained hesitantly, "as the man you choose can be linked to you, and therefore seen as a possible falsehood. Surely, it would be best to have an outsider spread the rumours. He will say that he came here expressly to bring goods you requested and overheard your guards speaking about the retreat!" Shajara noticed that Salih refused to make eye contact with her, and it shook her confidence.

"How do I know you are not in the employ of my brother, trying to bring ruin down upon me?" Salih barked at her.

Shajara felt as if she had been slapped in the face. How could he think these things of her? Where was the camaraderie that existed between them these countless nights before?

She had tried to fight against feeling anything for Salih but it was little use, she was in love. Furious and hurt, she answered back, "Because I chose to come here! Our Caliph gave *me* the choice." She saw the surprise register on his face and continued, "He showed me the gifts you and your brother had sent him, and he told me a little about you both. There were two gifts to send back – a jewelled scimitar or me, and he put the choice in *my* hands. *I chose* to come here, *I chose you*!" Shajara made a quick bow, turned on her heel and dashed out of the room before he was able to see the hurt in her eyes.

Shajara ran to her room and closed the door. Her mind raced and she scolded herself for having fallen in love with her master. She was no better than Hababa. She was a slave and was owned by Salih, if she did upset him, then she could easily be sold again, about this, she was certain. She had been given good advice by Soraya all those years ago, please your master and never let your emotions get in the way. The past months with Banuqa and Salih had been the best times in her life. She had felt secure and cared for, although the threat of attack from Adil loomed over them, she had simply not been able to fret. She had been blinded by affection, and more importantly, she had felt part of a family, something she longed for since leaving her parents all that time ago. Her thoughts were interrupted by a knock on her door. Shajara wiped the tears away as she opened the door. It was Banuqa's maid who conveyed that Banuqa was still bed ridden and requested her friend's presence. Shajara did not hesitate and rushed to her friend, glad to be distracted from the thoughts in her head.

Banuqa looked pale and gaunt, and Shajara's previous emotions were eclipsed by worry for her friend. But Banuqa waved her hand as if to dismiss her concerns.

"I am fine. I am only bored of staying in bed, although I know I must. I need a distraction. Come, sit and entertain me, Shajara."

"Of course, I will entertain you, dear Banuqa, but first give me a moment. I will return shortly." Banuqa needed entertainment, Shajara needed distraction and she knew just the thing. She raced back to her room, opened her trunk and pulled out her best dancing dress. She untied her hair and styled it as she had when she danced for the Caliph – two long braids down the side of her face and down to her waist and the back left loose. She put on her dress, her bangles, her anklets – both adorned with coins and two more tied around her bare waist and her forehead also adorned with coins. These tinkled and clinked with the movements of her body.

When she entered the room, Banuqa's face lit up and directed her maid to help lift her into a sitting position.

"Oh Shajara! You will dance for me?" Some colour crept into her cheeks, and she clasped her hands in delight.

"I have no musicians today, but I will sing a little to make up for it." It had been so long since she had danced, and she thought she hadn't missed it, but now as she stood ready, she felt the excitement rise in her body. She tapped her foot for a few beats and then started the slow movements of her dance, and the soft words of the song she sang, "He who has never loved has not tasted life's misery or bliss, for in love is sweetness and bitterness, go and ask those who taste it." Her body moved with the words, as if it knew both misery and bliss. She sang and danced for her friend and saw Banuqa smiling happily back. At the end of the song, there was still much more left of the dance which included many twists and spins, a faster beat with shimmies and shoulder accents. Shajara used her arms to accentuate hip movements. She knew that her arms could create shapes with her body which could highlight accents such as backbends and head tosses.

Shajara finished her dance, her heart racing and her breathing rapid, she looked to Banuqa, now quite pale, her eyes fixed, her smile gone. She followed her gaze to the doorway, and there stood Salih. His tall, strong figure taking up most of the doorframe, his eyes on Shajara, soft and sad. He turned and walked away.

Shajara's heart sank. The dancing and singing had made her forget everything for a while. Instead, she had focused on her movements and her song. Now, all the upsetting factors returned, the illness of her friend Banuqa, the looming threat of attack, and the obvious disappointment and anger which she could see in Salih, the man she loved. She went to her friend and squeezed her hand. Banuqa was at a loss for words, and so Shajara went to her room.

She carefully removed her clothes and accessories and put them away in her trunk. She sat on her bed combing her hair from the plaits and contemplating how she could rectify the situation she now found herself in. It felt like each time she started to feel comfortable in her new home, something arose which necessitated her to leave, and she felt almost certain that Salih would send her away from this new home of hers. There was a knock at the door, and she hastened to open it. There stood Salih.

"Meet me in the stables in 30 minutes. Wear clothes to ride."

Shajara watched him as he left. What could this possibly mean? A horse ride at night? Could he not wait until morning to have her out? Did he mean to do her harm? Irrational thoughts tripped through her mind as she put on her riding attire.

They left the palace stables on their horses both looking at the night sky. At first, they were both silent. Then Salih started to speak. Shajara listened politely as he spoke of astronomy, for she knew he had studied it with the best tutors in Cairo. Truth to tell, however, much of what he told her she had known for years. Long ago in the house of Osman, she had learned why Muslims contemplate the heavens. They rise to know the break of dawn, when the Dawn Prayers must be said, and at the end of day, they check the sunset to know the time of the Evening Prayers. The movements of the sun are studied to give the times of the other prayers, the new moon is welcomed as the time to end the Ramadan fast and the pole star points to *qibla,* the direction of Mecca. Did not the Holy Quran itself command Muslims to study the heavens? But she decided that it was best to say as little as possible.

Many of the stars to which Salih proudly pointed she already knew from her journey with Osman's caravan. Mohammed Eye for Eye would lead his men away from the campfire the better to see the stars. In case they should ever lose their way, he would teach them the stars used to navigate across the deserts. She had not forgotten his lessons. She had learned much in her life, and she told herself to feel grateful, but there was only sadness in her heart tonight. Salih too seemed to speak without feeling, only to avoid an uncomfortable silence where there used to be friendship and respect.

They reached a field where Shajara could see bushes planted row after row for as far as she could see. The moonlight highlighting what she thought were white blooms. She did not know the bush, or in fact where she was, as they had spent much of the ride with their faces towards the sky. Salih stopped and dismounted and came to Shajara to help her dismount. He opened his arms to her, and she slid into his large capable hands. He was gentle as he set her on his feet, but quick to remove his hands from her waist, turn and walk to the end of the field where she followed, her heart in her throat. What was all of this about?

Salih picked a blossom from the bush, smelled it and passed it to Shajara. She did the same and a glorious scent filled her senses. "Incredible," she murmured. With shaking hands, she passed the rose back to Salih.

"This rose is called The Damscene Rose – the rose from Damascus. It is what produces Rose water. All these roses will be picked and pressed and poured into the purest mountain water to produce the rose water that has become popular as far as China. It is the sweetest smelling rose in the whole Caliphate." Here he paused and looked into Shajara's face – the first time since he had caught her dancing in his sister's room. She saw kindness and also something else, sadness she thought.

He continued, "But would you believe its origins are actually from Central Asia?"

Silently, she shook her head.

"You will leave to go back to Baghdad, tomorrow," he said it simply but directly and Shajara felt her throat go immediately dry. He was sending her back to Baghdad. He no longer wanted her and would send her back with shame. She lowered her head lest tears started to form. She could not look at him anymore.

The night was clear and the moon large and bright in the sky. A warm wind blew and Shajara could smell the blossoms riding on the breeze but could not appreciate it. She was about to lose all that she cared for. She would leave Salih, leave Banuqa, leave Damascus and start again. The pain of it all overwhelmed her.

"Shajara" – Salih started gently – "look at me."

Shajara could not. She did not want to meet his eyes or look into his face. His voice was kind, but his words were cruel. He was going to send her back to Baghdad, and not to the slave market, but either way, it was the same. He wanted her gone.

She felt the warmth of his hand on her chin and he pulled her face up to meet his gaze. As he did, a tear ran the length of her cheek. Her eyes met his and she saw only sadness in them. Could it be that he was sad to see her go?

"Why?" was all she could whisper.

"Don't you understand?" he said sadly. "My brother is coming. We have very little chance of defeating him, although I will give it everything I have. You have been more than helpful in your efforts," he smiled. "But you are not safe here. He will not hurt our sister. Banuqa will be safe, but you...you will not be spared. He will learn that you have become important to me, and he will..." He did not continue, but slowly Shajara began to understand. Salih was trying to send her away to keep her safe. Thoughts began racing through her mind. She looked at him and he at her.

"You mean you are not sending me back because you are angry I was dancing? I thought you were upset with me?"

Salih laughed.

"No, Shajara al Durr, how can I be?"

"Because you were! You accused me of betraying you to your brother. And then you saw me dancing and you, you…"

He interrupted her, "I realised that I cannot allow you to stay here with me anymore, even though I enjoy the time we spend together, more than I imagined possible. But what I want even more is for you to be safe. For you to stay alive!"

Shajara wrinkled her brow. It was too much to take in – Salih cared for her safety.

He continued, "When I saw you dancing, I had never seen anything so lovely in all my life. You were astonishingly beautiful! I realised then that I was being incredibly selfish – keeping you near me because I enjoyed our conversations, appreciated your humour and intellect, delighted by your beauty, but also keeping you in the direct line of danger. If Adil knows how important you are to me, he may use that as leverage – he may kill or torture you or take you for his own. I cannot allow that to happen. Above anything, I must keep you safe, because you have turned everything upside down! I no longer care for taking the throne in Egypt. I care nothing for claiming back what is rightfully mine. I care only for you and making you happy." Shajara's eyes grew wide as she felt his arm wrap around her waist and pull her close; he looked hard into her tear-filled eyes and kissed her.

෪

Chapter 31
An Uncertain Future

The ride back to the palace was one that Shajara believed would be etched into her memory forever. All her worries had melted away. Her head spun with happiness and her heart danced. Salih loved her, and she loved him. Regrettably, there was already a clash. Shajara refused to leave Damascus, the palace and most certainly not Salih, nor Banuqa. She would stay regardless of imminent danger. Salih begged her to see reason. He promised he would send for her if and when he could. He offered her the choice of going back to Baghdad, staying in a safe house in Damascus, he even offered Konya. But Shajara would not be swayed. For the first time in her life, she argued against a direct order from her master. She would fight to stay with Salih, she would fight for love. She felt there would be no life without Salih. She stubbornly refused. As they walked to her room, Salih turned to Shajara, "Tonight, I can deny you nothing. You have made me the happiest man, Shajara. But I will not give up. You will *not* be here when Adil comes. When our spy tells us, he is on his way, I will send you away." Shajara raised a challenging eyebrow. "By *force* if necessary," he added. "And when our cunning plans deem me the victor, I shall take you as my wife. But until that happy day, we must wait and look to the future." He took her hand gently in his, brought it to his lips and kissed it tenderly. "Good night, my Shajara al Durr."

It was the practice of Salih and Rukn to ride every morning after prayer. So, several days after Banuqa's recovery, Shajara suggested to her that they might ride with them. Their customary route took them out of the city, past Salihye, down a wooded path to a stream. The men jumped their horses over the stream but, although Shajara was willing to follow, Banuqa was fearful. Instead, the women dismounted and ate a picnic breakfast while they waited for the men. Salih and Rukn galloped out of the woods into the open country by the Barada

River. Shajara and Banuqa, always had enough to talk about and enjoyed what would become a peaceful morning routine.

Since riding to the rose fields, Salih requested Shajara to entertain them in the evenings with her dances. She was tentative at first but found that Salih found more delight in her *Mamluk* folksongs and her Anatolian dances than in the more elaborate performances that had won her fame in Baghdad. She teased that he must have *Mamluk* blood running through his royal veins, and he delighted in her teasing. "In fact, my father made me governor of Amid which is in the province of Diyarbakir in southeast Anatolia, that is only 20 nights journey from your hometown of Konya! It was in Amid that I first had the pleasure of commanding a force of *Mamluks*. It is there that I learned to appreciate them as soldiers and admire their courage. I heard their songs as they sat by campfires in the evening. Of course, valiant as they were, they sang not half so well as you!"

"Sir, please, a moment?" Rukn had crept into the private quarters without their notice and Salih hurriedly went to him. He returned moments later stroking his beard.

"What is the news?" Banuqa worriedly asked.

"There is good news and bad," he informed them. Rukn informs me that Faris and his father have arrived in the city. They will come to the palace tomorrow. His tone was grave, all the love and teasing gone now, and he turned to Shajara, "your plan is to begin, let us trust in God."

"And the bad news?" Shajara asked.

"Rukn has discovered that a servant has stolen a horse from the stables and rode off in the direction of Al-Karak. Although men were sent after him, they failed to catch him. This is a disloyal man, one I believe may have been in the pay of Al-Nasir, my cousin." Salih sighed.

They confirmed the news by questioning other servants. Sure enough, the spy had been busily gathering information. Had he learned that Rukn had sent a man to Cairo who would tell of the mustering of Adil's troops? Would Adil find and kill the man who was their only hope of being forewarned? Was the spy even now informing his cunning master of Salih's lack of troops? Had the spy learned that the story of Salih's planned retreat was untrue? Was Al-Nasir even now learning of the deception? Before long, would enemy forces move on Damascus? They were horrified to think of the damage just one spy could do.

Later that night as Salih walked Shajara to her room, she sensed he had a great weight on his shoulders, before she could ask, he divulged, "I am a weak man who has achieved little in my life, Shajara. If I was stronger, I would send you away tonight with a few good Mamluks to keep you safe. But the thought of living without you makes me wonder whether life is worth living at all."

"I will not leave. If you send me away, I will only return. If all our plans have been dashed and Adil knows of our deception and has in fact discovered our spy, then we shall face what comes together," Shajara told him. "But I believe that great achievements lie ahead. God does not desert the pious and the brave!" She comforted him and put her hand gently on his bowed head. "You need only confidence in yourself."

"No," he replied, "I need only you by my side. Sleep well," he told her as he kissed her forehead goodnight.

The next morning, Shajara awoke with such a spring in her step! Today she would see Faris and Mohamed Eye for Eye. She had so much to tell them. She had spent much of the previous day writing letters to mother for Faris to take back. Salih had told her that she was not to leave the palace to see Faris, because they must maintain that this visit was solely business. There was sufficient worry about the spy that had left and what the damage would be, but he would send a messenger as soon as Faris arrived.

Shajara practically ran when the messenger came for her, and all but threw her arms around Faris, had it not been for a very stern looking Salih eyeing her closely. They smiled and laughed and exchanged stories as if no time had passed at all, while Salih and Mohamed Eye for Eye stood idly by. Aware of their discomfort, Shajara suggested, "I suppose we need to tell you our plan."

Salih cut her short. "Our business has already been completed, Shajara."

"Oh," Shajara murmured obviously disappointed.

"And we should not lose any more time," Mohamed Eye for Eye said. "It has been a great pleasure to see you again, Shajara. Faris and I often tell the story of you saving his life around the caravan campfires."

"And the story of saving the caravan from bandits and the sandstorm!" Faris added. At this, Salih's eyes widened, and he turned to Shajara whose cheeks blossomed pink.

"I would like to hear that story myself," Salih declared looking upon Shajara with complete admiration. "That is a story she has yet to tell me!"

"We shall have time later to catch up on all our news." Shajara smiled at them as they prepared to leave.

Salih made a gesture to usher them out and cutting her short said, "It's unlikely they will have time to spare, Shajara. They have a rather important mission ahead of them and must accomplish much before travelling to Cairo."

Stunned, Shajara stood helplessly as he thanked Faris and Mohamed Eye for Eye for their understanding and help. Before he exited, Faris turned and winked at her, and although confused why Salih had sent them away so quickly she couldn't help but to smile affectionately back.

After they left and Salih returned, she found it difficult to even make eye contact with him. Had he not promised to send for her as soon as Faris arrived? Had it not been her idea in the first place to send for them? Why had he sent them away so quickly after she arrived and why had he not agreed to let them come one more time before they left for Cairo?

She rebuked herself for having sulky feelings, for she had the love of Salih, wasn't that more than she deserved? She was his slave and had no claim on him. Men in his position could take four wives and as many concubines as they liked. And yet, he declared his love for her and had promised her marriage which was more than she had dared to dream. Perhaps she had not told him of the friendship that existed between Faris and her. Maybe he did not realise how important Faris had been to her in a very uncertain time of her young life.

But seeing his face now cleared up any misunderstandings, Salih was jealous.

"I have changed my mind, Shajara," he said calmly, "I think we should marry as soon as possible. We need no elaborate ceremony, by law we need only witnesses and to declare our intention to marry." Shajara stood stunned but smiled and held out her hand.

"But Shajara," Salih's voice became serious, as he took her hand in his, "there is something you must know, something important before you agree to marry me."

"There is nothing that would change my mind." But Shajara saw pain in Salih's eyes and was frightened by it. "What is it?"

"I will come to you tonight and tell you everything, things you don't yet know about me, and it may change your mind. I will find you after my work here is finished."

Shajara left him, her mind whirling from the meeting. She had been thrilled to see Faris and Mohamed Eye for Eye and hopeful about their plan, and then Salih's wish to marry was more than she had ever dreamed, what could possibly change her mind about Salih?

She decided to seek out her dear friend Banuqa and see what she may know.

It was clear to Shajara that Banuqa knew very well what this secret was, but continually told her, as soothingly as possible that it was not for her to say. So Shajara tried to take comfort in her words and wait for Salih.

He arrived at her door late that evening looking haggard and Shajara who had tried to keep her fears at bay felt them flooding back all at once. She rushed to him hoping for him to take her into his arms, like he had done before, but he backed away, and told her to sit.

"Shall I call for tea? You look absolutely worn out." But he shook his head and started to rub his jaw as he always did when frustrated and tired.

"Shajara, there is so much about me that you still don't know. Today, when Faris and Mohamed Eye for Eye mentioned the stories they tell of you on the caravan, I realised there is still much I don't know about you either." Shajara's heart dropped. *He has changed his mind about marriage.* She knew it was too good to be true. Had his feelings for her also changed?

"Many of the things that have happened to me in my life have been completely out of my control. My father and his advisors were in control of my life until the day he died. I was sent as hostage to the Crusaders at their request, but when I got back, as the oldest son, I was expected to be trained to be Sultan, and a Sultan has certain obligations he must fill in order to be successful." He looked longingly to her for understanding. She nodded.

"You are speaking to a slave, I know very well about not being in control of one's life, Salih."

"Of course, you do, my love, I'm sorry." He stroked her cheek with such affection she thought her heart would break.

"What I'm trying to tell you is that…I am, in fact, already married." He searched her eyes imploring her to understand, but all she felt was complete shock, she didn't know what to say or what she felt. He continued, "It was an arranged marriage, neither of us felt anything for the other and although I wanted to make the best of our union, it seemed my wife's heart belonged to someone else. She hated the very sight of me, and no matter how I tried, things only got worse. When a baby arrived eight months after our marriage, I knew the child was not mine, but the baby was a boy and the entire country believed I now had an heir."

Shajara still unable to say anything just whispered, "Go on."

"So, several days after Muazzam Turanshah was born, I confronted her. I made a deal with her. If she told me the truth, I would give her what she wanted. I told her that I would never breathe a word of this to anyone, which is why I never even told my sister the truth. She and I have not seen each other for several years now. She lives far in the countryside with distant relatives. She is happy with the man she loves, raising a son whom everyone believes to be mine. There was a fair bit of gossip at the time, but we covered it up by saying our son's lungs could not handle the hot, dusty air of Egypt, and that is why she had to live in the countryside of Syria." Salih sighed heavily. "After that, I vowed I would never again marry unless for love. I have wanted to tell you, and now that I have, I must beg you not to reveal this secret to anyone."

Shajara was pensive as she thought about the legality of marrying a man already married. She knew that the prophet Mohamed had allowed for polygamy to continue, as it had for most religions at the time. For a woman without a husband or a father was often left with no alternative but to beg for a living. It allowed for men to care for more than one woman, and the only stipulation was that no marriage was to be kept a secret from the others, and that he treat them all fairly. She loved Salih and knew she could not lose him over this so she said, "I never before realised that the life of a slave girl and that of a prince of Egypt could be so similar. You spoke of not being able to make important decisions about your life; I know how that feels. You spoke of being the victim of manipulation and deceit; I know a fair bit about that too. And lastly, you spoke of a dream to marry for love, and that, too, is my dream. We may not know everything about each other, that is true, but never before I have felt that we had so much in common! Surely, this is not an obstacle for us." She had barely finished the sentence before she felt his lips on hers and his strong arms envelop her in an embrace.

৪৵

Chapter 32
A New Beginning

The next evening, Banuqa arrived to Shajara's chamber with the dress she had commissioned to be made from the beautiful brocades that Shajara had presented upon their first meeting. A beautiful gown fit for even the fanciest of ceremonies had been made within hours and Shajara awed at the intricate pearl adornments which had been added all over the fancy golden threaded brocade.

Shajara fingered the pearls and looked incredulously at Banuqa.

"Where on earth did you find all these pearls?"

Banuqa shyly admitted, "I had a necklace of my mothers, that matched my aunt's necklace, the one my brother and I gave you. I had the pearls unstrung in order to sew onto the brocade. I hope you like it."

Shajara was unable to say anything but kissed Banuqa's cheek.

"And look what else I found!" Banuqa said as she pulled long threads of very small seed pearls. "We can use these to adorn your hair! You will be more beautiful than ever, my dear friend, and from today on, I will call you sister."

This was the happiest day of Shajara's life. She felt as if she were walking through a dream. She wanted to remember every detail so that tomorrow, the first day of being Salih's wife, she could proudly write to her mother and tell them the news that she herself could not imagine to be true.

Meanwhile, Salih asked Rukn if he would attend the small gathering in order to witness their union. He also asked his private secretary who although not privy to all his military secrets, certainly maintained most of his official correspondence, and he asked him to write up the marriage contract. Additionally, he would request the presence of the Imam from the Mosque. This would provide proof to anyone who questioned the union. For in Damascus, normally, there would be many guests invited, a long parade through the town, a huge feast – families and friends making a huge fuss over the bridal dress, the jewellery, the food etc. The expectation of the marriage of the ruler of these lands would be tremendous, and yet, he would not indulge those expectations. He could not afford the time or efforts. Most of the people of Damascus knew this. But would they forgive it? The only offering he could make would be to slaughter as many goats as he could and give out meat to the poor. The rest would be made into a public banquet for the Damascus elite, a party he and his bride might have to attend. He held his head in his hands, for he knew he would face much criticism, not only for not having done the marriage the traditional way, but for marrying his slave. Honestly, he didn't mind the reproach of the people, but Shajara would become the target of much unwanted and cruel gossip, and that was something he could not bear.

He would try to make up for this by giving Shajara something in return – her freedom. In this marriage contract, he had his secretary stipulate that she would enter into the union as a free woman. He did not want to own her. She was an extraordinary woman who should not be shackled by the rules of slavery. The fact was that slavery was so ingrained in the society it was impossible to eradicate completely, but Islam and thus Salih found it a loathsome trade.

Additionally, he told the secretary to add there would be a dowry for Shajara, as required by tradition. This he would give her and send some 100 gold coins to her mother in Konya, care of Faris and his father, of course. The contract was prepared and all that was left was for them both to sign it. This process would have normally been discussed by the families of the bridge and groom. Since that was not possible, he did his best to be fair. He asked nothing of Shajara to come into the marriage, as might have been the custom, had she not been a slave.

The traditional Damascene wedding contract would have been written on silk, but Salih was not interested in these frivolous wedding details. He took the paper contract in hand, stood up and squared his shoulders and strode off leaving instructions for the secretary and Rukn.

It was moments after Salih had left that Shajara came looking for him. Rukn and the secretary bowed and told her she had only just missed Salih, but she shocked them by telling Rukn that it was he she was looking for.

"I've been thinking who will be my guardian for the signing of the contract. Customarily, it is the father or brother of the bride who will sign on her behalf. My father is dead, and even if he were not, he would not be permitted, as he was also a slave. It occurred to me that you, as a man from the same lands as my ancestors, and one who understands what it is like to live in servitude, could stand as my guardian, and sign the contract for me."

Rukn's eyes smiled with understanding. It was a great honour to be asked by Shajara, but as a military slave himself, he knew he could make no agreement until he had asked permission from Salih.

Shajara knew the same, and prompted, "If, of course, Salih agrees."

"And why not just sign it yourself?" He smiled teasingly, as both of them knew this was unlawful. Shajara accepted the compliment by smiling back but wondered, Why if women are as intelligent and capable as men can we not stand for ourselves? Sign for ourselves? Wasn't Khadija, the wife of the Prophet, peace be upon him, a strong capable, businesswoman? Men like to protect women, but where is the line between gallantly protecting them and eroding their God given liberties? It was like Jalal used to say, Live your life! But how? when there were rules for slaves, and laws regulating women? *Perhaps,* she mused, there would come a day, when women would stand in any position a man could and do a job as well as a man.

The room that was chosen for the simple affair was not the grand hall of the palace, for that was far too large, but a room off to the side. Thanks to Banuqa, servants had turned it into a stylish parlour fit for entertaining royalty. Carpets had been brought in to lie one atop another until the whole floor was covered. The winter was coming, and the chill of the large gaping holes between the massive blocks of stone could be felt all over the palace. Carpets had been hung on the walls, for this explicit reason. Candelabras were lit and hanging from the ceiling in glass casings. Flowers and greenery swagged the table, chairs and the sideboard.

Rukn stood by Salih's right side, his secretary to his left. The Imam was a sizeable man, rubbing his prayer beads mindlessly was busy viewing the large platters of food which were to be served after the ceremony. A movement at the door engaged his attention and he turned.

Banuqa entered with a beaming smile, walking somewhat timidly behind her was Shajara. She stood for a moment till her eyes found Salih. The light from the candles caught the pearls around her neck, in her hair and around her dress, glinting and gleaming. Salih was transfixed by her radiance.

Rukn and the secretary made a little bow to her. Salih took her hand and led her to the head of the table. The Imam stood behind the chairs, Rukn to Shajara's left side and Salih's secretary to his right. All eyes were on Shajara as she started to read the contract. At the third line, she could read no further, she reread the line again. 'Shajara al Durr, slave of Al-Malik Salih Najm al-din Ayyub will enter into this marriage contract as a free woman'.

She looked at Salih for an explanation. She found him smiling back at her. So, it was true? She was a free woman? She tried very hard to hold back the tears forming in her eyes. She wanted to tell him how grateful she was, how much she loved him and how happy she felt at this moment, but the words would not come. Salih saw her struggle. "Do not thank me, Shajara, I feel the same. You are my soul. You are my life now."

᪥

Chapter 33
Happy News and a Catastrophe

A few weeks had passed since Shajara became Salih's wife, and the year since she first came to Damascus was coming to a close. It was, she decided, the happiest year of her life. Now, its happiness was complete, for she was carrying Salih's child. It was a fact she had not yet made known to him, but she had shared it with a delighted Banuqa. She had decided to wait until a happy moment to tell Salih. However, these days, Salih worried constantly about her safety and the upcoming attack by Adil. She was certain that this happy news would force Salih's hand and send her away for her safety and the baby's. She could not leave him, no matter what the consequences, so she delayed telling him.

The days had been warm, and they were all happy this morning to ride out of the city. The two women followed Salih and Rukn along the path through the cool woods. They came to the stream, watched as the men jumped their horses across it, and then dismounted for their picnic. The men galloped away and were soon out of sight.

They had been talking and laughing, when suddenly Shajara saw the colour drain from her friend's face. She looked over her shoulder and saw they were surrounded by archers and men with drawn swords. "One word from either of you," one of the men said, "and both of you will die."

Shajara's mind was racing, who were these men and what did they want? They stood watching them but waiting and she understood that they were waiting for her husband. She knew that at any moment, Salih and Rukn would return, but how could she warn them? Banuqa came closer to Shajara and she put an arm around her shaking sister-in-law. Banuqa had had a sheltered life, and certainly, this must be a shock to her. Shajara felt a keen feeling to protect her but instinctively she also placed a hand to her stomach. What could she do to keep the ones she loved safe? She looked around hopelessly. She opened her mouth to try to address the man on horseback in front of her. He put his finger to his mouth and then took the same finger and slid it across his throat. Banuqa inched closer and a small sob came from her mouth, "Don't worry, Banuqa dear. These men are not bandits. They are waiting for Salih." But this news did not allay Shajara's own fears.

It was no more than a few moments later in which when finally, she saw them cantering back, easing their horses after their gallop along the riverbank. There were archers in the woods with arrows pointed at her, but she must surely risk a warning scream. Then, galloping up behind Salih and Rukn she saw two dozen horsemen their lances levelled. As the horsemen caught up with Salih and Rukn, another two dozen archers emerged from the woods, some with arrows pointed at Shajara and Banuqa, others at Salih and Rukn. They were surrounded! It was too late for screams or, indeed, for anything but surrender.

Salih and Rukn drew their swords, wheeled their horses round and round, but they faced a ring of 50 armed men. There was no escape. Rukn was ready to fight, but Salih motioned him back and threw his sword to the ground. "So, tell me," he asked, "who is your master? In whose name do you come against me with weapons drawn?"

There was no answer from any of the men, and it was difficult to tell who was in charge. Salih and Rukn were made to dismount at swords' point, their arms bound at their sides, their hands tied behind their backs, and they were gagged. Shajara and Banuqa had only their hands tied at their fronts but they, also, were gagged. The four prisoners were mounted on horses, not their own, that were already roped together. This had been a well thought out plan and Shajara cursed herself that they had taken the same ride morning after morning. She turned her head to look at her husband, he too, looked if he understood that their routine had landed them as prisoners.

Quickly and as silently as possible, the fifty armed men led their four prisoners towards the riverbank. There they turned south. There could be no doubt: they were headed to Al-Karak. They were to be the captives of Salih's cousin Al-Nasir, the one who had joined with Adil.

It was to be a journey of seven nights. They were not roughly treated, and a careful degree of respect was shown to Salih. On the first evening, one of the men came to remove the gags and ropes so they could eat. Several armed men watched over them, with strict instructions to not speak. Rukn, however, was the target of much contemptuous jest and only his gag was removed. The plate of food was served, but as his hands were still bound behind his back, he only looked at the food.

"Look at the great *Mamluk* warrior, how easy he was to capture! He will now eat his food like a dog!" Rukn's face revealed nothing. It was Banuqa who went to Rukn. She picked the food and put it gently to his mouth. But their taunts continued, "How quickly he threw down his sword! Aren't you meant to keep Salih safe? It was like attacking a litter of kittens!" They laughed cruelly and gave him a good kick in the ribs. Their derision was false, since all knew that Rukn would have fought to the end if his master had not thrown down his own sword. Shajara knew, as well, that their true opinion of Rukn was shown by the fact that they kept him bound with an armed guard watching him at all times.

Banuqa was quite clearly suffering from shock and fright. Shajara was doing her best to comfort her without speaking loudly, but Banuqa was crying.

Salih spoke to the guards, "Please may I speak with my sister? She is the daughter of the last Sultan of Egypt, the sister of Adil who rules Egypt now. This treatment is not something she is used to."

"But we are told you are used to being taken hostage, are you not? Would you prefer if we were Christians taking you from your palace?"

Shajara thought it cruel that they brought up Salih's time as hostage to the Crusaders, something he rarely spoke of. But it seemed not to bother Salih at all.

"Of course, I would prefer it! They, after all were our enemies, come to take our lands. I certainly do not appreciate my own family to treat me this way. But that is beside the point. I have surrendered and I will speak with my cousin when we arrive to Al Karak, but until that time, I would like to comfort my sister and wife."

The man made only a small nod and turned his back but did not leave. He was still close enough to hear their every word.

Salih turned to Shajara and Banuqa. "There is nothing to fear, my dear loved ones. My cousin will not be unreasonable."

Banuqa stopped her crying with only the occasional sniffle. "But they are treating Rukn so cruelly!"

Salih smiled. "Banuqa, do you think Rukn cares about their taunts and a small kicking? He is a mighty Mamluk, trained for every possibility of battle. Do not worry yourself about him." Rukn, still gagged was not able to speak but his eyes met hers and she smiled.

At night, Salih slept close to Shajara and whispered comforting words into her ear. "I will speak with my cousin. He will surely show some kindness. He will let you go, God Willing, my love."

But Shajara could see that inside, he was cursing himself for allowing her to stay in Damascus. For the first time in her life, she realised there were lives more important than hers, namely this sweet life growing inside her, that of her husband, sister-in-law and Rukn. She would do what she could to protect them, but she feared more than ever, that she was powerless to change their situation. She too cursed the situation and vowed never to allow something like this to befall them again.

Al-Karak was little more than a huge castle or fortress overlooking a village of shanty houses. They first saw its battlements against an evening sky on the last day of their journey. She thought it a grim and ugly place and she was doubtful its owner would be any more inviting. She felt an overwhelming feeling to be sick. She was not sure at first if the nausea she had been feeling the last few days was fear for the future or the baby growing in her belly. Now as they approached, as worried as she was, she could not help but smile, for she had heard in the harem that the more nauseated the soon to be mother, the stronger the baby, and that made her very happy. She put her hand to her stomach and murmured quietly to her unborn child, that all would be well, she would find a way.

Al-Nasir greeted Salih when they entered the main gate of the great castle. "Welcome, cousin Salih! Welcome, cousin Banuqa! Your brother will be surprised to learn you are here." He came forward as if offering an embrace.

Salih stepped away and said, "So, it is true! You have given allegiance to Adil? I can tell you it is an arrangement that will not suit you in the end!"

He laughed. "As ever, your mind jumps to false conclusions," Al-Nasir told him. "Come inside, we will drink and have something to eat and bring your Mamluk companions with you. My sources tell me that you are rarely without them!"

Did his sources also tell him that she was his wife? Shajara wondered.

"Even now, as we speak, Adil may be marching to Abu Kamal on the Euphrates," Al Nasir told Salih. "Yes, your lightheaded brother is easy to deceive. I am not. I took the trouble to learn your every movement. You need to remember this little lesson for your future...if you are to have a future. A man who lives by routine, who rides each morning to the same place, is a man easily trapped." He laughed mockingly.

So, their plan had worked! Adil was possibly riding to Abu Kamal! Faris and Mohamed Eye for Eye had done their task. Shajara knew it made little difference now, but she felt powerful that her plan had an outcome that could change their circumstances. Cunning and courage can conquer every foe. Jalal had spoken many words of wisdom to her. Now she felt a jolt of strength, we can still win against Adil and Nasir, we must only think of how!

Al Nasir was giving instructions for them to be led away, when Salih said calmly, "Cousin, whatever you have in mind for me and for Rukn here, I pray you will be kind to my sister, Banuqa, and to Shajara, who is to be the mother of my child."

The shock of his words was almost too much for Shajara. She saw Al-Nasir nod assent to Salih's plea, but her mind was taken up with puzzlement. How could he know that she was carrying his child? For how long had he known? And could it be that he was bluffing to Nasir in order to beg mercy for her? But before she could speak to Salih, he and Rukn were led away from them and Banuqa and Shajara followed the two armed men up many flights of stairs.

&♥

Chapter 34
Overheard in Al Karak

They had been four nights in the castle, and their only human contact had been with a frightened servant girl who brought their meals, and who refused to speak with them. However, Banuqa and Shajara had seen the men from a distance. Each day, they were allowed to leave their room to go out onto the walkway at the top of one of the castle towers. Far below, they could see Salih, Rukn and their armed guards as they walked in the courtyard below. But if they looked west, they could see the waters of the Dead Sea sparkling in the distance. They spent their days worrying and comforting each other. Increasingly, Shajara felt the pangs of nausea and increased appetite, yet when the food arrived, she often couldn't stand the smell, and pushed it aside. Additionally, she longed for sleep, but worry stopped her from sleeping soundly.

"Shajara," Banuqa cried, "my cousin's ruthlessness is well documented. He will surely kill us all! He is only tormenting us by keeping us alive!" Shajara needed to soothe her sister and she sat down next to her and took her hand in hers. "My dearest sister, I have heard much about this castle from Qipchuk. Shall I tell you about this fortress we currently call home?" A weak nod from Banuqa and Shajara began to tell the story of the great castle of Al Karak, avoiding the urge to curl up and sleep.

"This castle was built by Crusaders over a hundred years ago. It can hold a thousand armed men and was thought impregnable until it finally fell to a year-long siege by your valiant relative Saladin and his forces!" Banuqa proudly became more interested. "Al Karak is built atop this massive hill, which gives it a strategic placement on the much-travelled route called the King's Highway. In fact, it has long been used by Muslims to travel to Hajj, Christians and Jews too, as it leads to Mount Nebo – the birth and death place of Moses, also a prophet of

Islam. Romans and Nabateans; Byzantines and Crusaders, whether for military, trade or religion, it is an important route."

Shajara stopped speaking as none other than Al-Nasir strode confidently into their room. They both stood, holding each other's hands more tightly than ever. Shajara had not seen his face clearly before, but now he came right up to her, much closer than she felt was correct and looked at her intently. "Yes, you are beautiful. But I must say, you have bewitched my poor cousin. He is quite mad parted from you!" He made a mocking bow. "And you, Banuqa, tell me, are you now regretting that you chose to support Salih and not Adil?" He laughed but made another bow, much more courteous than to Shajara. Banuqa said nothing. He continued, "Your brother and I have had many conversations," he told her, "and I find him pious but practical. Perhaps not all is lost for him."

"And now, I think it is time that you should be re-united with your riding companions." Shajara thought he boasted too much of his achievement concerning their capture. With a courteous bow to Banuqa and without even glancing at Shajara, he was gone.

"He has the blackest of hearts, Shajara." Banuqa wailed, but moments later, they were led by a guard to a small room with tapestries of Crusader fashion on all its walls.

The tapestries showed men, women and beasts in a way that Islam would not allow. The two women agreed that the tapestries were one more proof of Al Nasir's lack of piety. Salih entered with Rukn, who was hobbled with chains. Salih embraced both women and, when the guards had withdrawn, whispered to them, "I fear our every word may be overheard. There could be listening holes behind those tapestries. Al Nasir knows every cunning trick."

Shajara noticed Banuqa looking pitifully at the bloodstains on Rukn's clothes and so bent to see if his chains could be loosened, but they were tight in place. Salih smiled grimly. "They know that Rukn is the dangerous one. They want him shackled to keep him from killing our guards. Have you seen that Al Nasir always wears armour under his robes, holds his scimitar unsheathed at his side and is never without guards? He is a man who lives in constant fear of assassination, a fear he has earned by cruelty to all in his power." He walked to a wall lifted the tapestry and, finding no listening hole, beckoned towards them. "Perhaps it is safe to talk quietly here."

"From our room," Salih told them, "we have seen pilgrims returning from the Holy City of Mecca and merchants carrying goods from Damascus to Cairo and back. It is a place where many travellers must come, and Al Nasir gathers news from all of them. Moreover, as we discovered, he has spies everywhere, not only in Damascus but, as he has revealed to me, in Cairo, also. He knows everything that happens. He knew my every movement and now I find he knows every movement that Adil makes."

Whispering even more quietly now, Salih told them of his conversations with Al-Nasir. "He has heard that my brother, Adil, has had trouble with his troops and now some of the emirs accuse him of betraying them. My brother is too fond of his pleasures to be a good leader of men and Al-Nasir is no longer sure of him as an ally. It is a perfect opening for me. If I make him the promise he wants, I believe he may join with me instead." Banuqa was shocked, but Shajara nodded calmly and reassured her. "Blameless are those who make promises under threat of their lives," she said. "Abu Al-Darda, said we may smile in the faces of those who have us in their power even while we hate them in our hearts."

Turning to Salih, Shajara said, "Al-Nasir has trapped you by guile, he holds us by force of arms, and if you lose importance in his eyes, he will kill us all. Surely, a promise to such a man, made under threat of death, is not a promise in religion or in law."

"It is so," said Salih. "Yet, if I promise him Damascus, we may save our lives and it may even be that we will win Cairo. It is our only way to escape this predicament we find ourselves."

Within minutes, Al-Nasir came into the room followed by two guards. "Well, are we agreed?" he asked? "It sounds to me as if we are." They looked at him in surprise. How could he have overheard their whispers?

"There are no listening holes in the walls, but the ceiling is a different matter," Al-Nasir said gesturing upwards where they could see little slits in the domed ceiling. "Yes, this whole room with its clever ceiling is designed as a listening chamber!" He was chuckling with mocking laughter. "Don't worry, for I have heard only that you have rightly seen your predicament and your way out of it. You are tired of imprisonment, my friends, and your fear of death has made you wise."

"Now, don't you think we should go together to my evening entertainment? I have the finest dancer in all the Caliphate to delight you. Although" – looking sharply at Shajara – "perhaps she will not delight you all."

What could they do but agree? He escorted them cordially to the castle's great hall, although Rukn remained chained. It was gloomy compared with the

Caliph's and its stonewalls were roughly built and blackened by smoke from winter fires. Al-Nasir's chief men were there, tables were set for the evening meal and musicians were playing in the corner. It was a tune to which Shajara had often danced in Baghdad. And there was the woman Al-Nasir had described as the finest in all the caliphate. It was none other than Hababa.

෫

Chapter 35
The Secret Revealed

Her face was still beautiful, her figure slim and poised, and her step agile and graceful. As Shajara watched Hababa, she wondered if she herself could have carried off the intricate dances with such flair. She decided that Hababa would have remained top dancer at the Caliph's court. It was her character after all, not her lack of skill, that had lost her the position.

Hababa finished her dance to great applause. As she left the room, Hababa made eye contact with Shajara, carefully inspecting her Baghdad rival; she stopped cold as she as she noticed Shajara's very slightly protruding stomach. With a mocking smile, she flounced out of the room. Shajara knew that in the eyes of a dancer, even the tiniest weight gained around the belly could mean only one thing.

Banuqa leaned over to whisper, "Why is she looking at you so?"

"She and I were both dancers at the royal court in Baghdad."

Banuqa's eyebrows shot up, but Shajara could say no more.

Al-Nasir broke into her thoughts. "This is a time for a new beginning between us and a cause for celebration," he announced. "Salih, you are too pious to join me in drinking this good wine and your Rukn would probably spit it in my face. Yet I toast you all!" He raised a goblet to his lips and drank deeply. "You negotiate well, Salih! Even though I know what your *Mamluka* thinks about promises made to me, I have no fear that you will break our pact. It may not be a holy promise, but it is a promise in the interests of us both. So long as we have those shared interests, we can trust one another." He drank again from the goblet.

"Now here is a proof of my new trust," he told Salih. "We will send Rukn here on a fast horse to Damascus. Have him take his *Mamluks* from there to Amman, where some of your father's *Mamluks* are still stationed. I have reliable reports that they are loyal to you not to Adil. Then Rukn, come back with as many *Mamluk*s as will ride with you. Of course, I will have to have you unshackled first!" he laughed as a guard bent to take off the ankle chains. Yet, as the chains came off, Al-Nasir had his hand ready by the scimitar at his side. Without a word, bowing to Salih, but not to Al-Nasir, Rukn went quickly from the room. "There goes the one man I can always trust," said Salih to Shajara, "however, our interests may change."

"It will be another month before Rukn returns," Al-Nasir announced. "I expect your good company every evening. We need to know much more about one another, and we can have the delightful Hababa dance for us. She was our Caliph's favourite dancer in Baghdad. Isn't that right, Shajara?" Shajara hadn't the time to respond, as Salih saved her from doing so by asking, "The evening has been a success cousin, but I would very much like to take my wife and sister to their rooms." He did not wait for permission, simply took Shajara by the arm and escorted her from the table, Banuqa followed.

Salih whispered into Shajara's ear. "All will be well, my love, Thank God. I am so happy that my cousin is as clever as he is underhanded. He has seen that Adil is not a good bet. Tonight, I will hold you close Shajara and the previous weeks' worry will melt away."

It had been months since she had shared a room with her husband, and her affection for Banuqa made her wonder if she should. Banuqa had been truly frightened since the abduction and feared that Al-Nasir would have them both killed. "I can think of nothing I want more," she said, "but I think your sister will not be happy to stay alone. She has suffered so, Salih. Perhaps we should not share a room tonight."

Salih smiled and drew her close. "What have I done to deserve you?" But Banuqa, over hearing them, insisted she would be fine, and she knew it was time for Shajara to tell her brother the good news.

Although it was not the way she had planned to tell him, but circumstances being what they were, she had little choice. For the first time in months, they were alone. Salih came to embrace her and she took his hand and placed it on her stomach.

"You are to be a father."

Salih was bowled over with disbelief and delight, "Blessings on you, Shajara. Always, you surprise me! And this is the best surprise of all! Many fears fade before this good news." He embraced her lovingly and kissed the top of her head. "May God reward you with all goodness." His voice shook with emotion.

"So, you did not guess? I heard you tell Al Nasir that I was the mother of your child." Shajara questioned him.

"Ah, that" – Salih smirked – "was a ruse, a dream for the future, and now my beautiful and clever wife, you have made it a reality." He pulled her close and stroked her hair. Happiness flooded her heart as he folded her in his arms and kissed her passionately.

That night while lying in bed, looking at her husband asleep next to her, Shajara remembered Soraya in the Inn of the Golden Tree. So, she too was growing her own golden tree. She had her freedom, a husband, and now the most precious gift of all – a family. Her blessings overwhelmed her, and she stroked her belly lovingly, and couldn't think of a happier time in her life. The future was still uncertain, but she would face anything as long as she had her family.

The months passed quickly. Every morning, Salih joined with Al-Nasir as he drilled the troops in the castle courtyard and then out onto the field below for mock battles and competition in archery. Sometimes, as they had done in Damascus, Shajara and Banuqa would watch the polo games. Shajara would comment that the men were not so skilled as the *Mamluk*s of Qipchuk and Rukn. She pointed out that some of the horsemen could not manage tight turns and that, unlike the *Mamluk*s, the archers dismounted to shoot at the targets.

Al-Nasir offered horses to Banuqa and Shajara, but Salih was fearful for her health and pleaded with her not to ride. The women spent their days reading and dreaming of names for the baby which was growing bigger every day.

Salih was sure their baby was to be a son. "We shall call him Khalil and you, my dear Shajara, shall be known as Umm Khalil, the mother of Khalil."

ఴ

Chapter 36
Khalil

There was good news. Rukn returned from Amman with an even larger force of *Mamluks* than they had hoped. After a day's rest from their long ride, Rukn drilled them for a further week and practiced joint manoeuvres with Al-Nasir's troops.

Other good news came with messengers from five emirs of Egypt. There had been more riots against Adil's rule in Cairo. These emirs were ready to swear allegiance to Salih and willing to muster their troops for battle against Adil. With the emirs as allies, Salih and Al-Nasir were confident they would have the numbers needed for victory and so they would set out for Cairo in two short days!

"Shajara, will you for once, listen to me? Battle is no place for a woman. You cannot come with me. I cannot protect you there. Can you understand I will not be able to focus on the battlefield knowing you are in danger! Al Nasir has given his word you will not be harmed. You are with child, it is unwise, no *unsafe* to travel." He stroked his beard in frustration. "In fact, Shajara, I forbid it."

They were alone in their room, and after a long evening spent speaking with Rukn and Al Nasir about the future plans of attack, both of them were tired.

"You forbid it?" Shajara playfully teased Salih. "I see, so now I am your slave once again?" She pulled the pins from her hair and let her black tresses fall down around her shoulders. She saw Salih's eyes lose focus and approach her, his hands moving to her hair. She continued, "Do you think I trust what Al Nasir tells you? Do you think for one moment, I would be safe if something was to happen to you? I think not." Salih had his hands in her hair and his mouth near her neck and she felt his breath. "Don't argue with me tonight, Shajara," he whispered, "I am undone by your beauty, do not confuse me further with your intellect." His free hand pulled her close. "Just come to me, lay with me tonight and let us for a moment forget our troubles."

She had a family now, a sister, a husband and this baby was all she wanted, and she would not allow them to be taken away from her, whatever their fate on the march to Cairo, and the ensuing battle, they would be together. "Of course, my husband, as soon as you agree that I will join you."

Shajara felt the child moving and kicking in her womb and knew it was not long before its arrival, but she prayed it would not arrive until after they arrived victoriously to Cairo. She prayed with all her might for a strong and healthy baby. She longed for sleep much of the day, but at night, sleep became impossible with the baby twisting and kicking for space. It was the middle of the night when Shajara felt a terrible pain in her back. Salih was sleeping soundly and not wanting to wake him, she got up to light a candle. She wondered what was causing this terrible pain. Her mind wandered to dark places – she had been poisoned by Al Nasir or the baby was in trouble, and she was suffering a miscarriage. Now her mind began to race, as she panicked about the pain in her back. She rubbed her belly, whispering softly to her baby, "It's going to be all right, my baby." She moved her hand around her stomach, there was nothing, no kicking, no turning, perfect silence. She walked to the clay jug of water and poured a glass hoping the soothing cold water would wake the baby. Nothing.

Panic set in. The pain was mounting and becoming unbearable. Should she wake Salih? What could he do, other than worry? Her mind raced, and then she remembered something. She remembered Nermine, the young wife of Caliph Mustasim's nephew who spent two days in labour. The Caliph's doctors and midwives tried everything, and through the whole ordeal, was Hababa. She did not leave Nermine's side. From that day onward, whether out of some actual interest in midwifery or trying to earn favour from the Caliph's mother, Hababa was often at the side of women in labour.

Shajara was doubling over with the pain in her back. She was certain now – something was wrong. She had no time to think; she would go and find Hababa. She grabbed the candle, shut the door and went to the women's quarters. Panting with the pain and effort, she spoke all the while, "It's going to be okay, little one. I'm going to find help."

The pain came in waves, and when it came, Shajara could not walk. She leaned against the stonewalls and was grateful for the cool they provided. She was perspiring with the pain and effort, but it was worry for her baby which spurned her on. She knocked quietly on Hababa's door, and then more loudly. When there was still no answer, panicked and frightened, she yelled. Finally, the

179

door opened. Hababa did not look like she had been asleep. She looked at Shajara holding herself up by leaning on the doorframe, she took in the state of her and without saying a word, opened her door more fully.

Now the waves of pain were coming faster and more intensely. She was using all her strength not to cry out in sheer agony. Hababa yelled for her slave girl and sent her off for hot water and towels.

"With God's will, we shall have your baby sleeping soundly in your arms by morning," Hababa assured her.

"But it's not time, yet!" Shajara panted. "You've misunderstood, I am not in labour. There is something wrong! It's my back!"

"No," Hababa snapped back, "it's you who has misunderstood. You think you know everything now you have been schooled in the palace, but you are still the same stupid slave, as the one gawking at me at the tailor's shop back in Baghdad. Now if you want my help, you will do as I say. Your baby is telling you it's time, and some women feel the pain in their stomach, others in their back."

Surprisingly, Shajara was overcome with gratitude. She forgave Hababa everything, and was happy to be subject to her insults, just as long as she helped her deliver her baby safely. And it is that which it seemed Hababa was keen to do.

"Come here and lean forward on this chair. You don't need to do anything. Your baby is moving into the birth canal. When pain comes again, squeeze my hand."

The slave girl returned her arms bulging with linens and a pot of steaming water.

"It took you long enough, you wretched lazy girl. Now take a cloth, soak it in the hot water and lay it on Shajara's back."

Shajara, sick with the sweltering heat, could not imagine anything worse, but as soon as she felt the cloth on her back, she could feel her tense muscles loosen. Hababa started kneading her back and Shajara felt her body relax just slightly.

Shajara barely could take a restful breath before the next onslaught of pain shook her body. Hababa and her slave girl worked silently and well together, other than the occasional insult from Hababa. Shajara could not stand without aid, and so Hababa helped her get on her knees. Shajara cried out, sobbing and gulping. Hababa still massaging her and the slave girl wiping her brow with a cold cloth.

Hababa encouraged Shajara with kind words, "It won't be long now, Shajara. Soon, you will need to push, and the pain will be gone." She felt her back was breaking and pain radiated down her legs. She gritted her teeth and yelled and cried, but nothing helped her.

The door opened and in walked Banuqa, but Shajara paid no notice. "I heard screaming! Is everything all right?" Banuqa asked sleepily. She took in the scene and rushed to Shajara's side. Hababa ordered her to massage Shajara's back. Hababa checked Shajara by feeling her belly. "It's time, Shajara, it's time to push."

"I can't! I can't." Shajara cried. She anticipated Hababa to curse her and insult her, she almost welcomed it, but instead, Hababa started to sing. She recognised the tune instantly. It was a song they had both sung in Baghdad. It was an ode to mothers, to the pain and worry of motherhood and to pride and love which it accompanied.

Shajara remembered singing the song with particular sadness, believing she may never know the joys and sorrows of motherhood. Now she started to push, regardless of the pain which racked her body. She pushed again as Hababa sang and pushed until she heard the beautiful wail of her child.

Hababa briefly inspected the child before washing and wrapping her baby. "Your son!" By now, Shajara was weeping from joy mixed with pain. Banuqa wrapped her arm around her shoulders and cried too.

Shajara looked at her son who now stopped crying and looked at his mother. Then she lifted his right ear to her lips as was customary and whispered the call to prayer, as that should be the first words a newborn should hear. "God is great. I testify that There is no God, but God and I testify that Mohamed is the messenger of God. Come to pray." And then Shajara added, "Welcome, Khalil."

"I will go to Salih," Banuqa offered.

"Here, Shajara, let me hold Khalil while you get clean. It is not proper for your husband to see you in such a state."

Shajara's head spun when she stood but Hababa's slave girl helped her. She sat on the divan and looked at Hababa. She saw nothing but love in Hababa's eyes.

"A million thanks to you, Hababa. God bless you. I am so grateful to have found you in al Kerak!"

"Yes," Hababa said softly as if she were speaking to Khalil. He gurgled softly back. "You are indeed lucky, and I will not forget that you owe me a kindness in return." She handed Khalil back to Shajara whose arms ached for the moments he hadn't been in them.

Salih entered the room cautiously but when he saw Shajara sitting and smiling at the bundle in her arms, he heaved a sigh of relief. "Thank God, you are both well!"

"Come meet your son," she said without lifting her eyes from her son's face.

He held his son for a moment to look at his black curls and grey eyes before whispering the *adhan* in his right ear. "Glory to God, he is perfect. And you, Shajara, you have brought me more happiness than I ever thought possible." He reached out to stroke her cheek. Shajara was happier than ever she had known.

&❧

Chapter 37
March to Cairo

It was time to begin their march to Cairo. Salih commanded that Banuqa, Shajara and Khalil should be carried in a litter, since Shajara refused to stay in Al Kerak. Before they left, Hababa came to speak with Salih and Shajara. In her typical brazen fashion, she spoke directly about payment for her birthing services. "I wish to come with you to Cairo." Salih was quite taken back. He had only just finished telling Shajara that it was highly irregular that women accompany men into battle, and explained to her that the morning of battle, they could both be sure they would leave the column with some Mamluks to safety.

And now, the dancing girl of Al Kerak was requesting to join. Shajara had not spoken to Salih of Hababa's reputation back in Baghdad, she had simply told him that she had been an immense help during her labour with Khalil.

"I can be of great assistance to your wife and son," she persuaded.

"My sister, Banuqa, will be attending her."

Hababa scoffed. "She knows nothing of newborn babies, nor of breastfeeding mothers."

"And you do?" Salih questioned.

"I am the eldest of eleven children. Of course, that was before I was sold into service at the Palace of Baghdad, but there I often accompanied the midwife with her duties." Shajara saw pain in her eyes and for the first time felt pity for her. Hababa's pain was often disguised with scorn and arrogance, but she had more in common with Shajara than she had ever recognised before.

Salih remained pensive, but Hababa had one last card to play, one she knew Salih would be weakened with. "Your wife promised me she would help me, as I helped her, in her hour of need – when no one else could help her." At this, Salih immediately softened. "And what about Al-Nasir, have you forgotten that we came here as his prisoners? I am not in the position to demand you to accompany us. You are his slave, not mine."

"I can handle Al-Nasir, I just need your approval. He will see that I can be an asset to him on the way." Salih turned to Shajara and although she felt she might live to regret it; she nodded her head.

"Make certain you have Al-Nasir's leave, I do not need trouble with him over you." Salih said as he left. Hababa smiled as she left, and said, "It's a funny world, isn't it, Shajara?"

Salih turned to Shajara. "One day, you must tell me what passed between you two, but at this very moment, I want only to hold you." Shajara nestled in closer to him and wished the moment could last longer.

Salih and Al-Nasir led a long column of armed men. Shajara's litter was carried at the rear of the column. Banuqa's spirits were much improved since leaving Al Karak and Shajara suspected this renewed optimism came from heading back to her beloved Cairo, but she could also see the delight when Shajara would ask her to hold Khalil. She saw also how happy Banuqa was to see Rukn's release. Hababa had been given the necessary clearance from Al-Nasir and rode proudly on her own horse in front of Shajara and Banuqa's litter. Banuqa was not happy with the arrangement and asked questions about Hababa, including the one Shajara was thinking too... "Can we trust her?" The answer was unclear. Up until a few nights ago, the answer would have been no, but since Hababa had helped her, Shajara had seen another side to her. She did not like how Hababa had wiled her way onto the column but did still feel indebted to her.

The first two days passed with hardly a peep from Khalil. He seemed content to sleep through day and night. He fed happily for a few moments, but then fell back into slumber. But on the third night, Khalil was restless and upset. He cried bitter tears and Shajara could not comfort him. She was sharing the tent next to Salih's with Banuqa. He was awake most of the night and his men came and went with important matters – hardly the place for a mother and newborn! After a couple of hours of his discontent, however, in walked Salih. "What is upsetting my son? Where is the dancing girl who swore to attend the new mother and son?"

"I don't know! I have tried everything! He is restless and unhappy." Shajara was near tears with frustration and worry.

"Give him to me," Salih demanded. He walked outside with his son to show him the moon and feel the night air, all the while whispering to him. To Banuqa and Shajara's surprise, Khalil was quiet, and it was not long before he came back with Khalil sound asleep.

"You see, he was quite fed up with your ladies talk. He wanted to speak with his father about military matters!" He winked at his sister, passed Khalil to Shajara, kissed her and bade them good night.

On the sixth day of the march to Cairo, they saw a small force of *Mamluks* ahead. It seemed that they could not be hostile, for they waited until the column had reached them. Shajara, ever curious, stepped from her litter. She saw Rukn embracing one of the *Mamluks*. Who could it be? Her curiosity was soon answered. Qipchuk came up, bowing courteously. "How pleased I am to see you again Shajara. But I am told congratulations are due, Umm Khalil. I cannot imagine a greater motivation to victory!"

"Thank you, Qipchuk, but tell me, what is happening! I am not told anything at the back of the column." Qipchuk laughed.

"Yes, I imagine you would prefer to be riding up front next to Salih!"

He told her how Caliph Mustansir had sent him to gather intelligence on events in Cairo. He had heard that several emirs were massing troops. And how Adil had squandered his resources and lost the loyalty of some troops. "Of course, as we used to discuss on the banks of the Barada River, nothing is ever certain in war," he told Shajara. "So, since I promised to bring our Caliph the most recent news, I plan to join the battle with my *Mamluks*." Grinning, he called to her as he rode away, "Perhaps I can help assure that your son will be restored as the rightful heir to Sultan!" Shajara wondered if he knew that Salih had already an heir, but these thoughts didn't bother her.

That evening, Salih strode into Shajara's tent, bent to kiss her and put his hand on his sleeping's son's head. "How are you, the light of my eyes? How is my mighty warrior of a son?"

"I am well husband, as is Khalil, but tell me, what worries you?"

"It seems I can hide nothing from you." He kicked off his boots and sat next to Shajara. He reached for her hand, pressed it to his lips then started to speak. "We are only a day's march away but only two emirs of the five and their troops have joined our column." He stroked his beard. "I wonder whether we should wait for the three other emirs to add numbers to our forces? Will the missing emirs come eventually, or have they changed their minds? If we wait, will the delay dishearten the emirs who have already joined us?" Shajara understood the complicated position they were in, but she felt she could not advise him one way or the other. Her mind had been entirely focused on Khalil and his comfort. Her body still ached from the labour and she was still overwhelmed with her new role as mother.

He continued, "Or should we risk an attack after tomorrow?"

"What?" Shajara stammered? "Already?" Although Shajara had known fighting was an inevitability, she had not realised they were so close. It frightened her. She clutched his arm, "Oh God, Salih, please, I beg you, stay safe. I cannot lose you! *We* cannot lose you!"

Salih wrapped his arm around her and gently kissed the top of her head. "Where is my confident wife? You were the one to tell me that we can conquer every foe with cunning and wit! Have you changed your mind?"

"I have never had so much to lose, is all," Shajara admitted. Khalil stirred in her arms and smiled in his sleep. She did not want to lose her husband, nor did she want Khalil to lose his father. She did not know where her confidence had come from before, but she was certain now where her weakness lay – protecting her family.

"Well, I cannot back out now, Shajara, our only option is forward. The question is after tomorrow or in a few days." What a gamble they were taking with an attack against Adil! Salih took her face in her hands, "You will not be harmed my love, I have formed a plan with Rukn. If we are to lose, the fate of Banuqa will be well. Adil will forgive her. My fate is less certain; he could banish me, imprison me or kill me. But I am afraid, that your fate and the fate of our son would be certain death. He will not allow an heir to live. You will both be killed. And so, several Mamluks will stay with you, as we attack, you will head back with the Mamluks. They will take you to Amman, where there is a family known well to me and Banuqa. They will take you in. Banuqa has happily given me her solemn vow to stay with you. She loves you, Shajara, as do I. She has no loyalty to Adil. If all goes well, we will send the fastest men on horseback to carry you back."

Shajara opened her mouth to protest, but Salih silenced her with a persuasive kiss. He stroked her hair. "But that will not happen, because we will be the victors! You, my clever wife, will march into Cairo as Sultan's wife, mother to his child, and his most prized advisor!"

"Qipchuk's assessment is that Adil has more than twice as many men as we do," he told her. "But his troops are of poor quality, not well disciplined and Adil has stinted on their pay. Qipchuk's judgement of the soldiers' morale is low; he says they will not fight well. So, I believe we go to battle tomorrow!"

Salih left Shajara's tent, and although she felt confident, he was taking the right course of action, she decided to find Banuqa, to leave Khalil with her in order to join Salih. He had found her indecisiveness unsettling. She had always seen a clear path, but she had been distracted. It was not the time to abandon her husband.

He had gone back to discuss with Rukn and Qipchuk. The question at hand was how should they deploy their forces? Salih smiled at her when she entered, and she listened as the men discussed strategy. Al-Nasir favoured massing all their troops for a frontal attack. "The disloyal will run as we bear down on them. It could all be over in in less than an hour." Salih was dubious. "An all-or-nothing strategy," he murmured, "and if it does not succeed, any retreat would embolden the enemy. Win or lose on a single throw of the dice?"

Other than Al-Nasir, Shajara told herself, I am among friends here. Why should I hesitate to give my opinion? She harked back to the time Faris told her that it shocked him that women didn't take much interest in war, as they had as much to lose. So, she spoke up.

She addressed Salih, "We all know the skill of Rukn and Qipchuk's mounted archers. We all know how they can turn their horses around even at full gallop. What if the *Mamluks* were to lead the attack? What if they were to ride up to Adil's force, engage briefly, but then feign retreat? Such a manoeuvre would not deceive a wise general. But do we believe Adil is wise? Adil, deceiving himself with his own hope of an easy victory, might send his men in pursuit. A well-trained army could manage a tightly disciplined advance. But I trust Qipchuk's judgment. These men are not well trained and would come forward confused and undisciplined. Then, your *Mamluk* horsemen would turn and join the attack to your brother's surprise and confusion."

Although Shajara's words drew murmured disapproval from Al-Nasir, Qipchuk was nodding agreement and Rukn smiled knowingly at her. "It will take some practice at first light, and all our captains must know and understand the plan, but it is a good plan," Rukn told Salih.

Shajara decided on a last bold statement. "Al-Nasir has great experience in battle," she said, "and you must listen to him. Yet I think Al-Nasir himself must approve my suggestion, for if our feigned retreat fails to draw Adil forward, we still have Al-Nasir's option of a massed attack."

187

"I accept Shajara's strategy," Salih declared, "and I also accept Al-Nasir's strategy. Plans for both must be prepared. But I will tell you, my cousin," he said to Al-Nasir, "that I will pray for the success of her plan, for it could bring us victory at a lesser cost of lives."

All eyes were on Al-Nasir. He sat quietly, but finally said, "it seems your wife has been trained in more than just dancing." Although it was said sardonically, it received no reaction from the men, who still waited for some confirmation. "We will execute her plan if Rukn and Qipchuk think they can execute it correctly." *Tomorrow will decide many things,* Shajara said to herself on her way back to her tent. "I put trust in God."

&❧

Chapter 38
The Battle

It was still an hour before dawn prayers, but Rukn had already returned from a night ride to assess Adil's forces. He reported that they were, indeed, superior in numbers and encamped well away from Cairo on a rising stretch of land. Their distance from the city and the protection of its walls seemed to suggest their confidence in victory. Their choice of the rising stretch of land suggested to him that they planned to await attack and to take advantage of the terrain in a massed counterattack. Rukn emphasized that the enemy would be looking into the sun and that their own manoeuvres should take advantage of that fact.

Dawn prayers were said. Rukn and Qipchuk led their mounted horsemen in practice feints. Salih and Al-Nasir instructed the captains of their troops and gave assignments in the coming battle to the two emirs. With the rising sun behind them, they prepared to march towards Adil's army. Shajara was hesitant to set out in her litter with her Mamluks in the direction of Amman. Knowing that Salih's forces were short, she felt guilty that she was using a further three men to take her safely away from battle.

Shajara was ready to leave and Banuqa was with her holding her hand. Neither of them could say anything. Anxiety for the outcome of the next few hours overwhelmed them. The Mamluks assigned to her looked nervously around and she knew they were upset to leave battle and their comrades. They set out with heavy hearts. Banuqa let a few tears fall and Shajara repeated her old friend Jalal's words. "Banuqa, my dear, don't cry. We were not born to seek safety and comfort, but to fly, to dance, to sing and to live courageously. Be strong." But within the hour, a commotion was heard behind them. Two Mamluks were approaching fast. "Stop! We have news!"

"What news?" Shajara blurted.

"The three missing emirs have arrived with several of the commanders from the opposing army. Salih has ordered us to come retrieve you."

"But have they come with men? Or alone?" Shajara asked, but there was no one to answer her. The Mamluks eager for more information had already started to return. Could this mean they had come to swear allegiance to Salih, and battle could be postponed, or would they still go to battle today?

As they approached, they saw a huge crowd and shouting could be heard. Shajara holding Khalil waited while Banuqa started to push her way to find Salih. Shajara heard a most bloodcurdling wail from Banuqa, and followed her into the crowd, holding a protective arm around Khalil. At the centre of the crowd, she stopped dead a horrified gasp escaped her, she saw Banuqa, tears streaming down her face. Shajara pushed forward fearful of the worst, praying silently, 'please not Salih, please God, don't take Salih'! In their midst was a horse with a body slung across the saddle. Bloodied clothing could not hide the elaborate costume. It was Adil.

The emirs bowed before Salih and swore allegiance to him as Sultan. But he was looking at his dead brother. "Who killed him?" he wanted to know. The emirs claimed responsibility, but so did Adil's commanders. Salih put an end to a shouting contest over the killing. "Take his body to Cairo; let him be buried honourably at some little distance from the tomb of our father, Al-Kamil. Now, we will ride to Cairo." His eyes met Shajara's. In one glance, Shajara understood what Salih was telling her. 'We've won! We are the victors, and I am now Sultan of Egypt'.

There was no time to lose; Salih must claim his rightful place in Cairo. News of Adil's death would spread quickly, and Salih must be in Cairo. Everyone was exhilarated. The column was set up within minutes and from her litter, Shajara saw Salih gallop to head his army's triumphant ride to Cairo. Banuqa rode silently in the litter holding Khalil. Banuqa was mourning her brother, Adil. After some time had passed, she spoke, "He was not all bad, you know, Shajara. He could be very fun. He always made me laugh when we were children. I don't know how he became so greedy and malicious." Shajara sympathetically nodded, feeling the tragedy that had broken this family. "Salih promised me that if we were the victors, Adil would not be harmed! I never expected this to happen." She held Khalil close to her chest and cried.

As Shajara listened, she saw Al Nasir gallop past their litter. She turned to Banuqa and took her handkerchief to her tears. "Of course, Salih knew nothing of this, Banuqa. It was beyond his control. But it is good that you brought it up, because we should ask ourselves, who has ordered this?" Banuqa's eyes grew large. "But it was the Emirs!"

"Yes, it was either the Emirs or Adil's commanders, but who orchestrated them to do that? We must keep a careful eye on them, *and* on Al-Nasir. Remember, sister, he was the one to first align with Adil, then he betrayed him by making a pact with Salih. Perhaps he was the one to order to Emirs to kill Adil. He will have known that Salih would not be capable of killing his own brother." She peered her head from the litter. "Look now, he is in close conversation with the three emirs, the ones to bring Adil's body." Shajara continued, "Think, sister, we are near the back of the column, don't you think it unlike Al-Nasir's character to miss out on sharing the glory with Salih leading this victorious column to Cairo? What could be so important that they should lurk at the back of this column?" Banuqa remained silent, but Shajara could tell, she had made her fear for her remaining brother's life.

"We must turn our minds to the future. Do you think it likely that Al-Nasir will be content to live in Salih's shadow? What was his relationship with these three missing emirs? What arrangements has he made with them? What role have they, in fact, played in Adil's death? And if Al-Nasir and the emirs betrayed Adil, what loyalty can Salih expect from them?"

Banuqa wiped away her tears. She sat up and listened, "You're right my sister, he is bad news for Salih. My brother will be very busy, and we must look out for him." Shajara nodded but her mind was still fast at work, "And I would also like to know what part of this plan Hababa will play? I owe her a debt of gratitude, but I would be a fool to believe she is not working for her own benefit, even if it hurts another. That is her way."

"It is my belief that Al-Nasir will not be content with Salih's promise that he can rule Damascus. This man," she told Banuqa, her eyes narrowing with anger, "will stop at nothing to satisfy his lust for power. He will never be satisfied until he himself is sultan of both Jazirah and Egypt. At this very moment," she concluded, "he is probably plotting against Salih."

As they looked to see Al Nasir, they witnessed him clasping hands with the three emirs. It was the same handshake that men make when they are selling or buying camels. But camels were not the subject of this deal. It was a conspiracy!

Shajara reiterated what she had learned of the history of Damascus from Salih. "Al Nasir was the son of a brother of your father Al-Kamil. On his father's death, Al-Nasir succeeded as Emir of Damascus…"

"But," Banuqa interrupted, "my father made war on his nephew and took Damascus for himself. I know this, Shajara, but my uncle was a cruel and angry man, and my father suspected his son to be as bad. So, he took it for himself."

"And that is how Al-Nasir found himself isolated at the gloomy fortress of Al Karak, master of only the surrounding desert. And so, it seems, that Al-Nasir wants revenge against the sons of Al-Kamil. Already he has engineered the death of Adil with the aid of these three emirs. Now, Salih must be warned that he could be next in line!"

Banuqa gasped and held tight to Shajara's hand. "I will tell Rukn to station his best Mamluks to guard Salih at all times. We will have time enough tomorrow after we have entered Cairo to deal with Al-Nasir! My dear sister, our fight has not ended, even with Adil's death."

৪৩

Chapter 39
Cairo

Salih decided that they would enter the city through Bab Zuweila to the south of the city. This huge gate had been the ceremonial entrance for the Fatimid sultans who had ruled Egypt for two centuries before Saladin. The sultans would ride to it from their fortress in the Mukattam Hills, enter the city in state and pass along the Qasaba, the main thoroughfare, to the cheers of their subjects.

Shajara and Banuqa were to be carried into the city in their litter escorted by a Mamluk guard at the rear of the triumphant army. When they were still outside the city walls and a good way from Bab Zuweila, Salih rode up alongside them. He winked at Banuqa. "Did I not tell you I would bring you back home?"

"Oh brother, I did not imagine this day would ever come, though I would have liked to see you and Adil reconciled." Salih's smile faded, and nodded, "But I cannot wait to take Shajara around Cairo!" She turned to Shajara. "I will show you the most extraordinary things, sister. You will see the Pyramids and Sphinx; you will see our beautiful Nile set against the expansive Sahara Desert. And the markets…there you will see all the wonders of the world!"

"We will make the sebuah for my son Khalil. It is a tradition that dates back to our Ancient Egyptian past. When a child reaches seven days old, we celebrate. This will be a celebration to remember, Shajara, for you have given birth to a future Sultan! We have much to celebrate, my love. I promise you, you will love Cairo, and Egypt will be your new home."

Salih was just as giddy as his sister. He spoke of the great city's history. "Nearly two centuries ago," he told her, "the Fatimids came here from Tunisia to found a new city. The old capital of Egypt had long been Memphis in the south, but they wisely founded their city here on this stretch of the Nile."

Shajara asked, "Why did they call it Al Qahira, (Cairo) the Arabic for 'The Conqueror'?"

"To know that," Salih told her, "you must know your astronomy! They named it for the planet Mars, the planet of war and conquest, which was in its ascendancy at the time of the founding." He told her that the city walls, originally of mud brick, had been replaced by stone a hundred years ago. "Just like the pyramids, these stones were cut in the Mukattam quarries. The walls stretch around the city from the northern gate, Bab al Futuh, to the Bab al Nasr, and then around to the Bab Zuweila at the south!"

As they rode towards the great gate of Bab Zuweila, Salih pointed to some stones bearing strange hieroglyphics. "These came from buildings of the ancient Egyptians who worshiped dozens of gods. When we come to Bab Zuweila, we will see columns from the ancient Egyptian's pagan temples. What they built lasted for centuries and it is fortunate that we can make use of such long-lasting stones."

"Peep out carefully from your litter when we have entered the city and you will see the Qasaba, the road that runs from the Bab Zuweila at the southernmost point of the city walls to the Bab al Futuh at the north. Then we will go to the old palace, long used by my father, on the western side of the Bayn Qasrayn, across from an even older, tumbledown palace of the Fatimids, where I will house my commanders."

Salih told them that it was his plan to pray in three mosques in the course of his first day in Cairo. "I will pray at the Mosque of Al Aqmar, which I think is Cairo's most beautiful, with its carved stone façade. Then at the Al Hakim Mosque, with its two enormous minarets, and then at the Mosque of Salih Talai where I hope to see its imam. Prayer is good and blessed wherever it is said, but in these beautiful and holy places prayer is true worship. And, Shajara, in my city there are finer mosques, higher minarets and muezzins with stronger voices than there ever were in your Baghdad!" Shajara laughed at Salih for she knew he had never been to Baghdad but the pride he showed in his country was admirable.

Salih's excitement grew as they neared the time to enter the city where he had spent many happy years. He promised Shajara that they would see the sights together. "Tomorrow, I shall pray at the Mosque of Al Azhar and show you where I learned astronomy in its university. But now, it is time for me to lead our column through Bab Zuweila. How do you think I look?" His clothes had been a subject of much discussion between Shajara and Banuqa. They agreed he needed to look like the Sultan, but if his robes were too rich, it might suggest the self-indulgence and extravagance that had helped give his brother a bad name.

194

Following their suggestion, instead of court dress, he would enter as a warrior wearing a silver breastplate. Now Salih wheeled his horse around waving his scimitar in mock salute as he rode off to head of the column.

Shajara knew that for Salih to go to the three great mosques was not only a holy duty but a way of showing himself to the people as a religious leader. He was very mindful that his brother, Adil, had lost the goodwill of Cairo's ordinary people with a reputation for impiety and debauchery. Salih was determined, from the first, to show that he was a better Muslim. Shajara urged that, to build a good impression of piety and charity, he think about founding institutions in his name to help the poor. He told her that Cairo had one of the earliest hospitals or *bimaristans* in all Islam, founded more than three hundred years before by Ahmad ibn Tulun, and that his own ancestor, the great Saladin, had founded the Nasiri bimaristan. "To do good for the poor is a good in itself and is remembered for generations."

Suddenly, in their litter, Shajara and Banuqa heard loud cheering. The Sultan had entered his city! Soon, the Mamluks carried their litter through the huge gate and they could look out from behind its curtains to the Qasaba. When Shajara pointed to the crooked, narrow little streets that led off the thoroughfare, Banuqa told her that they were built to trap the cool night air before the desert heat invaded the city. Shajara saw mosques built atop shops, something she had never seen in Baghdad. The shops, Banuqa told her, were to assure financial support of the mosque. They saw minaret after minaret, huge stone pointers to heaven. "They say that our minarets are all modelled after the lighthouse at Alexandria," Banuqa told her. "But we have one mosque, that of Ibn Tulun, with a minaret copied from the great mosque of Samara, not far from Baghdad. It has a most unusual outer staircase and is said to be like the Tower of Babel itself, but in holy Islamic form."

His first day in Cairo had taken Salih to the houses of several city leaders where courtesy had required him to partake of the offered delicacies. He wanted only a very simple evening meal and, afterwards, he walked with Shajara to the palace balcony. They looked down to the Bayn Qasrayn and then across to the other old Fatimid palace. To their north, towards Bab al Futah, they could see a dozen minarets. The top of each showed against the night sky, bathed in a gentle glow of light cast by oil lanterns suspended from wooden rods. They had been lit in honour of the Sultan's return, just as they would be again in Ramadan.

Shajara was exhausted and could barely keep her eyes open, that evening. She and Banuqa had been welcomed in the Harem with huge fanfare. Banuqa had been sorely missed. Many of the women cried with her over Adil, many congratulated her on her courage for her support to Salih. Banuqa introduced Shajara to all as the Sultan Salih's wife, which shocked many, but they knew better than to make an enemy out of her on the first day, by questioning her authority. Khalil was crying and Shajara's arms ached. She needed a bath and wanted to stretch her legs, for she had spent too many days in the cramped space of the litter. But she did not want to take Banuqa away from her friends. And from out of nowhere appeared Hababa.

"There is the beautiful Khalil. Please Shajara, go take some time to yourself, or be with your husband. After all, it is my job to assist and I am here. I will take good care of Khalil."

Shajara wondered where Hababa had been the last few days, after assuring Salih that she would be of service to the new mother and baby, and she was tempted to hand her over, but she knew now more than ever that although she was once was able to trust Hababa, that time was over. She was in cahoots with Al-Nasir, and she was certain of this fact. Luckily, she did not have to think about an excuse, as Banuqa appeared directly, "I will be looking after my nephew while Shajara sees the Sultan. I believe the arrangement was for you to help whilst travelling, now that we have arrived, there are many women qualified to help look after Prince Khalil." There was little for Hababa to say, she had no support here and Banuqa had rightfully taken her place as the Sultan's sister.

After washing and praying, Shajara went to Salih. Salih was still exhilarated by his success, although it had been a long and stressful journey for him too, but he spoke with her about his plans and the future. He took her to the balcony and showed her the view. He waved his hand across the expansive view and said, "I am home! I am finally home. No," he corrected, "We are home." He wrapped his arm around Shajara's shoulder. "We are all home. Thanks to God."

෫෨

Chapter 40
A Castle in the Nile

Three cockerels crowed them awake! "These mosques each have their own cockerel." Salih grumbled. "They are supposed to awaken the muezzin, but they do their job too well for me!" He rolled over to face Shajara. She turned sleepily to face her husband. "I worry they will wake Khalil! He has been sleeping very badly the last couple of nights."

Salih got out of bed and sighed. "Having the baby in our bedroom is completely unheard of, Shajara, you know that! There is no reason for you to be woken. There are plenty of ladies in the Harem who can take care of him and would be honoured to do so! We look like peasants all sleeping in the same room!"

Others had tried to persuade Shajara to allow Khalil to have nannies and wet nurses, but she would hear nothing of it. "He is my baby and I want to look after him." The fact was that she was unhappy to leave him with anyone other than Banuqa. "Husband, I have told you the other reasons. I do not know these women; how can I trust them with the most precious object in my life? How can I sleep well if I know Al-Nasir and Hababa roam these palace walls?"

Salih left to make his ablutions but called back to her "You are impossible! And I love you for it. I leave it up to you, you must do as you will."

Shajara got out of bed and reached for Khalil nestled quietly in his crib by the bed. She looked at him sleeping. She was so grateful for her life and family. She made Du'a and asked for her son to have a long happy life. She wanted to pick him up and kiss his forehead, but she resisted knowing sleep was good for him. She kissed her forefinger and gently laid the kiss on his forehead. "Sleep well, my beautiful son."

After prayers, Salih poked derisively at the crumbling brick walls. He was dissatisfied with his palace. "This palace and the one opposite are tumbledown firetraps," he complained. "And what is more worrying, how do we defend against attack? Look there at the Bayn Qasrayn, how do we deploy in there? There is much strategic building to do."

Shajara replied cautiously, "Well, there is always the Nile!"

"What on earth do you mean?" asked a puzzled Salih.

"I mean that island in the Nile which we see plainly whenever we go near the river. It has the best moat in the whole world and water for the longest of all sieges. So far as I could see, it has room for as large a fortress as you would like and a splendid garrison for your Mamluks. Besides, did you not tell me that you were the best of all Nile boatmen! And you would surely not hear the cockerels crow from the middle of the Nile!" She laughed, but Salih was pensively stroking his beard.

That very morning, Shajara's suggestion inspired Salih to sail to the island with Rukn and Qipchuk. Her thought of a garrison for the Mamluks grew in his mind. With Rukn and Qipchuk, he paced out the ground on the island where a fortress and garrison could stand. There would be problems shipping stone, and problems, too, in building a defensible harbour. But he had only to turn his head to the west to see the pyramids, surely if they were able to transport and build such a monument, then he too could imagine a great citadel, strong against all attack, just as Shajara had suggested. He smiled at the thought of her green eyes flashing with intelligence and uncanny understanding, for she had found the best defensive position in all Egypt, within days of arrival.

Salih had come to love Shajara deeply. Everyone could see that, and he did not care, nor did he try to hide it. She knew his every thought and shared with him her own thoughts just as fully. They had become happily inseparable. He leaned on Shajara not only for companionship but increasingly for counsel. She had never lost her habit of questioning everyone and everything, of watching and listening, and now she was seeing danger where it did not exist. He was Sultan now, and she a mother. Times had changed since they were in Damascus, or even Al Kerak. Now she should take her rightful place as head of the Harem, as Sultan's wife. Although he would always value her insights into people and her predictions of the course of events, he decided, it was best to have her focus on raising their son to be as clever and quick witted as his mother. Smiling to himself as they sailed back from the island, he believed himself to be the very luckiest man in the entire caliphate.

Watching Rukn and Qipchuk skilfully handling the boat, Salih told himself that they, too, were part of his good fortune. Ever since Damascus, he had understood Shajara's bond with the Mamluks. He had long suspected – and now happily accepted – that it was to her, the Mamlukah, that they gave deep loyalty. Her bond with the Mamluks was an added guarantee of their loyalty to him. Yes, a Mamluk garrison and a Mamluk bodyguard would make him proof against the assassination that had befallen Adil.

Back at the palace, preparations were in progress for a celebration Shajara had never heard of – the Seboua, an ancient Egyptian celebration for newborns held on the seventh day of a baby's life. The number seven had cosmological symbolism in the ancient Egyptians' belief, and in Islam, the seventh day was also the time for the Aquiqa – the slaughter of lambs to celebrate the arrival of a child.

The whole palace bustled with activity. Khalil's hair was shaved and weighed, and the equivalent in silver and gold was given to charity. The Harem ladies organised clothes and gifts which poured in from all the great families of Egypt. The kitchens were slaughtering lambs and giving two-thirds to the poor as dictated by the Muslim religion. The meat that remained was being cooked into lavish dishes. The lamb was made fragrant with coriander, cumin, sumac and mint, and the smell of cooking meat filled the palace.

Shajara had been uncomfortable at first with her position in the palace, for she had not forgotten how cruel some women in the Caliph's harem were towards wives, sisters or mothers of the caliph, and although they smiled to her face, she worried they shared unkind lies and plotted behind her back. She also knew that Hababa was making more friends as the days passed. She worried constantly about what she and Al-Nasir were planning. But tonight, she heard the women laughing and teasing light-heartedly and felt the air of celebration and forgot her fears, and soon she was laughing too.

That evening, Khalil was brought into the great hall sleeping in a decorated sieve by Shajara, the significance of the sieve was to shake gently away the evil spirits. Salt was thrown to keep the evil eye away and guests mashed mortar and pestles and made loud trilling sounds. Khalil awoke and cried bitterly. Noise was meant to awaken the newborn into the loud and hostile world, having been in the company of seven angels for the last seven days. Shajara had to step over him seven times without touching him, which proved difficult as he was wide eyed and red faced. The love she felt for her son was mingled with fear and worry for his health, happiness and future. Mughat, a herbal drink meant specifically for the lactating mother was brought for Shajara to drink. After she finished, the other guests were also offered the healthy drink. And then, Khalil was passed around for all to see by his proud aunt Banuqa.

Salih stood at the far end of the hall, wearing a proud smile, behind him was Al-Nasir, and he was neither proud nor smiling. Shajara could not shake the feeling that there was a plot developing in their midst, and she was still unsure of how to deal with it. Al-Nasir had told Salih that he would remain in Cairo until Salih's coronation. Shajara had tried to speak to Salih about her worry but saw so little of him. He was busy as ever with administrative chores and continuous meetings. At night, when he came to their bed, he was asleep before Shajara had a chance to speak to him.

But tonight, he was still reeling with excitement from the Seboua. So, she decided to speak with him. "Husband, I cannot help thinking that Al-Nasir, clever, greedy and ruthless, will not be content with Damascus and Al Kerak." But Salih waved the topic to the side. "I don't doubt that he will try something, but it will not be soon, I have much support here, and become more popular by the day, the army sings my praises. At the moment, I am more worried about the religious leaders and mullahs. I have displeased them, and most of them did not attend tonight's celebration. That, indeed, is a sign of their displeasure. I will have to spend the next few days trying to win their favour again."

Shajara, knowing her husband to be a man who put religion above all else, could not understand. "Why would they do such a thing?"

Salih sighed deeply. "Muslim scholars frown upon the celebration, as it is not one rooted in Islam, and is instead a pagan tradition. It is a tradition celebrated by Egyptians of all religions – Jews and Christians celebrate their newborns in this way. It is a celebration that binds us and reminds us that we are Egyptians, not Arabs. On the Temple walls of Hatshepsut in Luxor, we can see the queen gently shaking her baby in the sieve, just like we did tonight for our son. We are the sons and daughters of the greatest civilisation that was ever known, and I will not allow our traditions to be lost. I will show the people that I am both Muslim and Egyptian, and proud to be both!"

&❧

Chapter 41
A Warning

A great ceremony was to be held at which Salih would formally assume the Sultanate in front of all the great men of Egypt. Banuqa and Shajara would be permitted to watch from a hidden balcony. "Remember you are a warrior sultan," she told him, "wear your silver breastplate and come in with a well-armed guard." Salih was amused by her fears but promised to do so. "No one would dare to spill blood at such a time," he reassured her.

As the ceremony began, Shajara saw Al-Nasir and the three emirs standing close to the throne on which Salih would sit. Salih entered in his armour accompanied by ten Mamluks, their scimitars held high as a ceremonial guard. Shajara watched Al-Nasir's every expression. She saw the vengeful look he cast at Salih and she saw, too, his angry glance at the ceremonial guard. If there were an assassination plot it would not be today, but she didn't doubt it was far away.

After the ceremony, Shajara again shared with Salih her growing fears of a conspiracy by Al-Nasir, but again he remained dismissive. When she spoke with Banuqa, she said, "Shajara, Salih has convinced me that an assassination attempt is impossible. Certainly, Al-Nasir is not happy with the situation, but there is nothing he can do. He will leave soon, and all will be well. You need not worry now. Leave these matters now, Shajara. We are no longer in Damascus; you can rest assured that the men surrounding Salih will make certain nothing will befall him."

Momentarily, Shajara wondered whether she would do as Banuqa suggested, and concentrate instead on being a good mother to Khalil. But why should she leave the future of her family to men she did not know, or trust? This was not her way, and so during the time after lunch where many women retreated to the cool to rest, she left Khalil with Banuqa and went to find a guard to send for Rukn. Her movements had become more restricted in Cairo than they had ever been in Baghdad or Damascus. She was the Sultan's wife, and although she was provided every luxury possible, she was encouraged to stay in the palace walls. Guards forbade her to leave, and when she asked Salih, he too, told her it was for her protection. "How would it look if my wife left without the proper entourage? There is protocol, my loved one, and we don't want whispers to turn into rumours."

Rukn was brought into a room outside the harem which was one of Salih's offices. He was accompanied with two palace guards left at the door. Shajara trusted no one, so lowered her voice and told Rukn to watch Al-Nasir closely. "I know in my bones that he is plotting against Salih." She was relieved that she did not have to persuade Rukn of the danger, for he too saw Al-Nasir as a thoroughly evil man who would stop at nothing.

"It has been over a week since the coronation and still Al-Nasir hangs around the court. Why doesn't he go to Damascus to take up his rule there?" he added. Shajara shared with Rukn the thought that a plot must even now be under way. "Don't let Al-Nasir or the Emirs out of your sight," she told him. "Has anyone told you that you think like a General? Leave it with me. We must not have any written communication, and speak of this to no one, even the Sultan, for he has expressly forbidden me to continue watching Al-Nasir, which I have done since you told me in the desert after our victory. I will put my best men forward to seek out all communication of Al-Nasir's." He stood up, bowed and left the room.

At the evening's meal, Shajara sat next to her husband for the first time since arriving in Cairo. Usually, he had been accompanied by his advisors, religious leaders and others, but tonight, he had requested Shajara to be by his side. After a sumptuous meal of roasted chicken with oregano and sesame seeds, music played and out onto the stage came Hababa, dressed in a fine blue dress embroidered with coins, but Shajara was unable to take in the finer details, for she was transfixed by her smirk.

"Husband," Shajara blurted, "you did not tell me that Hababa would be dancing in your palace!"

Inside, she could not help but feel betrayed, but Salih did not take his eyes away from Hababa's dancing and only answered her, "And *you* did not tell me that you were having secret meetings with Rukn!" Shajara's mouth fell open, so he *knew*. Shajara had known her husband to be occasionally jealous, but never had she believed he would also be vengeful. Was this a punishment for her meeting Rukn? She turned to explain, but he cut her short. "This is neither the time nor place to explain yourself, Shajara. You will simply stop whatever you and Rukn have been doing and you will focus your energy into organising the women of the Harem." He looked hard at her, and continued, "Banuqa has been doing your duty since our arrival, but it is time for you to do so. You are wife of the Sultan, and Hababa is a fine dancer. Nothing more."

The rest of the evening was a haze of applause and music, but she took no notice, she was calculating and imagining the conversation she was going to have with Hababa after the dancing was finished.

After the show, she politely excused herself and left Salih in the company of men all vying for his attention. She walked directly to find Hababa. She had seen so little of Hababa in the Harem that she did not even know where her room was. In the end, however, it was Hababa who found Shajara. "Are you looking for me?" she trilled innocently.

Shajara had been so intent on finding Hababa, that she had not entirely formulated what she wanted to say to her. Many angry accusations crossed her mind, but now that Hababa was standing in front of her, she stammered to find the words.

In the end, it was Hababa who spoke in a whisper. "We cannot speak here. The Harem has many eyes and twice as many ears. Let me take you to a place where we can speak freely." She took Shajara's arm and laced her arm through it. Shajara angrily removed her arm, she would follow but she would not pretend that she trusted this backstabbing dancing girl who put only herself first.

Hababa led her down several hallways and Shajara realised that she knew very little of the Harem as she was beginning to lose her way back. A sudden thought came into her mind, *What if Hababa is leading me into danger? It is obvious that she is in cahoots with Al Nasir.* But before her thoughts could develop further, Hababa stopped in front of a wooden door filled with cracks and rotting wood. Hababa looked around to make certain they had not been followed and opened the creaky door. Hababa opened the door and to Shajara's surprise, it did not lead to a room but to a spiral staircase. Hababa started to climb the narrow and high stairs, but Shajara had come to her senses. "What makes you think I will climb those stairs with you? I will go no further with you, Hababa. I only came to tell you that you will not be dancing in this palace again, and it is time for you and al Nasir to leave Cairo." Shajara was stunned at the anger that rose up in her. She did not want to admit it, but there was also much jealousy.

Hababa turned and put her hand on her hip. "You think I am leading you into a trap? It is me who is trapped. I am the one in danger if Al Nasir finds out I am with you. I know what awaits me, it seems it is my fate, and I am tired of trying to outrun it. I am here to help you Shajara…again! I don't know why, let us just say it is because I have brought your child into this world, and now there is a connection, which cannot be untied."

Something Shajara saw in Hababa's eyes made her believe she was speaking the truth. And so, she followed her up the flights of dark stairs until finally they came to a small spot in front of a window. There were remnants of bird nests and a few birds took flight upon their arrival. She knew the castle had many towers which provided excellent views and were often used as lookouts. "So, what is it? What is so important we have to come here?"

"I need to warn you. You must be careful. Let no one near that you don't trust. Al Nasir means to kill, and he always gets his way. He has not told me his plans, but I know, you and your son are not safe."

"You have wasted your time, Hababa. I am already aware of his plans." Shajara turned to leave, but Hababa grabbed her again by the arm.

"But your husband and his sister remain as fools. I expected as much from you, Shajara. You have managed to do in life what I failed, you have a powerful wealthy husband who loves you and a child. It seems my bad luck to always end up with the wrong man. But you are making a very big mistake by not persuading your husband to kill al Nasir. He is a very serious threat."

"But if Al Nasir succeeds in his assassination, he will become sultan and you will be the favourite woman of the sultan, why would you tell me this? How does it serve you exactly?"

At this, Hababa sighed heavily. "I have tried to outwit that man, to beguile him, force him to love me, but there is no love or kindness in him. The only thing he loves is power and control, even as his woman, his enjoyment only comes from watching me suffer, whether it is physical or emotional, he has an uncanny way of knowing what I hold most precious and then watching as he cruelly takes it away."

Shajara was quiet as she listened and thought this through. She had seen Hababa's acts, but the pain in her voice was real. She remained silent long enough for Hababa to become impatient.

"If you must know my hidden objective, it is to get your husband to do what I dream of doing every night." Her dark eyes flashed with hatred. "Putting a knife in Al Nasir's heart and watching him die."

§❧

Chapter 42

A Great Loss

"It is a fine breezy day today, Shajara, and I have decided to ride with a small group of Mamluks to inspect fortifications built by my father to the north of Cairo. It will be a pleasant ride, and I want you, Banuqa and Khalil to accompany me." Shajara was still annoyed from his rebuke the night before, and truthfully had not feel very well all morning, but she told him she would be happy to do so. Because of Khalil, they would travel in a litter, and he sat happily on Banuqa's lap holding one of her gold bangles in his pudgy fist.

After only a few miles, as they came up to Al-Kamil's old fortifications, they heard the sound of horses. Banuqa looking out behind them panicked "There are at least 25 horsemen armed with lances, Shajara." Shajara looked in front "And there are another 25 lancers in front of us, but let us remain calm Banuqa, surely there is an explanation for this." They heard the sound of Salih and his men drawing their swords. "No, not again, Shajara," Banuqa wailed as she drew Khalil close to her chest, "Al-Nasir had thrown a noose around us and there is no escape!" Shajara held her hand, and as soothingly as possible, "don't let us panic yet."

Both enemy groups approached slowly towards them lances levelled. Salih and his men threw daunts and dares, but there was no fire in their words, they were outnumbered. They saw the odds were stacked heavily against them.

"We will drop our arms, if you promise the safe surrender of the ladies and my son." Salih opened the barter, but his offer fell on deaf ears, the men and their lances steadily approached, one eager for bloodshed prodded his horse into a gallop. Khalil sensing Banuqa's fear, started to cry. Shajara took him from Banuqa. "Hush hush, my darling, all will be well." But even as she said the words, her voice faltered. She heard Salih pleading for the mercy of his family when they all heard the thunderous sound of many more horsemen galloping at full speed towards them.

"We are doomed, Shajara, there are more of them!" Shajara stepped out of the litter, Khalil clutching her tightly. "No, Banuqa, you needn't worry anymore sister, it is our friend Rukn and a large troop of Mamluks faithful to Salih." They heard Salih order the enemy men to drop their lances, or no mercy would be spared, and within moments, Al-Nasir, the three emirs and their men had dropped their lances.

"Cousin, you have outwitted my brother, and very nearly succeeded in killing me, but you have underestimated the intelligence of those who care for me." Rukn now had his horse next to Al Nasir's and his scimitar at his throat. "You will never cross into Egypt again. You will go back to rule in Damascus, you will not plot against me, you will rule, until I decide you do not. Do you understand?"

Shajara and Rukn exchanged glances, for they had believed Salih would not allow Al Nasir to live once he discovered his betrayal. Rukn pushed the scimitar further into his mark and Shajara could see droplets of blood running down Al Nasir's throat.

"Rukn, choose the men who will escort this failed group back to Al Kerak. You will advise al Nasir to pay the men for their trouble, and an additional tax to me for the trouble he has caused." Salih commanded Rukn without making eye contact with his cousin, although he was begging for Salih to listen to his pleas to return to Cairo to gather his entourage and his belongings.

"Rukn, join us when you have finished here." Turning to speak with his other men. "We ride on." Salih rode over to Shajara and scooped her up and Khalil up onto the front of his horse. Khalil squealing with delight.

After a few minutes riding, and bringing the horse to a slow walk, Salih whispered into her ear, "Tell me, Um Khalil, who was it that, without telling me, ordered 200 Mamluks to come to our afternoon ride?"

Shajara giggled at his use of her nickname. "I have not forgotten the last time we went for a ride and a picnic in Damascus. Al Nasir captured our small group in just the same way. I vowed back then, that I would never make the same mistake again. *I* ordered the Mamluks to follow us. Do not be angry with Rukn." Salih tightened his grip around her waist and kissed her neck. "How could I be angry with either of you. I truly thought that was the end of our lives."

Then, more soberly, he told her, "Of course, you were right all along about Al-Nasir. He is a snake and I will never let him rule in Damascus. I will make war on him and those faithless emirs. Come, we will have our picnic and then back to Cairo where we will plan our expedition to Syria."

That evening, Salih and Banuqa tried to persuade Shajara to come to watch the evening's entertainment, but she felt sick to her stomach and wanted to stay in bed. Within the hour, as Khalil also became feverish and sick, somewhere in her gut she feared the very worst. "Salih, this is the work on Al Nasir, I know it." "No, he persuaded her," his plans have already been foiled, he would not have felt it necessary to poison you and Khalil, on top of trying to capture us today."

Salih and Banuqa tried in vain to convince her otherwise, but by late evening when Khalil was visibly weaker and still feverish, they too prayed for the health of Khalil. "You see, Salih, he didn't know that I would join you this morning with Khalil, and so he has poisoned me, and I, have passed it through my milk to Khalil." She didn't say anything more as she saw that Salih finally understood what was possible. Shajara did not leave the side of Khalil all night. Doctors were called and tried their cures, by dawn in desperation, old women claiming wisdom of the ancient ones, were asked to visit the palace. One woman took one look at Khalil and told Shajara bluntly, "He has been poisoned. There is nothing to do but wait." Shajara ordered Hababa to visit her at once.

"Is this the work of Al Nasir?" Shajara demanded. Hababa lost all colour from her face when she saw Khalil. She fell to her knees and kissed Khalil's feverish forehead.

"God protect him, and so God is Great three times, Shajara, I do not know how." She looked into Shajara's eyes and said, "I know it was his plan to kill you all. He would not have allowed Salih's heir to live. But I saw that you kept Khalil close, and I warned you yesterday." The wise woman spoke, "It is possible the child was poisoned through his mother's food – not strong enough to harm the mother – but through the mother's milk, it is possible."

For three hours afterwards, Shajara held her son to her heart rocking him and whispering how much she loved him, promising that God would look after him. Banuqa and Hababa trying their best to aid his comfort, but there was no longer any hope. Khalil barely able to open his eyes nestled in her arms died minutes before the noon prayer.

No one dared approach her as she continued to rock her dead son and sing to his lifeless body the lullabies she remembered from her mother, the language now foreign to her own ears after years of speaking Arabic.

Salih racked with his own grief, was the one to take his son's body from Shajara. Banuqa hugged her and they wept together. Hababa left without saying a word. The body was buried in the section of Cairo dedicated as the graveyard for those who could afford grand tombs. Salih promised he would build a mausoleum in which they would both be buried with their son.

After the death of Khalil, Salih changed his mind about bringing Shajara to Syria with him. He would go to Syria with a large force, but he needed watchful eyes to guard his interests in Cairo. Shajara had proved herself again and again to be his most formidable ally. No one could outwit her and although it pained him to be away from her during their time of grief, he knew now her place was not as head of the Harem, but as Head of State. "I will name Rukn as the commander of my army in Egypt. You, Shajara, in all but name will be my regent in Cairo."

Salih pondered his decision for days before his departure. Rukn, even though a Mamluk, would be readily accepted as the army commander. But would Egyptians obey the will of a woman? Perhaps if she were truly Egyptian, they would be more accepting, after all their ancient history was filled with Egyptian queens. That time was long ago, however, and since the arrival of Islam, it would be unprecedented to have a woman's name on official decrees. It was true that people knew he trusted her. But she could never rule as Shajara al Durr. She had been a slave with no name; her only standing in the society was through her marriage.

In the end, he decided to solve the problem in two ways. First, he would hold a major public ceremony to which he would command the attendance of all the great men of Cairo, and state that she was his wife. The religious men of Al Azhar would bless their union. And second, he would have her sign the decrees in a special way. Everyone knew her as Um Khalil, the mother of his son. And Khalil was a royal name, a male name.

Yes, let her issue her commands as his wife and as Um Khalil. She would be obeyed!

෪

Chapter 43
The Bahri Mamluks

Shajara was not herself for many weeks following the death of Khalil. People tried to persuade her there would be more children, but this only angered Shajara. She wanted Khalil back, and knowing this could never happen, she decided to accept Salih's offer to be regent, while he was away in Syria.

The Citadel plans on the island of Roda in the Nile, led to many decisions which, in his absence, became Shajara's responsibility. Its foundations were dug, stone masons were brought in, and shipment after shipment of stones were carried across the Nile. Shajara drove the work forward, impatient to complete Salih's impregnable island fortress. At night, she had no taste for the entertainment that was on offer, nor the company of the Harem. She wanted to be alone, but Banuqa was always there for her, helping her out of her depression. Always comforting her in ways only a true friend and sister could.

In less than a year, the great Roda Citadel was finished. Known in the Egyptian dialect as Qal'at al-Bahr, from the use of the Arabic word for both the sea and the Nile, its defences were the best in military architecture. Its harbour would hold a dozen boats armed with Greek fire. On its battlements stood giant catapults. It had its own blacksmith shop and armourer. There was a pigeon house from which pigeons could carry messages to all parts of Egypt.

The Citadel now housed the Mamluk garrison, specially selected by Shajara for their loyalty. Next to the citadel was a polo pitch used both for games and for military drills.

Each year, she planned to request Salih to recruit more Mamluks until the garrison numbered nearly 1000, known to everyone as Bahri Mamluks. Salih delegated to Shajara and Rukn the task of assessing the qualities of each new Mamluk recruit. It was intimidating for the young Mamluks to be questioned by her: none ever forgot the experience. It was Shajara, too, who aided the advancement of those she thought especially talented: they, too, never forgot that they owed her their positions. Salih trusted her in the management, and with the fair maintenance of them, she earned their devotion.

Rukn never gave up his close supervision of the training of the Mamluks. Every morning, he would lead them through complex drills. His favourite was the one they referred to as Um Khalil's feint. Over time, it grew into much more than the simple manoeuvre Shajara had described on the night before battle with Adil. The Mamluks practiced charging in waves, then breaking into two groups to harass the flanks of an enemy army, charging again, retreating in feigned panic, and then reassembling in an all-out massed charge. "If we practice it well," he told Shajara, "one of these days, your name will be linked to a famous victory."

There was no doubt in Shajara's mind that Rukn should remain the personal bodyguard to Salih and on the battlefield his chief commander. She liked him not only for his strength and valour, but also because he had been captured by the Mongols and knew both their strengths and weaknesses. The nightmare that they faced was an alliance between Crusaders and Mongols. Nor was there ever a doubt that Qipchuk would remain her bodyguard. They had been through many trials together and she treasured him for his loyalty.

Shajara promoted another outstanding young Mamluk, a Turkman named Aybak, to be Salih's 'Jashnkir' or taster of Salih's food. Fakr ad Din was a handsome young Mamluk who shone in his studies almost as much as in military exercises. Shajara saw him as a future administrator, maybe even as an army commander.

One exceptionally skilled Mamluk, a Kipchak Turk, named Qalawun was known as al-Alfi ('the Thousand-man') because at Shajara's suggestion, he was purchased for a thousand dinars of gold. Although Qalawun barely spoke Arabic, his astonishing skill as a horseman was combined with great talent for administration. Shajara encouraged his rise in power and influence.

Shajara kept close watch over the Mamluks in the camp, careful to see that their allegiance would always be to Salih, but she had also another appointment to make, and felt it was a risky choice – Hababa. She had remained in Cairo after Al Nasir was sent back to Al Kerak and had found her way into plenty of Harem gossip. She boasted often of Shajara and her friendship in Baghdad and in Al Kerak, and many of the Harem ladies were mindful of the connection. Shajara did not see any reason to correct it, as she reminded herself of her aid bringing in her dear Khalil into this world and having warned her to the possibility of Al Nasir's murderous plots. Still, she felt that she needed a spy in the Harem, and although she could always count on Banuqa, she needed as many ears as possible. Habiba would be an asset, she hoped.

෨

Chapter 44
Ruling Together

Salih had returned victorious from his Syrian campaigns. His nickname was now Abu al-Futuh, 'the victorious'. He was greeted with loud cheers from his people lining the streets and already knew he must have urgent meetings with the Amirs, his advisors at court and the religious men of Al Azhar, but what he wanted far more was to see his wife. He dreamed of holding Shajara tight in his arms and looking into her sparkling green eyes.

Night after night in Syria, he had thanked God for sending him such a woman. He had expected to care and protect his wife, as is expected of a man. What he had not expected was for her to be the one to care and protect him. Yet she advised and protected him better than his politicians or military commanders. Yet, in her time of real grief, the death of their son, he had not been able to take her pain away and he had not been able to save Khalil. His guilt for leaving so soon after his death plagued him throughout his time away from her.

Her letters had worried him that she blamed him for his death, as she wrote nothing of him, nor of her desire for more children. Only she wrote about the building of the citadel and the growing danger in Cairo. The Mongol threat was real. Indeed, the greatest threat was that they might find themselves facing both the crusaders and Mongols. They kept spies at the court of the French King, Louis, as well as at the court of the Great Khan, Gayuk Khan in Mongolia. Shajara had been clever in her letters to him and knowing that most of her letters would be read, used code when referring to them.

Approaching Cairo, he could see the Citadel and a burning desire to see Shajara overwhelmed him. His eyes fell on her from a distance and he looked nowhere else. The cheers blurred out and he saw only her smile. He vowed at that moment; he would never be away from her again.

That evening after many duties were filled and a prolonged dinner, he was finally alone with Shajara. He had had a long exhausting journey, but he had yearned for this time with her. After many treasured hours together, the conversation moved to the impending problems surrounding the invasions.

"I am more worried about the Mongols then the Crusaders. Remember, I lived with the Crusaders when I was given as hostage in return for a noble Frenchman. My father told me to keep my eyes and ears open, and I did. I have a certain respect for the Christian knights but less so for their mounts. Their horses are as big and as clumsy as the oxen we use to pull ploughs. The knights can use them to good effect in all-out charges, but they are useless in fast manoeuvres. However, in the evenings the knights too often get drunk and boast of impossible feats. Only the French lords ride horses into battle. Our worst Mamluks ride more skilfully than any noble Frenchman."

When they talked of the Mongols, Shajara repeated the words she remembered from her conversation with Jamal in Konya. She told how the news had spread of plains littered with the skulls of the victims of Mongol terror campaigns.

"I remember shaking with fear after hearing that news. Then Jamal explained that it was part of their strategy, as fear is a powerful weapon. So, I began to understand that if I felt fear, then I was falling into their trap."

"You stayed strong instead." Salih kissed the tips of each of her fingers. "You have always given me strength when I, too, felt fear." He stroked her cheek lovingly. "And what did your friend Jamal tell you to do to defeat the Mongols? I would be interested in hearing that!"

"To beat them," he said, "we need courage and, then, we need to outwit them. Courage and cunning can conquer every foe."

"Well then, we shall certainly win, as you have both courage and cunning."

&❧

Chapter 45
Shajara's Great Deception

Shajara felt life with Salih back at her side made her feel whole again. She still missed Khalil every moment, but the pain seemed more distant now that Salih was back in her life. Unfortunately, after a few months of his return, she noticed that he had a cough that did not get better. He also tired easily and although he agreed to see the doctors, none of their treatments seemed to alleviate the symptoms.

As time wore on, his health steadily declined. She begged Banuqa to find the most skilled doctors, and they plied him with remedy after remedy, yet he began to spend less time with his duties, and more time in bed. Shajara was often at his bedside reciting their favourite Quranic suras. When he slept, she took control of the administration and, because everyone knew that Salih's decisions had always been made jointly with her, her every command was obeyed.

Speaking with Rukn and Banuqa about the future, she said, "Salih's illness could not have come at a worse time. Our spies have reported that King Louis has embarked on a fleet of 100 ships from Cyprus. It will not be long before they are on our shores. I am sure that the Crusaders' goal is the conquest of Egypt and that, as in the Fifth Crusade, they will besiege Damietta."

"Where is that?" Banuqa's voice was worried.

Rukn answered her softly, "It is a city on the Mediterranean, east of Alexandria. It is rich with agriculture; they will try to take the city and then head south along the Nile. But you have nothing to worry about." Shajara saw how he laid his hand softly on her's, and she smiled. Their relationship had continued to blossom and Shajara hoped there would be a wedding soon. She knew it would bring criticism from many, but she could not be happier for the union. These were two people she loved and trusted, and their bond had grown over the years.

He smiled. "Banuqa, they tried this before when your father was Sultan. They took Damietta after a two-year siege, you were only a small girl then, but your father defeated them at Mansourah. In fact," he told her, "the town had been called Island of flowers, but after al-Kamil's famous victory, it became known as the place of victory (Mansoura). He built a citadel in honour of the victory. They will not have forgotten that either, and it is to Mansourah that we will march and from there to Damietta."

"I wish my father was here," Banuqa said silently.

"He was a great man indeed, he was wise, brave and a good Muslim. The Frankish chroniclers, although defeated by him, still praised him." Banuqa raised her sad eyes to him. He continued, "It is true, Banuqa, they wrote about the defeat, when their troops were starving, and your father ordered them to be fed." This put a smile on Banuqa's face, as Rukn quoted what had been written by the Crusader chronicler. "Who could doubt that such goodness, friendship and charity come from God? Men whose families had died in agony at our hands, whose lands we took, whom we drove from their homes, revived us with their own food when we were dying of hunger and showered us with kindness even when we were in their power." Our Sultan Salih is a man cut from the same cloth, and his wife, he looked to Shajara knows what it means to be a good general.

Shajara smiled at her sister, but her heart was heavy. Could her husband survive the long journey north along the Nile? Should she insist he stay in Cairo? She knew that armies needed their ruler there with them, they fought more courageously, but what would the consequences be?

When Rukn spoke to Salih later, he insisted he would go, but agreed reluctantly to be carried in a litter at the head of the army. Shajara would set out with Salih towards Mansourah the following day.

"Rukn, Fakhr ad Din and their Mamluks are well capable of dealing with the French," Salih told Shajara. "We will send Fakhr ad Din to Damietta with half our army to hold it until we arrive." Shajara accepted his decision but warned him, "Remember the danger of dividing forces."

At Mansourah, Salih, wearied by the long journey from Cairo, became feverish. An ulcer spread the infection in his leg, and they feared gangrene would set in. Shajara was seriously worried for his health. He was weak, had sunken eyes and was ravaged by fever. His tall and strong physique had shrunken, and he looked old. She prayed for his recovery but increasingly worried that she would have to make the majority of decisions from now on.

Now, Shajara could see that the march to Damietta was plainly beyond Salih's strength. He rose from his sick bed to review his troops. He felt that he would never reach Damietta and he could see that his remaining troops were inadequate even to defend Mansourah. "Send a messenger to recall Fakr ad Din with his Mamluks. Let the governor of Damietta hold it with the garrison there. It was well fortified by my father and will be well able to withstand siege."

"Are we certain of that, my love?" questioned Shajara. "What if…"

Salih waved his arm at her. "Yes, yes it will be fine." Shajara helped him back into bed and could feel how feverish he was. She thought of pushing the matter further. Surely, there was another solution, but the tired look in his eyes quieted her doubts. Even though Shajara knew that his troops feared losing their leader.

It turned out that Salih's last military decision was a fateful mistake. Fakr al Din returned with his Mamluks, but the Damietta garrison fled without a fight, they were no match for the French. King Louis and his crusaders walked into the city without the loss of a single man.

Shajara was torn, she was desperate to stay by Salih's side and nurse him back to health as best as she knew how, but she could not allow her judgement in matters of state to be overshadowed by her concern for her husband. He would never forgive her, if she gave up on Egypt. If Salih survived this illness, Shajara would have to make sure that Egypt was not lost to the French. It was time for her to take control of all his decisions from now on.

That evening, Salih took Shajara's hand. "Shajara, you have been my guiding star. I met you when I was lost and uncertain in life. You have helped me achieve great things and have made me happy and proud to be your husband but now it is your time. You will now shine like the star you are. You must take over from me." He told Shajara to bring him a sheaf of blank state papers with his royal seal. With the last of his strength, he signed them and gave them to Shajara. "Now, Um Khalil, my beloved wife, you can finally, as you have long deserved, be Sultan. Egypt will be guided once more by a woman, like our great ancient Egyptian ancestors."

Shajara wiped the tears from her cheeks. "What are you saying? You will survive this illness, and we will fight back the French and return to Cairo triumphant *together*." But he placed his finger on her lips.

"No, Shajara, this is the end for me. I will not last more than a few days, and I welcome it. There is too much pain, and it is my time to join our beloved

Khalil." His voice was weak, and she wanted to argue with him about his health and laugh at his ridiculous request of her reigning over Egypt as Sultan, but there was something in his eyes begging her to accept. He was tired, and so she took the papers, smiled lovingly and kissed his lips. He had already fallen back to sleep.

The news of the fall of Damietta had been the last blow to Salih and after lying unconscious for some hours, he died in Shajara's arms. Shajara had loved Salih deeply since they first met years earlier in Damascus. Yet, now she had no time to weep for her husband. Damietta was lost and the Crusaders might soon be at Mansourah. She went immediately to find Fakr and Rukn and brought them into the tent to see the body. "You, and only you, know that our Sultan is dead," she told them, her voice shaking. "There will be no mourning and no burial."

The Mamluk commanders were shocked but they trusted Shajara's judgment. "We need reinforcements and we need a new sultan," she told them. "You, Fakr, will ride to Hasankey in Iraq where Salih's first born son, Muazzam Turanshah has his army. Yes, Fakr, we all know that he is nothing like Salih, but tell him that I and Rukn here will safeguard his inheritance. That should, at least, win us his gratitude. Tell him to march here with all his soldiers. You, Rukn, look to the defences of Mansourah and send spies to report on the French. Now send me Suhayli, the Master Eunuch."

The men left the tent having sworn to keep Shajara's great secret. They knew she was right: Salih's troops would be demoralised if they knew of the death and the French would seize the opportunity to attack. Her deception was for the best.

Within minutes, the Master Eunuch entered to see Shajara binding her husband's corpse in a sheet. "Help me, Suhayli, we must wrap up his body well, for I cannot yet bury it." Suhayli was shocked but he helped her bind sheet after sheet around the body.

"Now you, Salih, are one of only four who know this terrible secret. And I trust you, on your life, to keep it. I will stay in this tent day until Fakr returns with Muazzam Turanshah. Yes, Turanshah will be the new sultan. Go now and tell all in our camp that Salih lives but must be kept quiet and cared for in this darkened tent. Then, each and every day, bring me meals for two and tell everyone that Salih is recovering well. One dark night, you must take his body secretly to the citadel in the Nile. Let it lie there until we can give him proper funeral ceremony at his own tomb by the madrasa in Bayn Qasrain."

How long would it be before Fakr al Din returned with Turanshah? She knew he had never been a son to Salih, and she knew very well that he despised her as a Mamlukah. How would he treat her when he was sultan? Surely, he must thank her for keeping his inheritance secure. Moreover, so long as she had Rukn and her Mamluk guard she should be safe enough. She thought over her decision to send for him. Yes, better Turanshah than to be taken by the Crusaders!

৽

Chapter 46
The Battle of Mansourah

In February, Rukn's spies brought Shajara news that King Louis' Crusaders were moving slowly north along the Nile accompanied by supply boats from Damietta. Shajara recalled Salih's account of al-Kamil's successful campaign against the fifth Crusade. Then, too, the Crusaders had marched towards Cairo only to be halted at Mansourah. "History is repeating itself," Shajara told Rukn. "What can we learn from it?"

"Well, the French dependence on supplies from Damietta might be a weakness as it had been for the earlier Crusaders." He continued, "we could organise a special force with the mission of capturing or sinking the supply boats." Shajara nodded ascent and dismissed him.

The French King's spies had reported to Louis that Salih had not left his tent in two months. Surely, he was either very sick or dead. When Louis finally came up near to Al Mansoura, he decided on immediate attack before the succession to Salih could be decided.

The problem for the French was that Al Mansoura was defended by the Ashmoun Canal, and before they could reach the town and citadel, they must find a means of crossing it. Louis ordered his engineers to build a causeway or dyke across the canal. From the citadel, Shajara saw the French begin to dig. She called Rukn to her chamber. "Our men can dig just as well as the French," she told him. "Each day, as they dig towards us, have our men dig away the opposite bank." With this simple stratagem, she kept the canal unpassable.

The long days of waiting for reinforcements were nearly over. Fakr ad Din galloped into Al Mansoura with the news that Touranshah with a large Arab army was only a few days march away. Meanwhile, however, the French and Mamluk armies faced each other across the canal in stalemate.

Shajara and Rukn agreed they needed intelligence on enemy plans. Rukn promised to capture a Frenchman, and within the day delighted her with the trick he used to capture a Frenchman. He hollowed out a large watermelon, set his best swimmer to swim across the canal, his head in the huge fruit. The swimmer bobbed in the water near the sergeants' camp. A sergeant leaped into the canal to seize the melon but was dragged under by Rukn's man and taken to the other shore for interrogation.

What Shajara did not know was that a Bedouin had approached the French with an offer, in return for gold, to show them a ford across the canal at some distance from Mansourah. The French cavalry, led by the King's own brother, crossed the ford. Then, unwilling to wait for their infantry they attacked the Egyptian camp where the commander was caught wholly by surprise.

The French cavalry, after their successful skirmish, rode towards the town of Al-Mansoura. Some 1400 knights with no infantry in support galloped headlong into the little town. Rukn had seen the French cavalry attack on the camp and now stationed his men around the town in the hope that the Crusaders would charge in. The rash French cavalry obliged him. Once they were all deep within the town, Rukn ordered the Mamluks to counterattack. Even the people of the town took part, throwing down stones and pulling riders from their horses.

As Shajara watched the French knights struggle in the narrow streets below the citadel, she remembered what Salih had told her of their weaknesses: they were brave but rash and they rode horses that were good only for an all-out charge. Now, the best of King Louis' cavalry had ridden unthinking into alleys in which they could barely turn their horses around. They were easy prey for Rukn and the Mamluks. In less than an hour, Louis had lost his brother and the best of his knights.

This battle of Mansourah had engaged only Louis' cavalry but his infantry remained intact and he had enough knights left to make his army still formidable. Rukn's special force swung into action attacking the French supply boats, capturing some, using Greek fire to burn others, and barricading the Nile with their own armed boats to block passage from Damietta. There were reports of malaria in the French camp and Rukn promised Shajara that famine would soon make their misery complete. Finally, he reported a great victory on the Nile at which 30 French supply boats had been captured. Now, only the arrival of Turanshah with reinforcements was needed to bring Louis to his knees.

வ

Chapter 47
Whose Victory?

Shajara looked out from the Mansourah citadel to see Turanshah's army coming up after the long march from Iraq. It was a disappointing sight, for there were no more than 300 in infantry. Only Turanshah and his retinue of about 20 men were mounted. Nevertheless, they were valuable reinforcements and, calling Rukn to join her, she hurried down to the courtyard of the citadel to welcome them.

Turanshah rode up and, without even the simplest greeting, not even dismounting, he addressed her. "I hear you have been forging my father's signature and spending from his treasury. Soon, I will be wanting an accounting from you." Then, turning to Rukn, "You, Mamluk, and your horsemen will take orders from me and my commanders. As I knew would be the case, you have failed dismally against the Crusaders. Tomorrow, I will lead the army into battle and put the King and all his men to the sword." He dismounted and told Shajara curtly, "You, Mamlukah, go to the women's quarters and stay there until I call for you."

How foolish she had been to expect gratitude for her efforts on his behalf! What arrogance he showed in depreciating the Mamluk's destruction of most of the French cavalry! What folly to commit his infantry, tired after their long march, into battle the day after their arrival! What silliness to talk of killing Louis instead of capturing him!

Shajara beckoned Rukn to follow her. "Hide your anger," she told him. "Turanshah plans to go into battle tomorrow, but his infantry even combined with ours cannot break the French. Only you and our Mamluks can do that. So, before the battle, feign great humility and obedience. But once opposite the French, forget about Turanshah and his commanders. You know the Um Khalil feint by heart. Use it to trap the last of Louis' knights and break his infantry." Rukn bowed his obedience. "And one thing more, Rukn, bring the French king back alive. A royal corpse is worth nothing. Louis, if you take him alive, is worth his weight in gold."

The next day, Turanshah's army came up to the French force at Fariskur. The French shouted loudly, banging lances against shields and derisively questioning the courage of their opponents. Louis' remaining French knights, heavily armoured on huge chargers, pranced at the front. It was still a formidable army.

Turanshah's infantry stood in place waiting his signal to march forward. Suddenly from the rear of the army, without any signal from Turanshah, the Mamluk horseman emerged in a mass charge led by Rukn. They rode forward at breakneck pace but, suddenly, they stopped, the hooves of their horses skidding in the sand, just short of the French front line. Were they outside the range of the French crossbowmen?

Rukn had judged the distance well. Shower after shower of French bolts fell harmlessly short of the Mamluks. The French knights on their chargers were no match for the Mamluk horsemen, who could turn tightly on their smaller, much more agile Arabian horses. They darted in and around the French cavalry, evading their lances, and shooting arrows at vulnerable joints in the knights' body armour.

Now, still without casualties, the Mamluks divided their force in two. One group of Mamluks under the command of Rukn rode to the French left flank; and the other, under Aybak, rode to harass the right flank. The aim was to get the French flanks to waver, and it had some success. Next, the Mamluks came together in a frontal attack. Each horseman shot arrows into the enemy's front rank where the French had stationed their best men. Then, wheeling around, they rode back towards Turanshah's army.

It was time for Um-Khalil's feint. This time, the Mamluks again galloped fast towards the French, but only a few rode within range of their crossbowmen. The others hung back and then, as if mustering their courage, rode forward, but again, at the last moment, stopped short. Next, those in the first wave, pretending to be discouraged by their lack of success, called loudly for retreat. Finally, the whole Mamluk force, in apparent disarray, rode away as if in flight, disappearing to the rear of the army.

Most of the French force remained in place, but the mounted knights, sensing victory, rode after the Mamluks and many of the French foot soldiers ran following them. Um-Khalil's feint was working! Now, the Mamluk horsemen suddenly reappeared. The French foot soldiers who had broken ranks were now in the open and well out of range of their own crossbowmen. They were easy prey. So, too, were the French knights, weighed down by armour on their clumsy horses.

Once again, the Mamluk horsemen divided into two groups to harass both flanks of the French. Once more, the tactic brought confusion into the French ranks. Once again, the Mamluks wheeled to attack Louis' front rank, which was now badly reduced in numbers.

Turanshah had watched the Mamluk manoeuvres with astonishment and anger. They had ridden into battle without his command! He promised himself that they would pay dearly for their insubordination. Yet, it was plain that an opportunity was open for a successful attack. He signalled his infantry to march towards the French. As they did so, the Mamluks again attacked the French front rank before breaking again into two groups to harass both flanks. The French front remained unbroken, but the flanks now wavered badly, and some threw down their weapons and ran from the battle. When they did, the rest lost courage. Louis remained at the front, but all but a dozen of his knights had ridden off the field to save their lives.

Soon the whole French army was in disarray. Louis rode with his dozen knights to a small hill away from the battleground. He could see that his army was in its death agonies and prepared himself to make a last stand.

Rukn remembered Shajara's emphasis on taking the King alive. Would Turanshah see that the King could be captured? Or would he be carried away in the heat of battle to order an attack on Louis? Shajara had said that captured alive, Louis was worth his weight in gold. As a prisoner, he could be made to sign a peace that would end the crusade.

Rukn took twenty Mamluks and rode to the hill. There he offered the French King his life, promised to assure his safety and that of his nobles. As Rukn rode away with his captives, he could see that Turanshah was leading a senseless slaughter of the French.

Rukn smiled as he thought how pleased Shajara would be with his royal prisoner. It would be interesting, he thought, to hear Turanshah's account of who had won this victory.

Then, he thought again of Shajara, and his dead commander and Sultan, Salih. He had been more than that, he was his friend. Let Turanshah beware, he said to himself, if he touches a hair on her head, let him disrespect her in any way, and he will die by my hand.

෪

Chapter 48
A New Day in Egypt

Turanshah rode into the courtyard waving a bloody scimitar. "This blade of mine slew forty French today," he boasted. "I have won an even greater victory than my grandfather, Al Kamil."

Shajara was standing in the courtyard with the master eunuch, Suhayli. "I thought I told you to stay in the women's quarters," he roared at her. "Eunuch, take her where she belongs. And you," he shouted at Rukn, "take your Mamluks and start killing the French prisoners. There are too many to sell as slaves." Rukn made as if to object and Turanshah threatened him with his scimitar. "This blade is sharp enough for your neck, Mamluk. You are a slave and you will kill on my command or be killed yourself."

Shajara turned to Suhayli as they left the courtyard. "Your name means companion, and so I must trust you to be my friend. Rukn has taken the French King and his knights to a house in town. You must go there swiftly and make sure that all is in order." She stopped Suhayli's bow fearful that his deference would be seen. "Turanshaw is in the grip of blood lust and we need to stay well out of his way."

Rukn had made as if to obey Turanshah but went instead into the citadel after Shajara. "You know as well as I, Um Khalil, that this evil man must be stopped. He hates us all and will kill us all."

"True, dear friend," she replied, "but let us watch and wait a little longer."

As Rukn left, Shajara wondered what Salih would have wished. Surely, Turanshah was not the rightful heir of his pious father, nor his grandfather Al Kamil who had fed the defeated French troops. She recalled Salih's saying: "Always, the victor in battle must be merciful."

That evening, Turanshah, surrounded by his henchmen, celebrated with wine and revelry. He still had his bloodstained scimitar, declaring that the French blood would keep it sharp. As candles were lit at the table, he would slice off the top of each with his scimitar, boasting that he would cut off the heads of Mamluks just as easily. "Send for Shajara," he ordered. "They say she can dance, so let's have her dance for us. If she doesn't dance well, I'll slice her too!" It was a fatal mistake.

Instead of Shajara, it was Rukn with a dozen Mamluks who ran out of the citadel, scimitars drawn. Turanshah's henchmen made a feeble defence and fell quickly to the Mamluks. Turanshah had cowered behind his henchmen but now ran away. Rukn struck at him as he fled, but Turanshah countered with his bare hand. Dripping blood, his fingers severed, Turanshah ran into the citadel pursued by Rukn. Desperate to save his life, Turanshah threw himself from the battlements into the Nile waters below. Shajara saw Turanshah's body fall into the Nile.

What next, she wondered? Her silent question was answered as a mass of cheering Mamluks came into the courtyard. Led by Rukn, they were shouting, "Um Khalil, Um Khalil," time and time again. There was no doubt of their loyalty to her! But what of the Egyptian troops? Again, the answer came with shouts of "Um Khalil, Um Khalil," taken up by the whole army. Then not only the Mamluks and Salih's Egyptian infantry but even the Arab troops brought by Turanshah took up the cry. They seemed glad of Turanshah's death.

Rukn bowed low before her. "Only you can lead us, Um Khalil. Only you are Salih's true and rightful heir. You are our Sultan, our queen!"

Shajara's mind was made up. She addressed the crowd of men from her balcony in the citadel. "Tomorrow we will go to Cairo together," she told them. "Tomorrow we will begin a new day for Egypt." A huge cheer rose from the crowd. "Um Khalil, Um Khalil, Um Khalil."

৬৩

Chapter 49
Into Cairo

"We shall enter the city through Bab Zuweila," Shajara told Rukn. "Ride ahead, let Cairo know we are an army in triumph. Tell them that we have conquered the Crusaders, that the French King is our prisoner. Let them celebrate a great Muslim victory."

In Shajara's mind, there was still a doubt: would Cairo accept her as its ruler? She recalled Salih's entry into Cairo. Yes, she would wear his gold and silver armour! It would remind the people of their ever-victorious sultan. Should she even ride in on his great war horse? Yes, she would ride into the city! A warrior queen, the conqueror of crusaders, was entitled to ride a horse! And, yes, she would ride at the head of the army.

Shajara came through the great gate of Bab Zuweila to thunderous cheering. Never before had Cairo seen such crowds. "Um Khalil, Um Khalil," they were shouting. The ordinary people seemed to want her. But what of the great men of Cairo? Would they obey a woman, a Mamlukah?

Shajara came up to the old palace where Salih had first brought her years before. City leaders, emirs, and the governors of several provinces stood at the palace gates. She knew them all, but they knew her only as their sultan's wife.

She dismounted from her horse and strode towards them. The men bowed. As was the custom in the presence of a sultan, they remained bowing low until she greeted them. "Stand up!" she told them and then went courteously to greet each man by name.

The leader of the group, a man long trusted by Salih, stepped forward. "Great queen," he addressed her, "you come to us with a more glorious victory than we have ever known. Every Muslim will ever remember your name, Um Khalil. Your victory over the French is the equal of Saladin's great victories. No Crusader army will dare set foot in Egypt while you rule. Each and every man here will swear allegiance." Shajara had to make decisions on the disposition of the French prisoners. Louis had to be held to his agreement to pay 400,000 French gold *bezats* as his ransom. The *Mamluk*s who had fallen in battle against the Crusaders had to be replaced.

Shajara smiled happily. It could not have gone better. She remounted her horse and turning to the men told them to come to the Citadel the next day. "There are many things to decide," she told them, "and I will want your counsel."

In the Citadel, Shajara and Rukn discovered to their horror that Banuqa had died that day. She touched the pale, cold brow of her dead friend. She was the best of friends, her always-loving companion, and the woman to whom she had been closest in her adult life. Shajara determined that her body would lie with that of Salih, brother and sister together, in his mausoleum. So, few things are certain in this life, she thought, only death. All that we can do is obey the will of Allah, the compassionate.

᭐

Chapter 50
Ruling Egypt

Shajara took as her royal name *'al-Malikah Ismat ad-Din Umm-Khalil Shajar al-Durr'*. It was the name that appeared on her decrees, but everyone still called her simply Um Khalil. Her ambassadors liked to call her *'Walidat al-Malik al-Mansur Khalil, Emir al-Mo'ammin',* because it reminded foreign rulers that Khalil was (or would have been if he lived) Emir of the Faithful. The imams of Cairo's mosques knew her popularity and they pleased her with a decision to name her in the Friday prayers, either as *'Shibat al-Malik Salih'* or as *'Walidat Khalil'*. She knew perfectly well that all these titles were intended to impress men with the names of the dead men in her life, Salih and her poor, dead baby son. For herself, she liked it best when she was called *'Malikat al-Muslimin'*, 'Queen of the Muslims'. In all Islam, no other woman had been so named.

The men who really know me are happy to obey me, Shajara said to herself. It is only men who do not know me who want me to step aside for a man. And, although few things are certain in this life, I will never step aside. I am the rightful ruler of Egypt!

Chapter 51
Post Script

We shall leave Shajara now as ruler of Egypt, Queen of Egypt. What memories should we keep of Shajara al Durr? We might remember her as the Conqueror of the Crusaders or as the first in a long line of Mamluk rulers, a new Egyptian dynasty which ruled Egypt for nearly three hundred years. Rukn went on to defeat the Mongols and later become Sultan himself after Shajara's death.

Perhaps it is best to remember Shajara al Durr as a young slave girl, as Osman finished his story of Khorayzan, he asked her what she had learned from it. "Few things are certain in this life," she told him, "but many things are possible for a girl, *In Sha' Allah*."

"Capable and beautiful, [she] must have been one of very few women in history who commanded an army in a major battle, as she did against Louis IX, King of France."
Sir John Glubb, Soldiers of Fortune: The Story of the Mamlukes.